# The Year Growing Ancient

## Irene Hunter Steiner

Tonia Marshall is a spirited and stunningly attractive young woman whose capacity for pleasure seems limitless. She is engaged to marry a brilliant young doctor who adores her, and to all appearances her life will unfold in a predictable fashion.

Then suddenly, five days before her wedding, a man looks at her — a stranger with calm clear eyes and sun-streaked hair — and Tonia finds herself enmeshed in a love affair that is to bring her tenderness, ecstasy — and, ultimately, sorrow.

*The Year Growing Ancient* is a heartrending story of passion, betrayal and a love that defied convention.

T5-AFS-541

# The Year Growing Ancient

### Irene Hunter Steiner

ST. MARTIN'S PRESS • NEW YORK

Copyright © 1979 by Irene Hunter Steiner
All rights reserved. For information, write:
  St. Martin's Press
  175 Fifth Avenue
  New York, N.Y. 10010
Manufactured in the United States of America
Library of Congress Catalog Card Number: 78-14925


**Library of Congress Cataloging in Publication Data**

Steiner, Irene Hunter.
  The year growing ancient.

  I. Title.
PZ4.S8224Ye 1978     [PR9369.3.S78]     823     78-14925
ISBN 0-312-89619-0

To David,
who renewed my strength

# 1

The girl began to shiver.

She shivered because of what had been done that morning, and that which remained to be done in the afternoon. Because the hands of the clock told her that the afternoon had already begun. Because that which had to be done was the most desolate difficult task ever demanded of her; and she was afraid.

It was a new and bewildering sensation—an introduction to a hostile stranger—for she had laughed her way through the more difficult scrapes in life and had been prepared to go on laughing for quite some time to come.

But the laughing had ended abruptly, cut off as quickly as a hand over a mouth silences a scream. She had turned, to see a man with sun-streaked hair and calm, clear eyes. The laughter stopped, faded away with the last vestiges of girlhood, and in its place pulsated a solemn awareness of being a woman for the very first time.

She had stood quite still. For once there was no smiling invitation in her eyes. There was more—a great deal more—and when he slowly put down his glass and moved toward her, she saw reflected in his face all that was portrayed on her own.

Luke had been detained in the hospital. A child cried for him, and the destiny of a group of people was decided on that whimper of fate. Which was why she was now shivering. She was about to put into action that terribly harsh word *jilt*, and her mouth tightened despairingly at the thought.

How do you tell a man that you're not going to marry him, with the wedding a mere five days away? What words do you choose to cause pain and distress, to damage a life? And having chosen them, how do you say them? In stammering soft, sweet apology? In crisp decisive tones, as a surgeon wields a scalpel, cutting the man swiftly, cleanly out of your life? Or when the moment comes, will the words stubbornly refuse to leave a throat that is dry and rigid through fear?

If the love had wilted or died—or turned to hate—the burden of guilt would surely be less, and the task made easier. But when the man is still the dear quiet man whom you'd nudged none too gently into falling in love with you, the man for whom you retained the strongest affection . . .

Well, how *do* you tell such a man?

She didn't know. She didn't know how or where to begin or even if she had the courage to begin. Courage was another stranger, shadowy and remote, an indefinable something that remained an unknown quality until needed. And at the age of twenty-one, blessed with splendid vitality, an incurable optimism, and the sort of face that made people blink a little when they saw it for the first time, she had never needed courage before.

It was needed now. Desperately. She could close her eyes against the kindly old face of the clock, but her ears had never been so acutely sensitive to its ticking. Normally placid and reassuring, on this abnormal day it became an inexorable countdown to a moment of truth, a moment which would blast her into a new life and a new love, with the attendant aching knowledge that the new love could only begin on the devastated rubble of the old.

The wedding presents, arranged so proudly by her mother and displayed all around her, were not helping any, and it seemed that some mocked while others stared mournfully in mute reproach. Reproach. That was the operative word. *Self*-reproach. Lashings of it. Bitter and abhorrent.

The minute hand of the clock was advancing steadily, relentlessly. She began to feel sick, and the shivering was becoming uncontrollable. By now Luke should have left the hospital. He would be well on his way to her.

They had met by chance.

They met in a dusty lane on a hot afternoon at a point about midway between the village of Rivingham and the holiday resort of St.Michael's-on-Sea; and neither of them had any business being there in the first place.

Luke Howard ought to have been a hundred miles away, diligently pursuing his studies in the University where he was a fifth-year medical student. It was ironical, then, that the cause of his being sent home temporarily was this very diligence.

Other boys played—he won bursaries. Others went a-broad for holidays—he worked vacations. Students with whom he roomed stumbled in from many a hectic party to find him asleep with the light still burning, his head pillowed on his books. The teaching staff applauded his determination but were unhappy with the fanatical dedication.

The dean sent for the tall, painfully-thin young man, observed the gaunt pallor of his face, the bony wrists sticking out from the shabby suit, and the burning intensity in the red-rimmed blue eyes.

He spoke gently to him, "Mr. Howard, I am rather concerned about you. I am told that you work halfway through the night, every night. This is not necessary for a student of your caliber. You are driving yourself too far, too quickly. There is such a thing as moderation, and you must acquaint yourself with it."

Luke was astounded. "Is that all you wished to see me about?" It was not rudeness, but a genuine astonishment that the dean should waste valuable time on trivialities.

"Not quite. I am sending you home for two weeks. I suggest that you spend the time fishing."

"Fishing! You can't be serious, sir! My work . . . the seminar paper . . . the examinations . . . "

"Fishing, Mr. Howard. The registrar has a rail warrant ready for you, and I want you out of this faculty by lunchtime. Come and see me on your return. Good morning."

Luke projected himself out of the office and down the corridor. He was shaking with resentment and fury. Whether it was the anger or the fact that he had forgotten to eat for twenty-four hours—or a combination of both, he only just made his room in time. He managed to climb on the bed and lay there clinging to it while the room swung round and round. When it condescended to stand still, he was drenched with sweat.

He knew when he was beaten. He took himself home to Rivingham, and his widowed mother was glad to see him. There was a close bond between them. It was high summer, and the countryside was still and drowsy. Obediently he bought himself a fishing rod—thirteen years overdue—and spent long days sleeping in the sun. Consistently appearing in his dreams was a shining brass plate which discreetly stated: LUKE HOWARD, CONSULTANT.

He caught no fish.

But the two weeks were memorable, not because of the fishing, but because of his spat with a long-legged, willful honey-blonde.

He was driving his battered little car down a dusty lane when he saw her—a tall, slender schoolgirl in a dark brown gymslip and cream blouse—standing in the middle of the lane brandishing a hockey stick at him.

He stopped. She reminded him of a young colt. All legs and a mane of corn-colored hair that the wind blew across her face. Then her hand came up and parted the blonde curtain, and Luke Howard looked at the prettiest face he had ever seen, complemented with large grey eyes, simmering with mischief, set in the clearest white sky, and a wide, beautiful mouth.

"Hello! Are you going past King Edward's?"

"The boys' school?"

"Yes. If you are, will you give me a lift?"

Luke leaned across to open the door, and she climbed in. He thought the legs and the hockey stick might encounter a little difficulty in the confined space, but she managed to fold them together gracefully enough. The gymslip was shockingly abbreviated, but it didn't seem to cause her any concern. Anyway, he was practically a doctor and had seen plenty of limbs. Not like these, though. He kept his eyes on the road.

"Phew, it's hot. Thanks a lot for stopping. If you hadn't come along, I wouldn't have made my date."

"Are you playing in a match over there?"

She had a delicious giggle. "I haven't heard it described like that before."

He threw her a startled glance.

"The hockey stick is a blind," she confided ingenuously. "It might come in handy as a weapon, though. To fend him off—just in case!" Again there was that little gurgle of mischief.

"Fend him off?" He couldn't get the drift of her words.

"My date. I've just told you. The boy I'm going to meet."

Luke felt himself grow hot. She must think him dumb.

"Why ditch school?" he asked. "Can't you meet him in the evening?"

"Not a chance. He's a boarder, and they rarely get out at night. So once a week I go over there, and then it's his turn to come here. Neither of us has been spotted yet, and I've been awfully lucky with lifts."

He eyed the legs. He could see why.

"How old are you?"

"Nearly seventeen."

"That means sixteen and one month."

She laughed. "You're quick on the uptake. How old are you?"

"Nearly twenty-four."

She laughed again. "I said you were quick. What do you do?"

"I'm going to be a doctor."

"Really?" She sounded interested. "Why? Doesn't being with sick people give you the morbs? It would me."

"You might be sick yourself one day, and then you'd feel differently."

"Sick!" With the arrogance of perfect health she dismissed the notion as preposterous.

"Do you want dropping near the school? Where are you and this boy meeting?"

"In a field." She grinned. "We've found a super hollow right next to the rugby field. Saucy, eh? Especially as he's captain of rugby next season."

Luke looked at her. She was lying back in the seat with her eyes half-closed and an ecstatic expression on her face. He slowed the car down and did a U-turn, which threw her against him and made her open her eyes and sit up.

"Why are you turning round?"

"I'm taking you back to your school."

"But why? What's the matter?"

"I don't like to hear of kids smooching in fields. I've seen a few like you end up in the labor ward of my hospital—or worse, in casualty."

She was indignant. "You've got a beastly mind. There's no question of anything like that. Not in broad daylight."

"Famous last words. People have been known to do that sort of thing outside the hours of darkness."

"Well, not me! I don't like the way you think, doc."

"I don't like the way you talk."

She eyed him with exasperation. "Honestly, you're making such a fuss. As if you were sixty-three instead of twenty-three. Haven't you ever had fun with a girl?"

"Not in a field."

"What a lot you've missed," she said coolly. "Mind you, chance is a fine thing. I would hate to go out with such a pious . . . " She struggled to find an epithet scathing enough, and after observing the sticklike arms and the long, bony legs protruding from the shabby shorts, she produced it triumphantly: " . . . scarecrow!"

He jammed on the brakes. "Out!"

She sighed. "Oh, dear! Did we leave our sense of humor at home this morning?"

"Just get out," he said.

She pondered for a moment. "It must be at least two miles back to school."

"Yes."

"You're going to make me walk?"

"That's right."

She swung her legs out of the car. "So long, doc. I only hope I'm never one of your patients. I should either be sermoned to death or die of frostbite."

He started the car and drove slowly, watching her through the rearview mirror. She swung along with an easy natural stride, and every now and then took a swipe at the top of the grass with her hockey stick. He fancied she was laughing. He stopped the car. It was such a dusty lane and a cloud was enveloping her. She caught up with him and passed without a sideways glance. She was singing! He let out the clutch and the car rolled abreast of her.

"Come on," he said. "I'll take you back."

She turned her head. "Stick it," she said sweetly.

He roared past her with ears burning. Ten minutes later, while stopped at a red light at the main road intersection, another car came alongside, a sleek cream Jaguar, with a man and girl in animated conversation. When the light changed, the Jaguar leapt ahead, and the honey-blonde, without interrupting her conversation, put her hand out of the window and gave a perfect V-for-victory sign.

The memory of that sign, and the girl who gave it, often intruded between Luke Howard and his medical books. Maybe it was an omen. He graduated cum laude, and a brilliant career was predicted for him.

But the horizon of his dream had widened. It now included long blonde hair blowing in the wind, and a look of ecstasy on a lovely face.

# 2

It took Luke Howard four years to catch up with the schoolgirl. By then, of course, she was no longer a schoolgirl. Neither was he a scarecrow.

The nurses of the Queen Elizabeth Hospital in St. Michael's-on-the-Sea had their own description for him: intriguing. Physically, he had matured into a striking man. The thin frame had acquired a lean hardness, the intense blue eyes were now clear and penetrating, and the stoop developed by years of book-poring was much less pronounced and not unattractive as he carried his six-foot, one-inch frame with long eager strides through the wards and research laboratories of the hospital complex.

Intriguing he might be, but regretfully his indifference to women became a byword. He smiled his shy attractive smile at the sister who was kind to his children. He scowled and was rude to the clumsy nurse. He made an enemy for life by his sarcasm to the good-looking female physiotherapist who refused to put one of his theories into practice. He simply didn't see further than his work.

Until the day when Julian burst in on him just after lunch.

Julian Goldberg was the first close friend that Luke had made. The only son of an eminent Manchester attorney, his absorption in the study of gynecology and obstetrics was as great as Luke's interest in the field of pediatrics. Thus, despite wide differences in upbringing, faith, and background, the two young doctors found a harmony of thought and opinion that began on the day they commenced their internship and deepened steadily during the months that followed.

There was yet another difference between them. Julian found time to play. And it was his gay coaxing that was responsible for Luke's reluctant excursions into the social life of the hospital. Excursions that of late had become far too time-consuming, so when Julian burst in on him, Luke paused in his writing and, before the other had time to speak, said firmly, "No. I won't make up any foursome, or take a blind date off your hands, or meet your cousin twice-removed at the railway station. I'm busy."

"Oh, come off it, old son! Have you forgotten what's happening this afternoon?"

"I'd have to be blind and deaf to be impervious to the fuss. Our new maternity wing is to be opened. Specially for Dr. Goldberg, it would appear. *Mazeltov*, Julian. Now, leave me in peace."

"Who is performing the opening ceremony?" Julian spoke patiently as if to a child.

"No idea."

"Don't you ever read further than your medical journals? Princess Tonia herself! Luke, this you've got to see! When this girl goes into action she's a sight for sore eyes. Come on! Her old man is giving a party afterwards, and I've wangled an invitation for both of us."

"Who on earth is Princess Tonia? She sounds like some decrepit member of an exiled aristocracy."

Julian sighed. "How ignorant can one be? She's the mayor's daughter, and because his wife's health is not too good, Tonia often deputizes for her mother. She'll cut the ribbon, be gracious to the mums, and coo over all the babies. But she'll make it such fun that we'll have a ball. Quite a contrast to the usual dreary chore where we all stand in line, smiling stiffly, feeling bored as hell inside."

"I don't understand the 'Princess' bit." Luke spoke absently and wished he could get on with his work.

"The local newspaper once dubbed her that because she reigned so beautifully over some function or other, and the bright young things in St.Michael's have never let her forget it. I could go overboard for her in a big way. Come and watch her perform."

"Not interested, my lad. Sorry, I just can't spare the time."

Julian thumbed through the newspaper he was carrying. He found what he was seeking and placed the paper hopefully on the desk in front of Luke. "There she is. At least have a look at her." He jabbed a finger at the column. "A nice picture, but she's even better in the flesh."

Luke glanced at the photograph. Then slowly put down his pen. With both hands he picked up the newspaper, and studied the laughing face for a full minute.

"I'll come," he said abruptly.

The lines of bunting fluttered gaily in the stiff breeze, and the many-hued dresses and hats of the women stood out in brilliant contrast against the white walls of the hospital and the soft green of the grass. On the small raised platform the mayor was making his speech.

Luke Howard stood right at the back of the crowd, his height enabling him to view the scene with ease. With narrowed eyes he scrutinized the girl on the dais.

She hadn't changed a great deal. Not physically.

The blonde hair, long and flowing and startingly fair against the hyacinth blue of her shantung suit, was exactly the same. So was the beautiful, mobile mouth, now more clearly accentuated by the use of vivid lipstick. And as he watched, she turned her head and murmured an aside, and the microphone picked up the mischievous little gurgle. That hadn't changed, either. Nor had the legs.

"Well?" asked Julian softly. "How do you like Daddy's little girl? Quite something, eh?"

Julian straightened his tie and ran a hand through his hair. "Once more into the breach, dear friend. Expect me when you see me."

With a wave of the hand and an exaggerated leer, he was gone.

Luke stretched his cramped back in disgust. The correct words and phrases just weren't forthcoming, and his concentration seemed to be sadly lacking. He wondered how Julian was faring. Rising and walking to the door, he opened it and put his head out into the corridor. No sign of life. Treading softly, he went along to Julian's room and tried the handle. The door was locked. He looked at his watch. Two a.m. Some party, he thought. He returned to his room and left the door ajar. Half an hour later he heard footsteps, and the next minute Julian appeared in the doorway.

"How was it?" asked Luke.

Julian propped himself against the doorpost and grinned wickedly. "I hit the jackpot. Some girl! I'll feed you the grisly details in the morning. Hell, but I'm dead beat!" He yawned hugely.

"The competition wasn't too stiff, then?"

"Compe— Oh, lord, I couldn't get near Tonia. Instead, I found me a cute little redhead. Wow! 'Night, old son."

"Good night, Julian."

"Not bad," said Luke.

"Not bad at all, and tonight I intend to exert all my legendary charm and see how far I can get with her. I reckon I can give the smart set down in town a bit of healthy competition." Julian grinned as his gaze wandered over the girl in blue. "Look at that luscious figure. Just my cup of tea!"

Luke stared at the other man's dark engaging face and black eloquent eyes, eyes which at this moment held a decided predatory glitter. He became very aware of the casual elegance, the slim expressive hands, the easy sophisticated charm of his manner and voice. By contrast, he felt gauche and uncouth, a clodhopper with blunt, broad-vowelled speech. He scowled as he turned his head again to the platform.

"Not your cup of tea, obviously!" Julian remarked blithely. "I'm surprised, but not sorry. She's just the kind of girl to go for a strong silent type like you, and I've got enough competition to contend with without having more on the doorstep."

"Very funny. About tonight . . . do you mind if I cry off? I've still got stacks of work to put into that paper . . . "

A burst of applause interrupted him, and he saw the mayoral party preparing to leave the platform.

Luke undressed and got into bed. He lay still for quite some time. Then he switched on the light, reached for the newspaper and looked again at the picture of Tonia Marshall. With a sudden, violent jerk of the wrist he sent the newspaper skimming across the floor. For Julian, maybe. Not for him.

The following night he commenced a tour of duty in Casualty. A fire broke out in the kitchen of The Horse Shoe nightclub, and all might have been well if the distraught chef had not lost his head and rushed into the dimly-lit restaurant screaming "Fire!" In the ensuing panic, an exit door jammed, people were trampled on and crushed, and three patrons and a young kitchen apprentice were severely burned.

Dr. Howard supervised the unloading of the ambulances and tried to calm the clamoring of shocked relatives and friends. One young man knelt by a girl lying on a stretcher, his face drawn and frightened. As Luke's hand gripped his shoulder, he looked up at him and stammered, "Is she going to die? She won't speak to me. Tell me she's not dead."

The girl's face was blackened with soot and grime, and her long hair reeked of smoke. One hand hung limp and was badly discolored and swollen, as if it had been stamped on, but there was no sign of any burns. Luke correctly diagnosed that she had been close to asphyxiation before being brought out of the building.

Her eyes slowly opened and focused on him. They remained blank for some time, and then he saw the crinkling begin at the corners.

"Good grief! It's the scarecrow. Heaven help me!"

She began to laugh weakly and was still laughing when oblivion again engulfed her.

Tonia Marshall's stay in the Queen Elizabeth Hospital was brief but memorable. She was interviewed and photographed and many of the town's most eligible bachelors were among those who crowded into the room where the Princess, her bruised hand proving no handicap, gaily held court twice a day to an admiring and appreciative audience.

Dr. Howard was not impressed. Nor amused. He became pompous and officious. He delayed visiting the patient as long as possible, and when duty eventually prevailed, there had been time to plan a course of action.

His opening gambit was crisply delivered. "Good morning, Miss Marshall. Been in any nice fields lately?"

It was childish, and as a tactical move it was a mistake.

"So, you remember," she cooed.

He took refuge in silence, picked up her chart from the bottom of the bed and proceeded to study it carefully.

She went over to the attack. "Luke," she murmured.

"Dr. Howard," he corrected her.

"Boloney, doc. You and I share a dusty past. We might as well be matey."

"You have enough mates," he commented sourly.

She shrugged a very smooth, bare shoulder at him. "Always room for one more."

"An invitation which is declined with thanks. Your temperature is up this morning."

"See what you do to me . . . Luke . . . "

He slammed the chart down and glared at her. "You know what you need, don't you?"

"Jam the door for a few minutes," she suggested. "Then we can both enjoy whatever it is that you think I need."

He conceded the first round to her and beat a hasty retreat, leaving a peal of mocking laughter behind him, but as the laughter floated away Tonia Marshall became unusually thoughtful. The despised shabby scarecrow had miraculously been transformed into this lean, attractive man, and she promptly made it her business to glean a little more information about the fascinating Dr. Howard. Luke! She'd never come across the name before. Old-fashioned, but she liked the sound of it.

The friendly nurse was only too eager to satisfy her curiosity: no wife, no fiancee, and definitely no girl friend. "Such a pity," she added regretfully. "One of the nicest— and most eligible—men in the hospital, but I don't think the woman exists who could arouse Dr. Howard's interest."

"Get thee behind me," murmured Tonia.

"I beg your pardon!" The nurse looked startled, but her patient was lying back with eyes closed, a tiny smile playing round her mouth. As Tonia recalled that brief encounter on a hot summer afternoon four years ago, she distinctly remembered seeing a fishing rod on the back seat of the little car.

She laughed softly. And decided to go fishing.

She played Dr. Howard with a skill that would have

15

aroused envy from the most dedicated fisherman. She toned down the impudence and stepped up the charm; switched off the charm and turned up the impudence. She played him backwards and forwards with an expertise which, she modestly conceded, was not bad—not bad at all. And by the end of the week, Luke was emotionally hooked and lay floundering, within sight of the net.

Then came a temporary setback. Luke saw the net and panicked. His work suffered, and he made an error, drawing a severe reprimand from one of the Senior Registrars, for it could have had fatal consequences. Smarting with humiliation, he retired to his room and sat with his head in his hands, gloomily reviewing the situation.

He knew perfectly well what had happened to him. This girl's presence was doing strange things, disturbing his concentration and causing his body to rebel against its celibate state. And because he was an innocent kind of man that meant only one thing. Marriage. Involvement with a girl inevitably lead to marriage. He had seen it happen with others, and therein lay his problem. He was neither ready nor willing to take such a step. His aim was specialization, and only when that was achieved would he have time for less important things. Marriage at some time in the future, he supposed. But not yet. Definitely not yet.

Tonia Marshall sat in the middle of his careful plan like a smouldering time bomb which, if exploded, would blow him and his blueprint sky-high. He had no illusions about her. She had the reputation of being one of the wildest in the town's bright young set. He'd seen the procession of young men filing in and out of her room, and the appearance of some of them made him feel sick. His face grew hot as he recalled the conversation at lunchtime between two colleagues who were gleefully recounting some of her escapades. Especially the time she appeared at the Country Club swimming pool in a costume that outraged all decency. . .

Luke shook his head clear. To entertain any idea of this girl as a doctor's wife would be committing professional suicide. In any case, a certain sentence rankled in his memory: Chance is a fine thing.

He stood up feeling that a battle had been won. Tomorrow there would be no retreating. He would go over to the offensive and play her at her own game. Now that he'd managed to become objective, it might not be quite so one-sided.

Early the next morning he stalked into her room with a curt, "Good morning." For once she was not smiling. The smooth golden hair framed a serious face, and the eyes were not crinkling, but grave and enormous. She looked very lovely. She also looked too angelic for words, and he regarded her with suspicion.

"Good morning, Dr. Howard," she said quietly.

He frowned. "No impudence for me today?"

She shook her head. "Will you please arrange my discharge? I want to go home."

He was unprepared for the hollow feeling in his stomach. He looked at her chart, and a feeling of relief swept through him. Her temperature, which inexplicably had been shooting up and down like a yo-yo, was still above normal. There could be no question of her discharge, and he told her so.

"I want to go home," she repeated. "I'm not sick enough to be occupying a valuable hospital bed. Surely, you agree?"

"No. When your temperature is normal, you can go. Until then, you're staying here."

He walked out, knowing that he was delighted at the respite. An hour later, a triple-car crash on the highway filled the casualty ward and drove all thought of her from his mind. It was not until late afternoon that he found himself back on the first-floor corridor looking for one of the staff nurses. As he passed Tonia's room, he saw the door half-open and automatically looked inside. He was two strides past before his mind registered what he had seen. He retraced his steps and looked in disbelief at the stripped bed and the woman who was sweeping the floor.

"What on earth is going on?" he asked, bewildered. "Where is Miss Marshall?"

The woman was just as perplexed. "I don't know, doctor. I was just told to clean the room."

"Who told you?"

"Sister Ellis."

He stormed into the sister's little office. "Where is Miss Marshall, and who gave permission for her to be moved?"

She stood up, taken aback by the tone of his voice. "Miss Marshall was discharged this morning. She's gone home."

"Who authorized the discharge?"

"Why, you did, Dr. Howard!"

"Did she tell you that?"

"Yes. I noticed that her temperature reading was still high, but she said she'd promised to stay in bed at home, and that you'd agreed to this. I never questioned her for one moment."

"It didn't occur to you to question me?"

The sister looked decidedly uncomfortable. "I knew there was something big going on in Casualty. I didn't think it necessary to disturb you. I'm sorry, Dr. Howard."

"You'll be sorrier still when matron gets through with you," Luke promised coldly. "I want a full written report of your conversation with Miss Marshall."

"Yes, doctor."

He went to see the matron. She listened to him attentively and then spoke frankly.

"If she chose to discharge herself, there's nothing we can do about it. Tonia has always been a law unto herself. . . a delightful girl, but a disrupting influence wherever she goes. Now stop worrying, Doctor Howard. Her mother is a sensible woman, and she'll keep an eye on her. In any case, the Tonia's of this world bear charmed lives, you know!"

For the first time in his life Luke Howard became a clock-watcher. Another three hours on duty. Within seconds of the minute hand pointing to seven, he was out of the building and into his car. He had never been to the Marshall home, but Tonia's mother received him with a warm smile. During visits to her daughter, she had spoken with the young doctor and liked him. "This certainly is devotion to duty," she teased. "I didn't expect anyone to check up on Tonia until tomorrow. Go upstairs, doctor, her bedroom is the first room on the right."

He didn't wait for an answer to his knock but walked in and shut the door firmly behind him. The girl on the bed looked at him calmly. "Are you calling on me in your professional or your personal capacity?"

"Does it matter?"

"Yes. I want to know if I'm receiving Luke or Doctor Howard. Then I shall behave accordingly."

The hot words he'd intended to say went cold. He leaned back against the closed door and looked at her. The space between them was his blueprint, his specialization, his future. He knew little about women, but her expression told him that chance no longer came into it. The decision was all his. In the quiet watching on her face, he had a momentary vision of how she would look in ten years, the wildness exhausted, the laughing softened, the prettiness deepened into beauty.

The tension went out of him, and he felt weak with relief. He smiled, a little shyly. He said, "Luke."

She took a deep breath as if the waiting had been long, and then she was Tonia in the present again. "Then for heaven's sake, don't tell Mummy! She'll have you out of my bedroom in five seconds flat, and I want you in it. I'm

19

dying to kiss you, Luke. That's why I left the hospital. I couldn't stand the temperature chart between us any longer."

This time it was Luke who laughed. He put his head back and laughed for all the solemn days without this impudent girl. And Tonia joined in, not really understanding the depth of his laughter, but simply because it was good to hear him laugh.

Mrs. Marshall, about to come up the stairs, stopped with her foot on the first step and listened approvingly. She knew perfectly well that Luke had no right to be visiting professionally, but it would be a healthy change to have this nice young doctor interested in Tonia. Maybe he would calm her down a little. She needed a steadying influence, and he looked as though a little laughter would do him a lot of good. She turned back, chuckling softly to herself. They could have another five minutes together.

Thus the smouldering fuse of the time bomb called Tonia was ignited, fanned into flame by a little shyness, a great deal of impudence, and peal after peal of laughter.

# 3

Luke expected . . . well, what did he expect? There had been so many rumours, so much gossip . . .

His only knowledge of women was confined to his work and the social gatherings connected with the hospital, so he had no yardstick to guide him and little experience with which to make comparisons. And Tonia Marshall was a revelation to him in more ways than one.

He expected the impudence that was always bubbling on or near the surface, which manifested itself in the mischievous gray eyes, the quirky mouth, and the long hair that danced a lively jig whenever she tossed her head. He received it in full measure.

He expected the laughter that formed such an integral part of her makeup. It shattered his world of solemnity, a fact that was revealed in the little smile which played round his mouth each time he thought of her and her nonsenses.

He expected a spoilt, pampered girl. He found a refreshing candor as she openly conceded her faults, and her heartfelt sigh, "I do try. Really, I do!" seemed genuine enough. Certainly her hot flares of temper were followed by an equally quick contrition, and a strong willful streak was tempered by glimpses of surprising humility.

What he had not expected was the warmth. As an only child, with his one parent thrust into the triple role of mother, father, and breadwinner, he learnt early in life to become self-sufficient. But deep down he was a lonely boy. The mutual pride of mother and son had forged a deep love between them, but one which did not result in any outward show of affection. Ann Howard was not a demonstrative person. Tonia was. And the joyous uninhibited warmth that flowed from her took him by storm. It surged out and enveloped him and penetrated every part of his being, carrying him bewildered from an old world into a new.

Another thing he had not expected was the discovery of a deep-thinking intelligence submerged beneath the layer of impudence. It rarely surfaced, but when it did he was startled, and then impressed, by the rational thoughts so unexpectedly voiced by the laughing mouth.

"Why didn't you go on to university from high school?" he inquired on one such occasion. "A bright girl like you could have gotten in with ease."

"Because this bright girl has other plans."

"Such as?"

She became deliberately vague. "I'm going to go awandering. A wandering minstrel girl with my guitar tucked underneath my arm. Can you see me as a super gipsy, Luke? My trouble is that I have a fondness for soap and water, and I don't know whether even a super gipsy is allowed all mod cons. I shouldn't think so."

"Well, don't wander just yet, will you? I've only just found you, and I couldn't possibly spare you to any gipsy camp, however super."

"What an admission, Doctor Howard," she teased. "Whoever would have thought that a rude little schoolgirl and a disapproving scarecrow could form such a beautiful friendship."

"It is beautiful, Tonia. For me."

Impulsively she covered his hand with hers. "Yes, Luke. For me, too. Fate moves mysteriously, doesn't it? I think we both owe a vote of thanks to the schoolboy who was responsible for my being in that dusty lane." Her eyes sparkled. "Pity it's turned cold! I could have introduced you to the hollow in that field."

He shook his head at her. "You little monkey! If you only knew how much I envied your rugby captain that day. What happened to him, by the way?"

"Haven't a clue. I can't even remember his name. I got bored with him very quickly, he loved himself too much. The complete contrast to you. Have you any idea how attractive you are, Luke?"

"Tonia!" She embarrassed him when she talked like this.

"Well, you are, and not realizing it only makes you more attractive. When I was in hospital, the only bright spot in the day was when you stalked in and looked down your long nose at me. Do you know, darling, you're the only man who's ever looked at me like that. You were quite a challenge."

They were dining in one of the town's most popular night spots, and her attention was suddenly distracted by two people who had just entered. "Hey, there's Angela coming in with Roger. Doesn't the candlelight do magical things to that flame-colored hair of hers?" She stood up and waved wildly until the couple noticed and signaled in return. The man had a quick word with the head waiter, who looked across and nodded, and Luke watched approvingly as the two began threading their way between the tables toward them.

This petite, rather serious girl and her regular escort, Roger, were the only two people in Tonia's set for whom he could truthfully say he had any time. The girl, he specially liked. Tonia had insisted on his meeting her before anyone else, saying simply, "My dearest friend, Angela Morris. Luke Howard. Please like each other."

The liking had been instant and mutual, and they often found themselves quietly entertaining one another during the more exuberant occasions when Roger indulged Tonia in her current passion for dancing.

She greeted them now with the blunt familiarity of

long friendship. "Hi! Are you joining us, or do you want to be alone?"

"Joining you, unless Luke objects strongly," Angela replied.

"He's probably quite relieved to see you. I've just been making him blush by telling him how handsome he is. Mind you, handsome is as handsome does. And he still does not jive!"

Roger gave a mock groan. "Not again, Princess! My feet still ache from our last session. Angela, shall I humor her and get it over with?"

"Do," she said promptly. "I shall sit sedately with Luke and enjoy it just as much."

"Come on then, you pest!" Roger laughingly pulled Tonia to her feet and led her onto the tiny dance floor. They flung themselves animatedly into the beat, and while Luke watched Tonia, Angela watched Luke and saw in his face the familiar repetition of what she had seen a dozen times before. All Tonia's boyfriends wore this eager adoration sooner or later, but with this man she fancied it went deeper.

He turned unexpectedly and surprised her intent study of him before she could look away.

"Does it show so much, Angela?"

"Yes, Luke. Does she mean so much?"

"Yes."

"Well, I think she's quite something, too. I've known her all my life, and to me, she's always been that little bit special."

"Tonia told me that you've been friends since kindergarten. You two must have had a lost of fun together. She has the greatest capacity for enjoyment I've ever seen and a zest for living that never ceases to astound me. Just look at her!"

They watched the gyrations of the couple for a few moments in silence, then Luke asked abruptly, "Angela, am

I going to last with her? Will she get bored? These last weeks have been happy ones for me, and I'm terrified that sooner or later the bubble will burst."

She chose her reply carefully because she had witnessed the bursting of many a similar bubble. "I think you'll last a long time because you're so different."

"Meaning I'm just a novelty to her?"

"Oh, no!" She was a little distressed. "I don't mean different in that sense. It goes deeper than that. The other men she's known have all conformed to a certain pattern. You stand quite apart." A telltale tide of color swept into her face. "I hope you'll last a long time, Luke. You're good for her."

He grimaced. "Good for her! That's what I'm afraid of! Just think of the things that are supposed to be good for us. Aren't they usually dull and dreary? But the forbidden things, the ones on the wrong side of the fence—they're exciting and heady, and we reach out for them. Angela, you've placed me in the wrong category for the right reasons, but please don't tell Tonia I'm good for her. Otherwise, I won't last out the night! Here she comes."

Tonia flopped down beside them, hot and breathless and exhilarated. "That was simply fabulous. Luke, my sweet, if you don't learn to dance soon, I shall write you off as a dull doctor and find someone who can. You don't know what you're missing."

The affection in her eyes as they rested on him belied the words. Luke knew that she was teasing; Angela knew that she was teasing; but they carefully avoided looking at each other. And Luke decided he'd better learn to stumble round the floor.

Julian didn't like it. He didn't like it at all. In fact, he was uneasy about the whole setup. To his astonishment—

and not a little, to his consternation—he had become greatly protective of Luke, having recognized early in their acquaintance that this quiet, dedicated man was a walking anachronism. Here was a man who kept abreast of every modern development in the medical world, who was perfectly and naturally at home in a world of children, but who was lagging years behind in a world of sophistry and permissiveness and laughing women.

Not so Julian. Julian loved present-day life in all its shapes and forms, and if the shapes and forms were female, so much the better. He easily accepted that the world was not a clean, shining sphere of bluebirds and sunsets, with pots of gold waiting at the end of the rainbow, but a teeming, seething hodgepodge of saints and sinners—an incredible mixture that was half-good, half-bad. And with the honest identification of himself as such, went out gaily and unscrupulously to meet life, not on its terms, but on his own.

He played hard and worked hard, and reaped the benefits of both worlds. He disturbed his mother and pleased his father, in whose image he was cast. He also pleased woman; and women were all too ready to please Julian.

All except Tonia Marshall, whom he antagonized at first sight.

On the day that she was admitted to the hospital, Julian left to attend a medical congress in Edinburgh, and on his return, he spent a few days in Manchester with his parents. Knowing nothing of the events that had taken place, he walked right into them. Literally walked into them. They were coming out of Jackson's Department Store— Luke, and Tonia Marshall. And they were walking hand in hand. Julian came to a sudden stop and screwed up his eyes briefly as if the glare was hurting him. Except that it was a dull, dismal day, and there was no sun.

Walking hand in hand, which Tonia insisted upon, was the most embarrassing thing that Luke had experienced. The first time it happened they were walking in a country lane, and Luke Howard looked down on the silky fair hair, the hospital forgotten. Tonia turned up her face and smiled, and with the most natural of gestures took his hand, laced her fingers into his, and continued as though nothing untoward had happened. Which simply was the case, as far as she was concerned. Some people are born touchers, and with complete ease of manner, she touched. Luke felt a little dazed. From time to time, he stole surreptitious glances, to convince himself that he was strolling hand in hand with a girl, and a lovely girl at that. He hoped fervently, however, that none of the hospital staff would come along, and when one or two cars passed by, he went hot under the collar at the thought that Rivingham folk could well be inside.

Thankfully, however, they met no one who recognized him.

The next time she repeated the gesture, they were in a crowded thoroughfare in town, and Luke suffered further agonies of embarrassment. He withdrew his hand on the pretext of using it to point to something, but the moment his hand dropped, Tonia reached for it again. After a few more subterfuges, the message got through. She stood still in the middle of the pavement and looked at him coolly.

"Are you ashamed to be seen walking with me?"

He assured her that he was not.

"Then stop tugging your hand away. This is my way of telling the whole world that I'm with you, and that I like being with you. But of course if you don't like it, we can end it here and now."

Because he didn't know her very well, and was unsure of her—and of himself—he said, "I like it."

The odd thing was that deep down inside, he did! After that, they walked hand in hand everywhere, and once Luke actually made the first move, which made Tonia laugh. And then, during the second week, as they were leaving Jackson's, he saw Julian. His subconscious reflex was a quick attempt to withdraw his hand, but Tonia looked swiftly up at him, followed his gaze to the man who stood waiting, and instantly tightened her grip. As they reached Julian, Luke saw his eyes linger pointedly on the clasped hands before his eyebrows shot up in their sardonic, mocking way.

"Congratulations, old son. I must go away more often if this is the kind of lovely mischief you get into the minute my back's turned."

As he spoke, his eyes raked Tonia from head to foot in a studied appraisal that raised two brilliant spots of color on her cheekbones. He gave a mock bow. "Your Royal Highness! Salaams!"

"Cut it out," Luke said uncomfortably. "Tonia, Dr. Julian Goldberg. You could call him the opposite number to Angela. He's just as nice, too, when he stops fooling and behaves himself."

Julian grinned. "Behave myself? What a wicked waste of time. Now this Angela girl sounds promising. Is she as gorgeous as Princess here?"

"The name is Tonia," she said icily.

Julian put his head on one side and surveyed her through amused eyes. "The way you look right now, Princess couldn't be better, believe me! Luke, I can't linger, I'm late as it is. See you back at the salt mine." He gave Tonia an odd, derisive little smile. "A pleasure meeting you."

Her eyes snapped angrily at his retreating back. "What an objectionable man. What could you possibly have in common?"

"Work. He has a brilliant brain. I don't know why he puts on such an act with women, because he's not like that in the hospital. I'm afraid he's given you the wrong impression."

"Wrong impression, my foot! I know his type through and through. He reminds me of the rugby captain—the one who loved himself to bits. Just don't include me in any outings with him, or the fur will really fly. And now let's change the subject."

Later, back in the hospital, Julian cornered Luke. There was no amusement in his eyes now.

"How the hell did you get linked up with her? Don't you recognize dynamite when you see it?"

"I'm in love with her," Luke said quietly.

Julian snorted. "In love! In love! After living like a monk for years, you're ripe for the plucking by any woman who flutters her lashes at you. But you should have graduated via your pure village maidens before taking on someone like her."

"Is that a veiled hint that I'm straying out of my class?"

"Hell, no! Not in that sense. Don't always act so bloody sensitive about your background. Anyone would think you were ashamed of it. Look, old son, when you were a first-year student, you'd have been a bit floored to have had to cope with surgery when you hadn't even completed anatomy and physiology. Right? In the same context, I'm suggesting that it would be wiser to have your first romantic dallyings with someone on your own level. A rank amateur, to be blunt."

"You can keep your suggestions to yourself. In any case, haven't you altered your tune a little? In the beginning, you were very keen on her for yourself. It was you who begged me to go and watch her at the opening ceremony. You, who couldn't praise her enough. You, who said she was just your cup of tea. Now she's with me. Sour grapes, Julian?"

The two men glowered at each other, until Julian burst out laughing and clapped Luke on the back. "That's probably what it is, old son. I'm jealous as hell, and I can't even fight you for her. You're much bigger than I am! I'll have to fall back on my opposite number—the Angel. What about an introduction?"

It was Luke's turn to laugh. "Angela? Nothing doing there, I'm afraid. Still, you never know!"

A week later, Angela and Roger were invited to attend a concert at the hostpital. At the last moment Roger was unable to come, but Luke could see no reason why Angela should forego the entertainment and said so. When she demurred, "Two's company, three's a crowd," he pleaded with her to come.

"I want you to do me a favor. Tonia has taken a most unreasonable dislike to my one close friend, and I've asked him to join us tonight, ostensibly to escort you, but really to give Tonia another opportunity of meeting him. Maybe this time, they'll get on better." He looked anxiously at her. "You don't mind? I assure you I'm not trying to interfere between you and Roger. That's the last thing I'd want to do."

"I don't mind at all. I'm only too glad to help, but when Tonia gets a fixation about something—or someone. Well, you'll see!"

He saw only too well. Julian was at his charming best, not only toward Angela but Tonia as well. It made not the slightest difference. Her patent hostility did not lessen, and she made no effort to hide it.

When Angela remonstrated with her, she reiterated doggedly, "I just don't like him. I can't put my finger on it, but there's something about him that puts my back up. Thank goodness we shan't meet often."

Her surmise was wrong. The hospital circle was a small one, and she and Julian were thrust constantly into each other's company. They attended the same gatherings and danced at the same parties. They were invited to the same homes, and for Luke's sake, because he was genuinely distressed by the friction between them, she hid her antagonism beneath an outward air of banter, which fooled everyone except Julian himself.

She refused to alter her first opinion of him.

# 4

The year turned. And February brought the snow, together with an influenza epidemic that spread rapidly through the town, paralyzing businesses and schools and reducing the hospital staff to an alarming figure. Luke was on of the lucky ones who escaped, although *lucky* was a debatable word. He found himself doing double shifts of duty that left him bone-weary and swaying on his feet with fatigue, wanting nothing more than to reach his room and fall asleep until the shrilling of the alarm clock brought him upright again, with the feeling that a mere six minutes had elapsed instead of as many hours.

Tonia was not behaving well. Both her mother and father succumbed to the flu, but it passed her by, with the result that her energy and vitality were as boundless as ever but sorely frustrated by being cooped up indoors.

The weather was shockingly bad, and monotonous gray days dragged into long gray evenings that began as early as half-past three in the afternoon, when the leaden skies forced the electric lights on, ushering in the lonely interminable hours. Hours without Luke. Therein lay the real source of her frustration. From their first meeting, all his spare moments had been spent dancing attendance on her, and now she had to sit and wait while he attended others. It was a new experience for her, and she hated it. She also hated herself a little for resenting having to take second place.

She scolded her spoilt half: Don't be so unworthy of

him. He can't help it. He's doing a good job.

It retorted: Surely he could manage to slip away for an hour? That isn't asking the impossible. And why can't he at least telephone?

Her mother, still confined to bed, interpreted the arguments by the petulance on her daughter's face. "I know how much you must be missing Luke, dear, but is it really necessary to make such a martyr of yourself?"

Tonia blew up. "Ten whole days I've been hanging around waiting for him. Is he so indispensable that the wretched hospital can't manage without him for just one evening?"

"Grow up, Tonia," her mother advised quietly. "Luke is a man, not an irresponsible boy. I'm quite sure he's missing you just as much, but while this emergency lasts, he's not the type to get his priorities mixed. He's got a tough job of work to do. When it's finished, there'll be time for you again."

The girl steadied herself. "Sorry, Mummy. I'm behaving like a spoilt brat. I don't know what's wrong with me."

"Could it be that you're in love? Really in love for the very first time?"

"I've been wondering . . . Do you ever really know? When you met Daddy, did you know straight away?"

Her mother sighed reminiscently. "Yes, I knew. He was the right man for me, but it took three years to convince him that I was the right girl for him."

"Three years! That's a small lifetime. If I had to wait so long for someone to make up his mind about me, I'd lose interest. In any case, I've always dreamed that one day love would walk up to me and sock me right in the eye. Wham! I'd hear music playing and bells ringing and *know* I was in love."

"You've been seeing too many romantic films, dear. It doesn't happen that way at all. It's a gradual process—first the liking, then the affection, and finally the dependence on each other, which leads to love."

32

Tonia shook her head. "Too long-winded. I'll stick to my dream."

"Does Luke fit into your dream? The bells ringing and the music playing?"

The telephone rang before she could answer, and she smiled at her mother. "Bells ringing, it is! If it's Luke, then I'll take it as an omen."

She picked up the phone eagerly. "Yes? Luke! Yes, yes . . . fifteen minutes."

Her mother looked anxiously at the window. "Darling, it's throwing it down. You can't go anywhere in this weather. Why don't you stay in the lounge where it's nice and warm. We won't disturb you, and it will be a welcome change for Luke after the staff residence."

Tonia was determined. "We're going out. I need a change, too. Now don't fuss, we're not going to walk in the rain, just drive in it."

She was in the doorway watching for him, and in his car almost before it stopped. Not only in his car but in his arms, saying incoherently, "Oh, Luke, Luke, Luke . . ." After the enforced separation, he was just as eager for her, and they hugged and kissed and nibbled at each other with a hunger that had never manifested itself before. When they eventually came up for breath, he said unsteadily, "Just as well we don't have to endure being parted too often."

He put her from him and started the car. "Where would you like to go?"

"Nowhere. I just want to be like this with you."

"You mean . . . in the car? We can't drive around in this!"

"I don't want to drive." Her eyes crinkled as she pressed close to him again. "Let's go and find a parking place on top of Fisher's Hill."

He took a deep breath. "No," he said.

"Why not?"

He knew the answer but was too shy to admit it. The

33

fever of their reunion had made his body tingle with anticipation; he dared not trust himself to sit with her for a
couple of hours in a parked car. But his muttered excuse
sounded feeble even to his ears: "Someone might come
along and see us."

"Oh, for crying out loud!"

The scorn in her voice made him wince. He said,
"There's a film showing at the Odeon that's supposed to be
good. Shall we try it?"

"As you please." She kept her face averted for the rest
of the journey.

The film had already started when they took their
seats, and it was difficult to try and figure out what had
gone before. In any case, it was mediocre, and Luke was
conscious of Tonia twisting restlessly in her seat. Halfway
through the showing, she nudged him. "I've had enough of
this. It's ridiculous sitting here for sitting's sake. I'm going."

She got to her feet and began picking her way over the
stretched-out legs with a series of "Excuse me's." He had
no option but to follow. They stood in the foyer and looked
through the glass of the revolving doors at the rain, still
coming down heavily.

"What now?" she asked. "I do wish you had a place of
your own, Luke. There's a fish-and-chip shop somewhere
near here. Do you fancy any?"

He wrinkled his nose, and she noticed it.

"Oh, don't be so superior," she told him sharply. "Better people than you have eaten fish and chips—out of a
newspaper, too, with their fingers. You should try it."

She walked through the doors onto the pavement and
peered down the road. "I think there's a coffee bar or
something down there. At least, we'll get out of the rain."

With her head down, she began to run, and again, he
followed.

The coffee bar was tatty and none too clean, and when
the waiter brought the coffee, Tonia eyed the thick white

cups with distaste. Gingerly she tasted the brown liquid. She shuddered. "Ugh.".

Luke said nothing. The longed-for evening was proving a miserable fiasco. He knew that he should have planned to take her somewhere nice, but with the uncertainty of off-duty hours, it hadn't been possible. Where on earth could they go?

Tonia glared at him and banged her cup down with such a force that the coffee splashed into the saucer.

"Why can't we be honest with each other? You know .perfectly well what we both wanted tonight. We could have stayed in the car where it was warm and cosy and put some music on and snuggled up to each other and caught up with all that's been happening these last ten days. But, no! The dignity of the medical profession must be upheld, and nice up-and-coming doctors don't neck in parked cars. So we sit through a lousy film. We don't eat fish and chips because Doctor Howard would look down his long nose and think it wasn't nice. And we end up in a dirty dump like this drinking undrinkable coffee." She stood up. "I'm going home. By bus!"

She was through the doorway before he could stop her. With his raincoat only half on, he was going after her, until a startled shout from the waiter made him realize that he still owed for the coffee. Cursing under his breath, he almost threw the coins into the man's hand, then hurried into the street. Tonia was already some distance away, practically at the bus shelter, and by the time he reached her, the misery had given way to anger.

"That's the third time you've left me tonight, and I'm sick of chasing after you like a blessed puppy. Don't you dare go home on the bus. I brought you out, and I'll take you back. Stay here while I fetch the car."

She stared stonily past him, and he made an exclamation of annoyance before swinging round and walking away. He had gone about ten yards when the bus came round the corner. He stopped and looked back. She had moved to the edge of the pavement and was holding up her hand to request the bus to stop.

"The little . . ." He had to go back.

"Tonia, don't go home without me. Please!" The bus drew alongside, and the driver looked inquiringly through the cab window. The girl slowly lowered her hand, and Luke shook his head at the man who gave a brief salute of acknowledgment before the bus trundled away.

"I'll go and fetch the car," he said. "I'll be as quick as I can."

She still wouldn't speak, but he was relieved to see her move back into the shelter. Fretting inwardly, it seemed an eternity before he returned with the car, and only when she was inside it once more did he breathe freely. Instead of heading for where she lived, he turned the car in the opposite direction.

"Home, please," she said haughtily.

Ignoring her, he drove the car up Fisher's Hill and parked it well off the road. The he turned to take her in his arms, but she struggled and tried to resist him.

"Don't touch me," she almost spat at him. "I practically had to ask you to make love to me, and I don't want it now."

"Just be quiet," he said. "Keep still."

"Let *go* of me. We're through!" She strained furiously away from him and attempted to break his grasp, but he held her firmly until she went limp and subsided against him, trembling. He stroked her hair until she was calmer, and they remained like that for some time listening to the rain drumming on the roof. Then Luke reached out with one hand and fiddled with the radio until he got some music.

"Tonia?"

"Mmm?"

"Are we through?"

"Yes." But it was a very half-hearted little murmur.

"No. Tonia, I want to kiss you."

"You don't have to," she said.

He smothered a tiny sigh, but she heard it and was ashamed of her childishness. She sat up and shook her hair back and gave him a wan smile.

"Sorry, Luke. I've behaved badly. I'm all right now."

"You are always all right to me," he said.

He pulled her to him, and she turned her face up willingly. He kissed her gently. "What you said was true. I've been longing to do this." He kissed her again, not gently this time, but with an ardor that was eminently satisfying to them both.

"Now it's your turn," he said. "See if you can better that."

"Huh. Nothing to it." She returned the kiss in full measure, and they smiled radiantly at each other.

"I could do this all night," he said.

She snuggled even closer. "Let's." He loved the feel of her arms around his neck and the warmth of her body pressing against his.

Suddenly the kissing was not enough. Not for Luke. A longing surged through his veins, and he knew what he craved. It was the warmth. It filtered through the thick, winter clothing as a tangible thing, and he wanted to reach out fearfully and wonderfully and trace it to its source.

He had never touched a woman intimately, with love, and his sensitive hands lingered with delight over the sweet places of her body. The softness of her he found unbelievable. He could feel her trembling, and it made him very tender. He looked at her enraptured face and was exultant.

Outside the rain ran down the windows like a slow, continuous curtain, but the car was an island in the midst of the water.

The music on the radio ceased, and from afar they heard a series of pips and the calm, measured tones of the announcer informing them that the time was ten o'clock and inviting them to listen to the weekly play. The voice shattered the spell. As they reluctantly moved apart, it was Tonia who voiced the protest for them both.

The drive down the hill and through the town was a silent one. It was still raining when Luke brought the car to a halt, and as he took his hands off the wheel to open the door, Tonia stopped him.

"Don't get out. There's no point in us both getting wet. I can see myself in."

He didn't offer to kiss her. Instead, he did something he had not done before. He took hold of her hand, turned it upwards, and bent and pressed his lips into the curved palm.

He said, "Thank you, Tonia."

She didn't pretend to misunderstand. Sudden tears filled her eyes. She replied, "You were very welcome."

He watched her run up the garden path, unlock the door, and enter the house.

Driving back to the hospital he was stern and unsmiling and very thoughtful.

The next afternoon Luke managed to get another couple of hours off duty. He did not go to see Tonia. Instead, he went home to talk to his mother.

# ✼ 5 ✼

Luke liked going home. He liked Rivingham. In a changing world, Rivingham appeared changeless, and the reassuring permanency of the cobblestoned market place always produced a glow akin to putting on a warm coat on a cold day.

It was not a pretty village; pretty was a word the inhabitants would have scorned. In a sober hard-working community there were no modern concessions, the stolid folk remaining faithful to a traditional way of life, doggedly resisting change.

Luke ruefully acknowledged, however, that at times this resistance was carried to excess. He still remembered the furor when his mother's decision to allow him to study medicine became known.

"Doctor? University?" His Uncle Will's eyebrows shot up into his hairline, and his Auntie Mary said bluntly that Ann Howard needed her head examined. That this was what came of letting the lad go to grammar school, where he mixed with those who talked posh and gave him ideas above his station. Both her lads had been taken out of school at fourteen and put to learn an honest trade, and what was good enough for them ought to be good enough for Luke.

But his mother was quietly adamant. If Luke had it in him to become a doctor, he was to be given the chance. From somewhere she found the money for the initial fees, and only when he was older did he appreciate the magnitude of that decision and the sacrifices made by her on his behalf.

Now he was to discuss another, equally momentous decision, and although no longer a schoolboy, it was with a schoolboy's trepidation that he turned his car into the familiar street where his mother lived.

She kept a little shop. The blinds were down, and remembering that it was early closing day, he put his finger on the bell marked "Private" and was relieved to see a shadow behind the lace curtains at the upstairs window.

His mother's face lit up as she answered the door, but once she'd greeted him, she drew back and examined him critically. "You look as though a good night's sleep wouldn'd do you any harm. Have you had this wretched flu?"

"Now who's the doctor?" he teased. "Go and put the kettle on. I've come to talk, and you know it's impossible for you to listen without a cup of tea in your hand."

"True enough." She led the way upstairs to the flat and he followed, sniffing appreciatively the familiar smell of homemade baking.

"What do you want to talk about? Something special?"

"Yes." Luke reached for a scone. "These yours? I thought you told me your baking days were over."

"Oh, I have fits and starts when I feel like doing a bit. I must have known you were coming. What's so important to bring you over here in the middle of an afternoon?"

"Wait until the kettle's boiled and we can sit down and concentrate. While we're waiting, I'll give you a tune."

"That'll be nice. No one ever touches the piano nowadays."

She stood in the doorway and watched him straddle the piano stool and idly run his fingers over the keys. Now what's coming, she thought. Something's bothering him, and it isn't only lack of sleep.

A few minutes later she carried the tea through to the sitting room, seated herself, and eyed her son expectantly. "Right," she said. "What's up, Luke?"

"Mother, I want to bring a girl home to meet you."

Her mouth fell open. "Well, not before time! I'd

begun to think I'd be in my dotage before you made me a granny."

"Hang on," he protested in mock alarm. "I haven't got her to the altar yet."

"You must be halfway down the aisle all the same, otherwise you'd never be asking me to meet her."

"Look, I know that in your day, if a boy brought a girl home, it automatically meant wedding bells . . . "

"It still does in Rivingham," she said darkly. "If one of my neighbours sees you bringing a girl in here, I'll be asked the date of the wedding the minute you've gone."

He grinned. "I'd better smuggle her in after dark, then."

Her eyes were as bright and as unwinking as a bird's. "Who is she, Luke? A St. Michael's girl?"

"Yes." He took a deep breath. "Her name's Marshall. Tonia Marshall."

"Marshall?" She puckered her brow. "Don't know any-one of that . . . . Luke! Not the daughter of the mayor?"

"Yes. Do you know her?"

"I know *of* her. Is there anyone round here who doesn't?"

"She's an extremely nice girl."

"And an extremely wild one, so I've heard."

"Don't believe all you've heard. You've always kept an open mind, Mother. At least reserve judgment until you've met her. It's important to me."

"Is it?" Her fingers tightened round the handle of the teapot. "Are you serious about this girl?"

"Yes."

"Oh, son . . . " Her stunned voice faltered into si-lence, and the atmosphere was suddenly tense. She poured herself another cup of tea and was annoyed to see how her hand was trembling. She hoped that Luke wouldn't notice. Making an effort to appear natural, she said, "You'd better tell me about her. How old is she?"

"She'll be twenty-one in May."

"How long have you known her?"

"I met her toward the end of last summer. She was slightly injured in that nightclub fire."

His mother's lips tightened. "Nightclub. Not a very suitable place for a girl of twenty to be found in. Have you started going to such places?"

"Occasionally. They're not all dens of iniquity—and I'm not twenty," he reminded her.

"More's the pity in a situation like this."

"I don't understand that remark."

She looked at him sitting rigidly on the edge of the couch, his long legs drawn up, the cup of tea in his hand untasted, his face wary and defensive.

"How many girls have you been out with, Luke?"

"That's irrelevant. I know my own mind."

"I don't think you do. So you can listen while I speak my mind and tell you what's wrong with you. You're going through a bad dose of puppy love, that's what! By rights, you should have got this behind you and learnt a bit about women in the process. But you'd more important things to do when you were twenty—like finding the money to put yourself through medical school." Her voice became urgent. "You've always been a sensible lad, son. Don't make a fool of yourself now! This Marshall girl—all Rivingham has hummed at some time or other about her goings-on, and there's no smoke without fire. A doctor's wife is supposed to have a certain discretion, a standing in the community. How much standing d'you reckon she'll give you?"

She paused for breath. "I'd better fill the tea-pot. I can see I'm going to drink gallons."

Her stiff back bristling with disapproval, she left the room, leaving Luke silent and miserable. When she returned, he said, "Now it's my turn. Will you listen, Mother? Really listen, without interrupting?"

"Well, I'll try. Go on. Let's hear what you've to say."

"Tonia may have been a bit wild in the past. I've also

heard some of the stories and I don't like the sound of them any more than you do. But she's young and very lovable, and people tend to spoil her. Give her time, though. As she gets older, she'll settle down, but at the moment I wouldn't want her any different from what she is. Mum . . . " He hesitated and then pleaded, "Mum, I love her. Please try to understand!"

Mum! He hadn't called her that since he was quite small, and the grown man's lapse into the childish term affected her greatly. She got up and poked the fire vigorously.

"Is she a church-going girl?"

"No," he said bluntly.

"Religion?"

"Same as us."

"Well, that's one blessing, I suppose. When's the wedding to be?"

He let out his breath. "I haven't asked her yet."

She straightened up, still holding the poker. "My, but you are old-fashioned, Luke. Not many men would tell the mother before the girl. I appreciate that. Well, when am I going to see her?"

"Sunday afternoon?"

"I'd better do a bit more baking, then."

He rose to go. Their glances met, and Luke put his arms round his mother and hugged her silently. She stayed in his embrace, startled, before breaking away. "You big softie," she murmured. "Go on with you. I'll be ready for you on Sunday."

He was halfway down the stairs when she called to him. "Luke?"

He looked at her. "Yes?"

"I hope this Tonia girl realizes how lucky she is."

He grinned. "I'll ask her, along with the other question."

He didn't get the chance.

Sunday afternoon came, and they got off to a good start. Tonia was bubbling over with high spirits, and once she knew that Luke was free for the rest of the day, there was no containing her. Her dancing vitality had never been more evident, and she looked particularly lovely in a figure-hugging, gay-striped sweater, with a cheeky tam-o'-shanter perched at a ridiculous angle on her blonde hair.

He held her at arm's length, and they appraised each other eagerly. "I've been counting the minutes since last Wednesday," he said.

A tenderness crept into the smiling gray eyes. "Me too."

Hand in hand they walked down the path toward his car. As they drove away, she said, "Angela's just phoned. Roger's turned up with some new records, and they want us to go over and stay for supper. Isn't that nice?"

"Yes, but we're not going. I've got a V.I.P. meeting lined up for you this afternoon."

"Really? That sounds intriguing. Someone special?"

"I think so. I'm taking you to meet my mother."

He was unprepared for her look of panic, and took a hand off the wheel to squeeze her knee reassuringly.

"It's all right. I've prepared the ground. I hurried over last Thursday to tell her all about you."

She went very quiet, and with her transparent face, he could almost see the gaiety evaporating. Puzzled, he wondered what was going through her mind. They were well clear of St. Michael's before she spoke, jerkily, "Luke, please stop the car. There's something we've got to get straight between us."

He felt bewildered and a little chilled. "Can't it wait until afterwards? We're late already. You're not nervous about Mother, are you?"

"No, I'm not nervous. I just don't want to meet her."

Luke took his hand off her knee. "What a peculiar remark to make. Are you being difficult again? Like you were last Wednesday?"

Tonia shook her head. "On the contrary. I'm trying to avoid the difficulties that may arise if you take me to your home."

"I've been to your home and met your parents, and that hasn't created any difficulties."

"That's different."

His face darkened. "I don't see why. If you're not being difficult, are you by any chance being snobbish? Are you worrying as to whether my mother and my home will rise to your social expectations?"

"What a beastly thing to say! I have a lot of faults, but up to now no one has ever accused me of being a snob. I'd hate to have your village inferiority complex. You can stop the car. I'm getting out."

"I promised my mother I'd bring you for tea. Do you want to add discourtesy to your list of faults?"

"Make some excuse. Say I've gone down with flu. You can drop me at a bus stop, I'll go back to St. Michael's, and you go on to your mother."

At that, he did stop the car. So suddenly that she nearly hit the windscreen.

"Sorry," he said shortly. He switched the ignition off and turned to her. "So now you want me to lie about you. Let's have it, Tonia. Why won't you come home with me?"

"Because of the implications. Because I know how Rivingham people think. If I go home with you, your mother will think we're going to become engaged."

"And aren't we?"

"No."

Luke felt his stomach muscles bunch. Tonia saw him look sick, and her anger fled.

"Luke . . . darling . . . I'm sorry. I've been afraid of this moment. I think I'd better try and explain."

"Yes, I think you'd better," he said.

"Your mother . . . she'll be waiting."

Luke started the car and drove along until he saw a telephone booth. Tonia sat and watched him go inside, feeling a little sick herself, at the sight of his pale, set face and with the nervous knowledge of what she intended to tell him.

She watched him replace the receiver and return to the car. "Where to?" he asked. "Your favorite hunting ground on top of Fisher's Hill?"

She flushed. "My parents are out. Let's go back home."

They were both silent for the rest of the journey. As they entered the house, Tonia asked hesitantly, "Would you like some tea?"

"No, thanks."

They went into the lounge and sat down in the armchairs, facing one another. He noticed that she pointedly avoided the couch. She pulled the tam-o'-shanter off her hair and began to fidget with it, and then burst out defensively, "Why spring marriage on me so suddenly? We've never discussed it before."

"Let's discuss it now. I'm asking you to marry me."

"Luke, I'm sorry. I don't want to get married just yet."

"Did last Wednesday night mean nothing to you, then?"

"Yes, of course, it did."

He said very quietly, "Let me tell you what it meant to me. You let me touch you in a very intimate fashion, and I interpreted your lack of protest as an acceptance of me as the man you intended to marry. Now I learn that marriage didn't enter your mind."

"No, it didn't. I don't automatically assume that every man who makes love to me wants to marry me. Or I him."

"Is such love-making a customary practice in your so-called smart set? What about Angela and Roger? Do they indulge in that kind of thing?"

She hesitated, and then honesty compelled her to admit, "Not Angela."

"Maybe she's old-fashioned. Like me."

"Maybe she is."

"Or could it be that she's just fastidious? And prefers to keep herself decent until the right man comes along?"

Decent! Tonia had been listening with an ever-growing sense of incredulity. She burst out, "I didn't know that men like you existed any more! For the life of me I can't see anything indecent in what happened between us. I thought it was wonderful beyond belief. And so did you."

"Only because I thought you were going to be my wife. I wouldn't have touched you otherwise."

"Oh, for heaven's sake!" Her patience snapped and her temper flared. "You were born in the wrong era, Dr. Howard. The Victorians would have lapped you up, and the Puritans would have welcomed you as a gift from heaven. You're steeped in your narrow village morality—and, personally, I find it boring."

Luke stared aghast at the stormy face.

"I had no idea I was boring you. We've been going around together for how long? Five months? You've never shown any signs of boredom before. I thought you enjoyed being with me."

She drew in a long, slow breath. The hurt in his eyes dispersed the storminess and made her gentle.

"Dear, dear Luke. You're such a nice man. But you're not with it! In this day and age two people don't have to marry just because they indulge in a little serious love-making. Did you think that we had?"

"I think it would be advisable," he said stiffly. "What has happened once, could happen again. I think we should get married."

"I don't. Luke, be honest. Do you really want to get married at this stage in your career?"

He was a little taken aback at her insight. "I . . . six months ago I would have said 'no.' But now . . . "

"Now, because of what happened last Wednesday—and because you know as well as I do that we'll want more and more until the inevitable happens—you feel obliged to offer marriage."

He flushed. Her calm appraisal of the situation came uncomfortably close to the truth, and he was resentful that an ex-schoolgirl should play psychologist and put into words that which he refused to think. His was the maturity, yet she seemed to have assumed control.

"Poor darling," she said. "I've put you in a spot, haven't I?"

Her gentleness disarmed him. She was rarely gentle. With simple honesty, he said, "Tonia, I want you."

"Yes, but that isn't quite the same, is it?"

"Meaning?"

"Wanting me and wanting marriage are two separate things. Don't confuse them."

"But they're automatic! They go together. I can't have one without the other."

She sighed. She knelt down by his chair and sat back on her heels, hands tightly clasped in front of her. "Darling scarecrow, I want to talk. Really talk. We've had lovely times together, and I haven't been bored. I shouldn't have said that. But I've always avoided serious conversation, and now I've got to talk, and you're not going to like what I have to say.

"Luke, when I said you'd been born out of your time I said it in temper, and it came out like a taunt. It wasn't meant to be, it's simply the truth." She gave him a faint smile. "I can just picture you as a stern, handsome Puritan, walking straight and tall in a wide-brimmed hat, bringing up your children in the fear and admonition of the Lord, with a sweet-faced, submissive wife hovering in the background who would attend your every need and never contradict you or go against your wishes in any way."

She paused, and Luke was amazed to see the dawning of tears in the wide, gray eyes. This was indeed a new Tonia, and he leaned forward and touched her face wonderingly. She put her head on one side and rested her cheek against her hand.

"You know what's coming, darling, don't you? I don't fit into the picture. I don't conform, and I never will. The sad part is that I don't want to, because if you were born too late in time, then I was born too soon."

That was when he felt the first cold finger touch him, and she must have seen the shadow on his face because she went on hastily. "Please listen. We're not ready for each other. You have a dream to realize, and marriage to me would slow that down. I would demand time and attention from you. I'm not prepared to sit quietly at home, while you concentrate on your studies, not at the ripe old age of nearly twenty-one! That means you'd be caught between your career and me and end up by not doing justice to either.

"Also, I have a dream of my own. All my life I've wanted to travel, to get out of St. Michael's. I can't bear to stay in this dreary little town, when outside the whole world is waiting . . . beckoning . . . "

She caught her breath with excitement.

"Oh, Luke, there's so much wonder I want to see. Switzerland! Can't you just visualise the mighty Matterhorn, sharply etched against a brilliant blue sky? Rome! I want to stand in the Colosseum with tears in my eyes. To watch the white Lippizaners waltzing in Vienna. Luke, do you realize there are countries where the sun smiles down on you from morning to night? Where the skies are a perpetual blue and the sea is warm and the sand unbearably hot under your bare feet . . . "

Her voice trailed away, and her eyes closed in rapture as she was caught up in the ecstasy of her dream.

And for one searing moment, he shared her vision. He could *see* her running along the water's edge on a deserted beach, wearing the outrageous costume about which the men had sniggered, see the beautiful body tanned to a warm gold, a thousand sparkling droplets turning the wet sheen of her skin into a gleaming iridescence, turning her into a golden girl—a faraway unobtainable golden girl. He felt a stab of fear. He had to bring her back. To break down the dream, which inexplicably did not include him.

He spoke harshly and deliberately, "Daydreams. Just daydreams that can never come true. If the name is Rothschild, you can go dreaming into the sun, but if the name is Howard and you have four weeks leave a year, you cut your cloth accordingly. Tonia! Are you listening?"

Reluctantly she opened her eyes. "Yes, I'm listening. They're not daydreams. I intend to make them come true."

"How?"

"Do you know that this bright girl can speak three languages fluently? Three and a half, if you count a smattering of Russian! Well, for my twenty-first, Daddy's promised me a tour through Europe to help me brush up on conversation. When I return, I want to look for a job as courier with a travel agency. I wanted to do this when I left school, but Mummy's health was worrying us even then, and with Daddy just commencing his term of office, it was hardly the time for me to go away. But his term ends this year, so as soon as we have an ex-mayor in the family, I'm going job-hunting. It'll be a piece of cake, Luke! Something marvelous is always waiting round the corner for me! I'll find something super, and away I'll go on my magic carpet."

Looking at the confident glowing face, Luke said bleakly, "I had no inkling of this. I never imagined you as a career girl."

She hooted derisively. "I'm not! Believe me, darling, I'm not! I'd much rather do my traveling the lazy way instead of having to work for it. But I do want to get the travel bug out of my system, and while I'm waiting for you to become a consultant, this is as good a time as any." She reached out and hugged his legs and laughed up at him. "I'll tell you what! Let's make a date to meet in front of the altar three years from now. Do you think you'll be through by then? Imagine it! Your ambition realized—and my itchy feet stilled. Who knows, I may even become an ideal Puritan wife, and together we'll raise hordes of children. That would confound you, wouldn't it?"

He couldn't raise an answering smile. "It might take longer than three years. Supposing it's four?" His voice became hoarse and pleading. "Tonia, I'll be over thirty by then. I can't wait that long for you."

"You don't have to, Luke."

He stared blankly into the level gray eyes that met his so unwaveringly. "What are you trying to tell me?"

"We're not children. You said you couldn't have me without marriage. Luke, darling, you can."

The silence that followed filled the room and was painful to them both. In disbelief, he asked, "Do you realize what you're saying?"

"Yes. It wasn't said lightly—or easily. I've thought about it very carefully."

"Oh, you have, have you? That's interesting. How long has this careful thought been going on?"

"I think, subconsciously, from the day I walked out of hospital. When you came here that night, I watched the struggle in your face—your ambition versus me. I realized then what a nice person you are. Most men I've known would never have allowed the struggle in the first place. My alternative would have been their obvious solution."

"Your alternative!" He towered over her, his eyes blazing. "Tonia, I would never have asked you this before, but I'm asking now. How many men have you made this offer to? The truth, please."

"You're the first." There was the ring of complete sincerity in her voice, but he missed it. He was fighting a tide of disappointment and fury, which threatened to overwhelm him, and it made him contemptuous.

"With your reputation, I find that hard to believe."

"There have been a few near-misses," she said steadily. "My fault. I have a passionate nature. But I never liked anyone enough to go the whole way. Maybe because most of them expected it. But you're different. You never expected a thing. That's why I like you enough, Luke."

The fury erupted. "What the hell are you? One minute, you're still a slangy schoolgirl; the next, you're propositioning me like a woman of the streets. I just don't understand you."

"I know you don't. That's why I won't marry you just yet. I've told you—we're not ready for one another."

"And we never will be! Exactly where did you visualize our beautiful encounters to take place? On the back seat of a car? Or in a field?"

Her cheeks flamed. "You give me little credit for intelligence. I wouldn't want it that way, either. My field days are over."

She caught hold of his hand. "Luke, think about it. When you've calmed down. We will be married, but not yet. Get me out of your system and then settle down to . . . Luke, don't go away looking like that! At least, talk about it . . ."

"I'm not interested. If you're expecting me to thank you for your generous offer, then I must disappoint you. In Rivingham, we have a word for girls like you. I happen to have ideals about the woman I want for my wife. I want proximity of mind as well as body. I want my ring on her finger. I want the privileges of marriage, but I won't take them without the responsibilities."

He looked down at the girl on the floor and, in a cutting voice, asked, "Can you take your mind back to that dusty lane? The second time I offered you a lift you made a shockingly vulgar remark. I won't repeat it, but that's what I think of your alternative."

The front door slammed behind him.

"You know something?" Tonia addressed the silent

room defiantly, "he's coming on! That last crack was definitely not the sort of thing a Puritan would have said. There's hope for him yet!"

She tried to laugh, and then her face crumpled, and she buried it in her hands.

Julian was the first to find out. Even before Angela. He was wining and dining his redhead, but she was not living up to expectations, and he was decidedly bored. He couldn't figure out why he'd ever thought her cute, and as the evening progressed, his attention wandered more and more.

So that, when a couple went onto the dance floor, the redhead lost out completely. She might have been invisible. His eyes were riveted on the stunning fair girl.

She was with a youngster of about twenty-one, who kept his cheek ardently pressed against hers all the time they were dancing. Julian observed that although the boy kept his eyes shut, his partner's were wide open, and there was a look of utter boredom on her lovely face. Also that the boy held her in a tight embrace, which she suffered passively but which which evoked no answering response whatsoever.

For quite some time he watched the repetitive pattern. They danced, returned to their table, ate, and then danced again. The redhead became petulant and distinctly annoyed at his monosyllabic replies to her chatter. She sighed. She knew the fair girl. So Tonia Marshall was back in circulation again!

Julian tensed. The couple returned to their table, and the girl picked up her evening bag, obviously intending to visit the ladies room. With a muttered apology to the redhead, he left the table. His footsteps made no sound on the thickly carpeted corridor, and Tonia was startled to hear a harsh voice saying, "Just a moment, Princess."

She turned to see Julian facing her, his black eyes narrowed and glittering.

"Oh, it's you," she said ungraciously. "Don't call me by that idiotic name."

"Your friends all call you that."

"But you're not my friend."

"The lady is shrewd," he remarked dryly.

"What do you want, Julian?"

"I've been watching that cheek-to-cheek demonstration with great interest. What does it mean? Why aren't you with Luke?"

"Mind your own business." She pushed to open the door, but his hand shot out to grip her shoulder and swing her round roughly.

"Luke *is* my business. Would you by any chance be double-crossing him?"

"No, I wouldn't. Take your hand off my shoulder. If you're so concerned, why don't you ask him what it means?"

Slowly he relinquished his grip. "I intend to."

"I'll save you the trouble. Luke doesn't need a nursemaid, he's perfectly capable of looking after himself . . . "

"Not when he's involved with someone like you."

"Well, he's not involved any more." She held her head very high and faced him squarely. "He's given me the push. Dropped me. Which should fill your ears with delight, Julian."

"Wha–at?" He gave a jubilant laugh. "Hoor–ray! So he's regained sanity at last. That's the best news I've heard for quite some time. Princess, you've made my night!"

She caught him completely unawares. Her hand swept up and smacked against his cheek with a force which rocked his head sideways. He kept his face averted, and she saw his eyes close for a moment. Then slowly, almost in slow motion, he turned towards her again, and his expression frightened her.

54

She pressed the back of the offending hand to her mouth to prevent the incoherent words from tumbling out, but the anguished apology in her eyes was plain for him to see.

He ignored it. In a voice made brittle by anger, he told her, "One of these days, someone is going to give you a bloody good hiding, and when that day dawns, I hope I'll be there to applaud."

He was halfway down the corridor before she tried to call his name. "Julian!" But the agonized whisper was a mere thread of sound, quite impossible for the man to hear.

Nor did he witness the tears that fell in the blessed sanctity of the ladies room.

The redhead thought disgustedly that she must be losing her touch. Julian dropped her at her home well before midnight, kissed her perfunctorily, gave her bottom an absent-minded little pat, then drove off without a backward glance.

Arriving back at staff residence, he went along to Luke's room, and saw the slit of light under the door. He tapped, and felt the handle yield. Luke was sitting up in bed, reading a journal.

Julian wasted no time. "I've just seen Tonia having dinner with a besotted-looking kid. She tells me that you two have broken up.

Luke glanced at him briefly. "Yes."

"Want to talk about it?"

"No."

Julian hovered for a moment. "All right, old son," he said gently. "Just remember, though, if you should want an ear, mine's available."

Luke went about tight-lipped for a few days and finally sought out Julian one evening.

"Look," he began belligerently, "I don't want sympathy or soft-soaping. Just give me a plain answer to something. I asked Tonia to marry me. She refused, but offered to have an affair with me. Am I some kind of sexual freak because I blew up and said 'No'?"

Julian bit off a quick exclamation. "Some people get all the luck," he said lightly. "I have to work damned hard to get my women into bed, and you get it handed to you on a platter! But dear, dear, no wonder the Princess came unstuck. She didn't know her man, did she?"

"Be serious," Luke snapped. "How would you have reacted?"

Julian went very still. "I'd have called her bluff," he replied very quietly.

"Bluff?" Luke shook his head. "She wasn't bluffing. She meant every word, I assure you."

"Well, there's a simple way of finding out. Take her up to the lakes for a weekend. Then she'll either have to swallow her brave suggestion or spit it out."

Luke's face was a study. "And if she isn't bluffing?"

Julian walked to the window and peered out into the darkness, one hand in his pocket jingling some loose change.

"Well?" demanded Luke.

The man at the window kept his back to him. "Then you, old son, will be a very lucky man, because either way, you win. If she sleeps with you, then I defy you to say that the experience could be other than wonderful. If she doesn't, then she'll marry you."

"It's marriage or nothing," Luke said doggedly.

Julian turned and surveyed the disconsolate figure, his stoop very pronounced tonight as he hunched forward in the chair, his clasped hands hanging loosely between his knees. He drew a chair forward and sat down facing him.

"Luke", he began. "I think a little plain speaking is called for. You fell for the Princess with a thud that echoed throughout the entire hospital building. Have you ever analyzed why? From the day you entered the Queen Elizabeth, women looked twice at you. Of course, they did," he said irritably, as Luke tried to protest, "most of them calm sensible women, as dedicated to their calling as you are to yours. But did you fancy any of them? No! You deliberately chose the most unlikely incredible contrast. If you scoured Britain, you couldn't come up with anyone less suited to you than Tonia Marshall.

"But hooray, it seemed to work! She made you astonishingly happy. She transformed you. She put a look on your face that was sadly lacking. And then what happens? You have your first serious clash of thought and surprise, surprise! You suddenly discover she doesn't conform to Rivingham rules! In fact, she's damned un-Rivingham in her ideas, and you're shocked! Disgusted! Luke, how naïve can you be? Didn't you anticipate this? If you wanted a Rivingham-type bride, then why the hell did you start something with her?"

He pushed his chair impatiently from him, and the scraping of the legs on the wooden floor set Luke's teeth on edge and added to his already taut nerves. He watched Julian go back to stare at the blackness outside.

Then he himself rose. "I can see that you think I'm an utter fool. Sorry I troubled you, Julian. Good night."

"Just a minute, Luke." Julian sounded tired. "Knowing what you know now, has it made any basic difference? Do you still want her?"

"She's in my blood," he said hopelessly. "I'll always want her."

# ❀ 6 ❀

"Making any headway?" Mr. Marshall entered his daughter's room and eyed the disorder on the carpet. Tonia sat on the floor surrounded by glossy travel brochures and an atlas. She looked up at her father and disinterestedly flicked another page over.

"Not really. I keep changing my mind. I'm going round in circles."

"Hm. Been in rather a lot lately, haven't you? Unusual to see you at home night after night."

"Catching up on my beauty sleep."

He frowned at the listless face. "Doesn't seem to be doing you much good. How about a trip to Manchester tomorrow on the mayoral expense account?"

"To do what?"

"A couple of months ago the Board of Trade put out feelers to several northern resorts about potential facilities for receiving trade delegations from overseas. London is losing its appeal, it seems. Costs are exorbitant, and many have been there before. Well, you know me! Anything they do down there I reckon we can do better, so I told Alan to reply promptly and paint a glowing picture of our amenities, and what do you think the damn fool did? Went down with flu and forgot all about it. That man will drive me daft."

Tonia suppressed a smile. Alan Miller, the mayoral secretary, was forever in her father's black books.

"So you'd like me to deliver the reply, and do a bit of smarming while I'm about it?"

"Will you?"

"Yes." She scrambled up from the floor. "I can do something for myself at the same time. I've been wanting to make on-the-spot inquiries from large travel agencies about the possibilities of courier work. Manchester is just the place."

Manchester wasn't. Her charm opened the doors of several managers' offices, but all she emerged with was a handful of application forms, each containing a blank page ominously headed: PREVIOUS TRAVEL EXPERIENCE (*give full details*). True, she received one offer to guide a party of students through the Lake District, but she was strongly tempted to tell them what to do with it.

Which inevitably turned her thoughts to Luke. Was he missing her? As she was missing him? Miserably she faced up to the fact that she was badly shaken by his abrupt exit from her life. The contempt in his face had hurt, and his continued absence hurt even more. She, who had triumphed over so many, had been defeated by one quiet, old-fashioned man.

Her eyes began to water. Damn this wretched city smog, she muttered fiercely, and stuck up her chin, fixed a smile on her lips, and invaded the Board of Trade offices. The officials were delighted. Both with her and her father's reply.

It was a dreary afternoon. The shops failed to please, there was no cinema or theater show to tempt her to stay, and eventually she made her way disconsolately back to the station for the 5:10 PM train.

She stood in the main hall, idly checking the departure board, and then stared in disbelief. Somehow she must have misread the timetable, becuase the train to St. Michael's was scheduled to leave at 5:00 PM and the one following not until 7:30 PM. She looked at the clock. One minute to five! For crying out loud! She raced across the hall, down the subway, and up the steps to Platform 10, just as the guard was raising his flag. He saw the girl come

59

flying up the steps and obligingly held open the door of the last compartment for her.

"Only just," he said.

"Thanks so much," she panted.

She subsided breathless in the corner seat, vaguely aware of a man who sat in the far opposite corner, his head and shoulders hidden behind a newspaper. As the train drew out of the platform, the man lowered his paper. It was Julian.

"Oh, no!" She started up from her seat, but there was no escape. It was not a corridor coach. Feeling trapped, she sank back on the seat and looked apprehensively at him.

Julian fingered his cheek meaningly. "Afraid of reprisals, Princess?"

"Of course not." She turned her back on him and gazed loftily through the window.

"Now let me see . . . " He sounded amused. "This train runs nonstop to St. Michael's, so we shall be quite undisturbed. The journey takes just over an hour, which gives me ample time to put her across my knee . . . "

She swung around sharply. "Oh, don't mind me," he said, "just talking to myself."

She turned again to the window and addressed his reflection. "Don't play cat and mouse with me, Julian. Take your revenge if you must, but get on with it."

With a swift movement, he stood up and came toward her. She pressed back against the hard upholstery, very conscious of the quickened blood coursing through her. He looked down at the defiant flushed face for several seconds before seating himself opposite her.

"Shall we declare an armistice?" he asked quietly. "We're stuck with one another, so let's make the best of it. An hour's truce in the middle of the Marshall-Goldberg hostilities?"

He held out his hand.

Warily she stared first at the hand, and then at his face.

"Take it. It won't bite! Neither will I!"

Hesitantly she put her hand in his. "Do you always behave so magnanimously?"

"Always. Heaping coals of fire on an enemy's head is the most subtle form of revenge. Or so I'm told."

"And I'm the enemy." It was not a question and he let it pass without comment.

"What took you to Manchester?" he asked.

She explained about the errand performed on her father's behalf and, much to her surprise, went on to tell about the negative results of her travel inquiries, even to producing the application forms.

Julian took them from her and perused them before saying unexpectedly, "If I'd known this a couple of months ago, I could have helped you."

"But how?"

"Contacts. Dozens of them. Alternatively, we could have done a lot of homework." He smiled at her puzzled face. "I'm the modern version of the Wandering Jew. You name a country—I've been there. I could coach you about hotels, restaurants, bars, foreign exchange, local customs. We could fill these pages with some very convincing and impressive data."

She was wide-eyed with envy. "How on earth did you manage to do all that traveling?"

"Ah! Belonging to a dispersed people has its advantages. We have relatives scattered all over the globe. Uncles and aunts in San Francisco, Montreal, and Adelaide; Tel Aviv and Johannesburg; Philadelphia and Prague. Cousins in Belgrade, Rio de Janeiro . . ."

"Oh, stop it! Stop it!" Laughing she covered her ears. "Do you mean to say you've actually been to all these places?"

"Nearly all. I spent a couple of years wandering before I entered medical school, and many vacations since have been spent abroad."

"Luke had to work through his vacations," she found herself blurting out.

"Yes, Luke came up the hard way, not like you and me. Everything he wanted had to be worked for. Nothing came easily, certainly not freely. That's why he guards so carefully the standards—and the relationships—that he holds dear. He's quite right. Things of value should never be taken lightly. Or given lightly, for that matter."

Their eyes met and held, and it was she who dropped hers first. He knew! Either Luke had told him or he'd guessed. She peered through the window at the passing landscape and was appalled to see the miserable face drooping hazily back at her. Determinedly she brightened up and changed the subject.

"What have you been doing in Manchester?"

"Spending the day with my mother."

"Your mother!"

He raised an eyebrow. "Aren't I entitled to have a mother?"

"I'm sorry. I wasn't being rude. You're simply so full of surprises. You doctors get so little free time, and you're the last man I'd expect to spend a whole day with his mother."

"Depends on the mother, doesn't it? Mine happens to be interesting and delightful. More so than many a woman half her age. Present company excepted, of course!"

She looked at him suspiciously, but his face was quite serious.

"Actually, my mother is of Russian descent, way back, and when my grandmother was alive she could keep us enthralled for hours on end by telling us what *her* mother had related about life under the Czarist regime. One of these days my mother intends writing a family history—not for publication—simply to preserve memories which she feels should not be allowed to fade."

"I should think not!" Tonia was enthralled. "Tell me more, Julian."

He laughed at her eager face. "Well, let me see. I think that Great-Grandfather Rudi would have fascinated you . . ."

The time flew by. Julian talked well and amusingly, and she lay back in her seat, thoroughly relaxed, watching his dark mobile face with interest. She had never really looked at him before.

"Tonia?"

It was the first time he had pronounced her name, and she felt her face go as serious as his.

"When you offered to sleep with Luke, did you mean it?"

So he did know! She bounced up angrily on the seat, her cheeks flushed, eyes hostile.

"Does Luke have to tell you everything?"

"No, he doesn't have to. He wanted to. It's good to confide in someone occasionally. You have Angela. I'm the opposite number, remember. Answer the question."

"Certainly. My life is my own, to do with as I please. Just as my body is my own, to give to whom I please. Does that satisfy you?"

"No. That was an evasion, not an answer. You're a coward, Princess . . . " quickly adding, as he saw the temper rise in her face, "and don't slap me again, because if you do, I'll slap you back. Promptly and hard."

Involuntarily they had both risen to their feet, and the sudden stopping of the train caught them unawares and jerked them off balance. Startled, they looked out at the familiar platform of St. Michael's-on-the-Sea.

"The end of the armistice," he said. "Now we can go back to being enemies again."

He opened the door and stepped back to allow her to leave first. She made no immediate move. "I don't want to be your enemy, Julian."

His expression was enigmatic. "You haven't given yourself any choice."

"I don't understand what you mean."

"It's not important that you should. Concentrate on understanding Luke a little better. That *is* important."

She went home deep in thought. She could only interpret Julian's last remark to mean that Luke had not written himself permanently out of her life. Her steps quickened. As she let herself into the house, her mother called, "Tonia, is that you, dear?"

"Hello, Mummy." She ran up the stair and popped her head inside her mother's room. "Daddy's letter went down well, but no luck with the courier job. Application forms to fill in by the dozen, but no definite promises."

"Oh, I'm sorry. You must be disappointed."

"You've got a big smile on your face for someone who's sorry," the girl teased. "Don't you want to get rid of your daughter?"

"Darling, you know I don't. Tonia, Luke telephoned. He's coming round at eight this evening."

"Oh." Her legs felt hollow, and she sat down quickly on the bed. "He didn't say anything else?"

"No." Her mother gave her a searching glance. "As we haven't seen Luke for a couple of weeks, I take it that something is wrong between you."

"He asked me to marry him. I told him I didn't want to get married just yet."

"Well, that was a straightforward answer and no reason to quarrel. If you enjoy one another's company, you can still go around together, surely?"

Tonia stood up. "That isn't quite the whole story. I

must rush. The train was so dirty that I need a bath before I do another thing."

The door bell rang promptly at eight, and Tonia, brushing her hair in front of the mirror, allowed herself a little smile. Dear scarecrow, with his obsession for punctuality!

She opened the door and looked a little defiantly at a stern-faced Luke. Her heart sank. They exchanged stilted greetings, and she took him into the lounge.

His opening words stunned her.

"I'm taking you up on your offer. I've booked a room for the weekend at the King's Head, a rather nice hotel on the Ambleside road. Can you be ready at noon on Saturday?"

Her mouth went dry, and her heart began to race.

"I . . . I suppose so. You . . . " Her voice suddenly went, and she gave a convulsive swallow. "Why have you changed your mind?"

His voice was flat and hard. "I want you in any way I can have you. Does that answer you?"

This couldn't be Luke speaking! She stood appalled. She felt a little sick. Not this way, her heart cried. Not in cold, unsmiling hostility. Oh, Luke, *this* isn't what I had in mind!

"Shall I tell your mother I'm taking you to visit friends? Or will you tell the necessary lies?"

She winced. "I'll tell her."

"Right. I won't sit down. There's a visiting lecturer speaking at the hospital whom I particularly want to hear." He looked pointedly at his watch. "As it is, I shall have missed half of it."

He turned to go. "By the way," he said, as an afterthought, "Julian will be joining us. He's bringing a woman, too."

"*Julian* coming! Bringing a . . . a woman!"

He regarded her obvious distress with surprise. "Oh, don't worry. They'll be on the same errand as us. I don't suppose we'll see much of them."

Tonia would have sworn that Luke was incapable of leering, but the look on his face was a passable imitation. Her hand went to her throat. She felt as if she was choking. "A *woman!* Do you think that Julian is saying that about us, 'Luke's bringing a woman, too'?"

"Well if he is, does it matter?" He seemed genuinely puzzled. "After all, you're not my fiancee—not my wife—how else would he describe you?"

A suspicion leapt into her mind. Became a certainty. "This is Julian's doing. He's at the bottom of this. He's a . . . a . . . Oh, how I hate that man! And at this moment I hate you, too. Just go! Do you hear me? Go . . . "

She whirled on her heel, but he caught hold of her. "Not so fast. What are you getting so het up about? I've capitulated. I'm agreeing to your terms. This is what you wanted."

"It isn't! You know it isn't! I wanted it to be beautiful and magical and you've made it . . . Oh, how could you? Just go away . . . "

He paused for a second at the door, saying gently, "I was brought up to call a spade a spade. I'll be waiting when you want me, darling."

Darling. Luke had never used the word before. She drew a deep, quivering breath and went slowly upstairs. Her mother was wrapped in a warm dressing gown, sitting in front of the electric radiator, and her head turned in surprise as the door opened.

The girl walked to her mother and sank down on her knees beside her. She buried her face in her lap. "Oh, Mummy . . . "

Back at the hospital, Julian was waiting.
"Well?"

"It worked," said Luke grimly. "It worked only too well. She hates you. She hates me. I only hope your psychology is right, Julian."

"You'll see," he said.

# 7

The hand upon her head was reassuring. "Can you tell me about it, darling?"

Her voice was muffled. "You'll be so shocked."

"I doubt it. Talk it out, dear."

All during the faltering recital, the girl was conscious of the hand stroking her hair, pausing only once fractionally before continuing steadily, each stroke radiating a wave of comfort, which helped her to carry on to the sorry end. Then there was silence. She had kept her face hidden, but now she sat back on her heels, remembering with a stab of pain that the last time she had knelt like this had been before Luke. Hesitantly she looked up. Her mother was smiling!

"Aren't you thoroughly disgusted with me?" Tonia's flushed face was astonished.

"No, darling, just very thankful that fine young men like Luke and Julian still exist."

"Julian isn't a fine young man," she muttered. "I met him on the train this afternoon, and he pretended to be so nice, yet all the time he must have been laughing, knowing what was going to happen tonight. I'm quite sure that he'll go with his . . . his *woman!*"

"Obviously he's quite sure of you, too! He's very effectively prevented you from being just that with Luke. He sounds interesting. You must bring him to meet me one day. And now, Tonia? What now?

"But . . . aren't you going to say anything about what I've just told you?"

"I don't think so, dear. It's obvious that you're not very happy with yourself, and that's much more meaningful than anything I can add. As a matter of fact, I'm rather proud of you."

"Proud? *Proud?*"

"I'm proud that you had the courage to tell me. So many daughters wouldn't have done. I hear many mothers complain that their children never confide in them. You and I seem unique in that respect."

"Angela can't talk to her mother. She's told me so."

"Then I'm sorry for them both. What a lot they're missing."

"Mummy, can you understand why I did it? You see, I know myself so well. I couldn't possibly give Luke the quiet hours he needs, and so I wanted to give him wonderful moments to compensate. I did say I'd marry him later." Her voice trembled. "He was so scathing, said there was a name for girls like me . . ."

"He was disappointed. He loves you, dear, and wants all the things that go to make up the whole of you, not one minute little part. I think I will say something. Oh, no reproaches! Just a fond mother thinking aloud."

Her face took on a sweetness that was tinged with sadness.

"The man to whom you eventually give yourself will be a man to be envied. All your life, from when you were a little girl, you've been blessed with a shining happiness, which is a wonder to behold. And this precious gift—and it is a gift—you will carry with you, and there will be great beauty in your giving.

"What a pity it would be, then, to hide such beauty in dark, secret corners, unable to let it blaze forth into the full light of day. For you, my darling, will wear your moment of surrender as a shining badge for all the world to see. But if you're compelled to hide it away, why, it would break your heart."

There was a raptness in the girl's face.

"Go on, Mummy."

"If you were to go with Luke this coming weekend, you'd have your magical moments. With your warmth, how could it be otherwise? And then Monday morning would dawn. Far too soon. You'd come back here, with that revealing face of yours carefully controlled, terrified of wearing your happiness. You'd greet me a little too brightly and walk slowly upstairs to your room, which astonishingly, amazingly, is still the same, although you're so different. And you sit on your narrow little bed, with your body feeling strange and already so lonely away from his, and suddenly, resentfully, you feel dreadfully lost, dreadfully cheated . . . "

"But . . . " Tonia was frightened by something she couldn't fathom, "a narrow little bed? You and Daddy have always teased me about clinging to Granny's big one."

There were tears in her mother's eyes. "So we have, my darling. I was getting a little carried away."

"No, you weren't," the girl whispered. "You couldn't possibly have described those emotions unless . . . Oh, Mummy, darling Mummy!" The gray eyes were misty as she cupped her mother's face between her hands.

"I couldn't bear to relive it through you, Tonia."

"Mummy, was it . . . ?"

"Yes, dear, it was Daddy. There were reasons why we had to wait, mainly economic, but it made a mockery of our wedding day. Those beautiful vows, they weren't said with the same sincerity . . . "

"You know something?" Tonia interrupted fiercely. "I'm proud of you, too. Can you imagine Mrs. Morris telling Angela what you've just told me? Never! You know something else? You're going to have all the thrill and joy of my wedding, just as soon as I can get Luke to fix the day."

"Oh, no, dear! No!" Her mother became agitated. "You mustn't let my story determine your future. It would be like marrying on the rebound. You must sleep on it, Tonia. Please!"

"Shush! You have no say in the matter." She threw back her head and laughed excitedly. "Now I know what's been wrong with me! I must have wanted this all the time, despite my silly modern ideas. Oh, Mummy, life is good again. Shall we have a wedding on my twenty-first? I really couldn't choose a more appropriate date, could I?"

"Tonia, please listen, dear." She strove to remain calm. "You are not to rush into this on a wave of emotion. I feel so responsible . . ."

"What rubbish! You've been wonderful. Simply wonderful! Oh, I can't wait to tell Luke. He would be at a wretched lecture! Won't Daddy be pleased? And Julian Goldberg will be livid!"

She leapt to her feet and, with outstretched arms, spun round like a top, the blonde hair swinging wide, the lovely face radiant. "Whee! I feel quite light-headed now that I've made the decision. I'll phone the hospital switchboard and leave a message." She stopped her pirouetting and looked anxiously at her mother's white strained face. "Be happy for me, Mummy. Honestly, you haven't pushed me into this. Luke will be good for me—you've said so yourself."

Her mother made one last attempt. "The traveling . . ."

"Oh, that!" It was dismissed impatiently. "When Luke's a famous consultant, which he *will* be, he'll do a lot of traveling, and we'll go together." She knelt again, and her expression was sweet. "You've straightened me out, darling. I'm glad you're my mother." She reached up and kissed her.

Mrs. Marshall managed a smile. "I've gone tired all at

once. Silly of me. Help me into bed and then off you go to make your call. And bless you both," she whispered.

It was nearly midnight, and the house was in darkness. The front door bell rang once, sharply. Mrs. Marshall smiled and turned over to settle into sleep. Her husband, fast asleep, didn't even stir.

Tonia leapt out of bed and ran down the stairs. She switched the outside light on, unbolted the door, and held out both her hands to the man on the doorstep.

The sweet penitence in her face melted his bones. For one fanciful moment he saw a Puritan maid, heartbreakingly tremulous, soft, gentle. Then she moved forward a little into the light, and the scolding he'd prepared, the apology he'd resolved to demand, the sternness he'd intended to apply, they all fell away.

Not because she said, "Thank you for coming." But for what she didn't say. For in her eyes he read the promise of what he had never dared expect from a woman. A promise that no Puritan daughter could ever have made. A promise which assuaged every lonely moment of his twenty-eight years.

He pushed her gently back into the shadowy hall. He held again the precious warmth and laid his cheek against hers.

"Please be sure," he begged. "Marriage to me would have to be forever."

"I'm quite, quite sure," she said.

And she meant it with all her heart.

The wedding day was originally set for the tenth of May, the date of Tonia's twenty-first birthday, but before arrangements could be finalized, a mayoral crisis occurred. Her father came home one day with a terse "Where's your mother?"

"Lying down. Why, what's wrong? You look worried."

"I am. Come into the study. I want to show you something."

Tonia followed her father, who stood at his desk rummaging through the contents of his briefcase. He took out his diary, opened it, and handed it to her. "My engagements for the month of May. Look at them. It's obviously going to be the most crowded month since I took office. The first week, as you can see, is busy enough. Then the second week, of course, we'll be up to our eyes with your wedding. But look at the last two weeks. Every day there's something that requires an appearance from your mother, including that infernal 'At Home' business. And now, to cap everything, listen to this!"

Delving again into the briefcase, he produced a letter and stood scanning through it. "That visit of yours to Manchester certainly paid off. We've been invited to host a trade mission from South Africa, only a small group but an influential one; an international toy fair, which should attract a large number of exhibitors; and a party of hoteliers from Switzerland. Hmm, coals to Newcastle, that last lot, I'm thinking!"

He put the letter down and looked across at her. "Tonia, you'll be away on your honeymoon when these events take place. How's your mother going to cope? Even cutting civic hospitality down to a bare minimum, she'll be exhausted before we're halfway through. Whereas June, by contrast, is a very slack month, and my term of office finishes shortly afterwards . . ."

His voice trailed away, and he looked hopefully at his daughter.

"If I postpone my wedding until the beginning of June, it will help you and Mummy tremendously. That's what you're asking me to do, isn't it?"

"Yes, love. There's no point in beating round the bush. Will you think about it?"

"I don't have to. A June wedding will be just as nice as a May one."

Her prompt answer surprized him. "Good heavens! You're agreeing? Just like that, with no explosion, no hitting the roof? My goodness, Luke is improving you!"

She pulled a face at him. "That's if Luke has no objections, of course."

Strangely enough, Luke had. A peculiar little shiver traveled down his spine, a presentiment . . . He recalled one of his mother's expressions: "Someone is walking over my grave." He shrugged it off. They were discussing a wedding, not a funeral. But he wasn't too happy. He had a moment of panic. "You're not changing your mind, are you?"

"Luke! I simply want to help Mummy. I'm seeing her for the first time as a person. She's nice—I like her."

"And I like you. Tonia, I don't want to change that date." He could look awfully stubborn, she thought.

"Darling . . . it's only a matter of waiting three extra weeks!"

His hands reached for her shoulders. "It's a matter of . . . Anything could happen. I don't want to wait."

There was an intensity in his voice that was new, and the wide gray eyes met his, startled. She pretended to joke. "Hey, I'm supposed to be the passionate one, remember?"

"Only until we're married."

Her eyes danced. "Threat or promise, Dr. Howard?"

"The end result will be the same," he said.

She wound her arms around his neck. "Please, Luke? A June wedding? To help Mummy?"

He sighed. With such a lovely, pleading face in front of him, what could a man do?

Suddenly it was spring. A soft, green banner unfurled across the countryside, and the lilac was in blossom for Tonia's twenty-first birthday.

She hung out of her bedroom window, one arm outstretched to touch a heavy scented branch, still wet with dew, and the perfume drifted up into her face causing her eyes to close in rapture. The fragrant earth was stirring, restless in sympathy with her young eager blood, which throbbed in an ache of anticipation. But for what, she didn't know.

She heard the garden gate click and opened her eyes to see Luke standing on the path, laughing up at her.

"Happy birthday."

Dreamily she looked down at him. "All my life, even when I'm an old, old lady, the scent of lilac will remind me that once I was twenty-one, on a laughing morning that sparkled the way I felt inside, and life waited for me outside the garden gate."

Again he felt that odd momentary panic. "*Inside* the garden gate," he corrected. "Come down to earth. I've got a double birthday present for you."

She flew downstairs to let him in, vital and glowing in every line of her strong young body, and an unreasoning resentment plucked at him. This should have been their wedding day. She was puzzled by the hint of sullenness in his face, but it was chased out of her mind by his gift. A slim bracelet of heavy silver, delicately patterned with engraved scrolls and flowers and bearing inside a simple inscription: TO TONIA, FROM LUKE.

She was quite taken aback, for secretly she had expected a much more mundane gift.

"Why, Luke, it's beautiful! And exactly what I'd have chosen myself. Darling, you've surprised me. You know me better than I thought you did!"

She was more than surprised. For such a practical man it was an unusual choice of gift. Luke could have told her that the choice was Julian's, that he would have preferred a gold watch, solid and satisfying, similiar to the one his mother had given him for his own twenty-first. But Julian had snorted and swept him off to Manchester and into the sort of shop Luke would nervously have avoided, a tiny elegant jeweller's shop tucked away in a select arcade. Now, looking at her ecstatic face, he was thankful for Julian's intervention.

He asked, "Aren't you curious as to the other half of your present?"

"The other half?"

With an indulgent smile, he handed her a letter. "Read it. The first trip on your magic carpet."

He had been offered a two-year fellowship with the Johns Hopkins Medical School in Baltimore.

"America! And I can go with you? Oh, Luke, Luke!" She flung her arms round him and hugged him excitedly. "What a wonderful twenty-first birthday! What a wonderful year! Everything I've ever wished for is going to come true."

# ✿ 8 ✿

The busy fortnight was to begin with the arrival of the trade mission from South Africa. Mr. Marshall had sweated out two of his war years on the Cocos Islands, and on his way home to Britain the homeward-bound troopship mysteriously dallied for three weeks in Durban, to the unforgettable delight of all on board. The hospitality extended to them had been overwhelming. Now, on learning that the Durban Chamber of Commerce had organized the impending visit, Tonia's father hailed it as a long overdue opportunity for personal reciprocation and thus was instrumental in persuading the local officials to plan a more extensive itinerary than was usually offered to the town's visitors.

He briefed his daughter. "This delegation from Durban . . . let's have a look who's coming, the vice-president of the chamber of commerce, the regional branch manager of a building society, head of a real estate firm, member of the publicity bureau . . ."

"Oh, do get on with it!" Tonia stifled a yawn. She was feeling strangely listless. "I couldn't care less what these people do, or who they are. Where do I come in?"

"Patience! Patience! Our itinerary is included somewhere if you'll just give me the chance to get to it."

He skimmed through the next paragraph. "Ah, here we are. They're traveling up to St. Michael's by train on Thursday, and a meeting with the press has been laid on for them after they've settled into their hotel."

"Where are they staying?"

"The Savoy. Might as well give them the best. On Friday morning, a tour of the town, buffet luncheon. In the afternoon, they're to be introduced to their local counterparts as far as possible."

"Do a straight swap. The mayoral secretary for the publicity bureau man," she suggested dryly. "You can't lose on the deal."

Her father grunted. "Don't tempt me. Now, Saturday sees the start of the cricket season, and knowing that most South Africans are cricket fans, I've arranged for them to watch the match as guests of the Cricket Club. Afterwards a party is to be held in the pavilion, and the secretary has asked us to pop in officially. Do you think you could persuade Luke to take you for an hour? You wouldn't need to stay longer."

She doubted it. Luke abhorred cocktail parties, regarding them as an empty frivolity and an extravagant waste of time; but whereas the occasional hospital party was made bearable by having Tonia continually at his side, the civic function afforded him no such consolation. He usually ended up in a corner, making stilted conversation, eyeing Tonia gloomily as she flitted from group to group and covertly watching the clock for an end to the whole wretched business.

Her doubts were confirmed. "Impossible. I'm much too busy," he told her impatiently.

She gnawed furiously at her lip and thought crossly that he wouldn't have refused so promptly—or so flatly—a few months previously. Before their engagement, in fact. She almost blew up—she'd been on her best behavior for so long that it was wearing thin—but stopped herself just in time.

"Are you on duty Saturday night?"

"No," he had to admit, "but if you're going to be tied up with your father, then it's a good opportunity for me to

do some reading. There's a lot I want to get through before we leave for America."

"But I don't have to stay all evening! Daddy says an
hour will be enough. Luke . . . please . . . don't let's waste
a Saturday. Pick me up at the clubhouse, and we'll go on
somewhere from there."

He thought quickly. First of all, knowing Tonia, the
hour would stretch to two. The opening match of the season was always well attended, which meant that most of her
old set would be there, and once they latched on to her, it
would need some mighty good persuasion to prize her
away. He said hopefully, "Roger plays for the club, which
means Angela will be there. Why not go for the whole
match and keep her company? It's ages since you two had a
girlish session, and when the party is over, she and Roger
can bring you home."

She regarded him coldly. "Girlish sessions were never
part of my scene. Julian also plays for the club. Maybe I
should have a session with him, and he can bring me home
afterwards."

He looked down his nose. "Don't be childish. Is that
supposed to be funny?"

"If your sense of humor will rise to it. Which I
doubt."

"Tonia, you're being difficult," he accused her. "You
postponed our wedding in order to help your father with
occasions such as this one. I was dead against the idea, but
you pleaded and got your own way. Now you're stuck with
it, and you're grumbling. You don't know your own mind."

She looked at him oddly. "Maybe I don't."

The sudden constraint between them made Luke uncomfortable. What was the matter with her? When she got
into one of her awkward moods, he never knew how to
cope.

Angela, when telephoned, sounded most offhand. She

said she wouldn't be attending the match; she'd promised to help her mother with something. Tonia banged down the receiver. Luke, Angela . . . She could feel herself becoming increasingly irritable.

It was arranged that she should go to the party with her father and Roger would see her home. A few minutes before she was due to leave, Luke telephoned. "The reading has gone much quicker than I expected. Would you like me to pick you up about eight o'clock at the club?"

"If you like." She sounded disinterested.

At the other end of the line, he frowned. "I thought you wanted me to come."

"Just please yourself, Luke," she said. "I must go. Daddy's waiting. Bye."

The match had obviously finished early, for the party was in full swing, and as they walked up the steps to the pavilion, the secretary appeared. "Hello, Mr. Marshall, glad you could make it. You, too, Tonia. It's been a real humdinger of a match. We won, and the boys are on top form."

Her father lingered to talk with him, and Tonia went on ahead. As she entered the room, the noisy exuberant atmosphere hit her and sent her spirits soaring skywards. Her head went up, and her eyes sparkled. For no apparent reason, a heady breathless excitement shot through her. With no inhibiting Luke beside her, she had a curious feeling of freedom, a child let out to play, a bird on the wing . . .

She saw Julian, whom she completely ignored, and then Roger came towards her, his face beaming. "Am I glad to see you. I was beginning to think you were also a deserter. What a miserable pair of partners we've got! Do you think they've eloped?"

She giggled. The mere thought of Luke and Angela indulging in anything so improbable was hilarious, to say the least. Then a girl shrieked, "Tonia!", and the next moment she was the center of a laughing crowd, most of whom she hadn't seen in months. The minutes flew, she was vibrant with the sensation of being gloriously, wonderfully free.

All at once she had the most distinct feeling of being closely watched. Not merely an over-lingering look in passing from some casual admirer, but a scrutiny so intense that she could feel it boring into her back. She tried to ignore the sensation, but it persisted. The back of her neck was prickling, and she passed a hand over it, wondering whether she'd been bitten by some insect.

The clubhouse stood in a clearing in the midst of a heavily wooded area, and the warm, sultry evening was full of myriads of midges and tiny flying insects, a host of which had swarmed inside. One, more persistent than the rest, hovered round and round the top of her glass, and she was trying ineffectually to brush it away when Roger whispered in her ear, "Don't look now, but you've made quite a conquest. One of the visiting firemen can't take his eyes off you. The packages in South Africa must come in different wrappings."

She spluttered over her drink and whispered back, "Don't tempt me. Now that I'm practically walking down the aisle I must behave myself." Then her eyes danced. "Is he worth turning round for?"

Roger squinted sideways. "Mmm. Don't know. Hefty specimen. Wouldn't care to tangle with him. Good shoulders."

"Never mind his shoulders, you idiot. What about his face?"

"Nice tan. Obviously didn't get it over here. Tough-looking. Craggy, outdoor type. If looks could kill, I'd be stone dead!"

"You are a fool, Roger. I'm going to miss all your non-senses."

"The same goes for me. This town will be decidedly dull without you, Tonia. Your glass is empty. Same again?"

"Please."

He turned, and Tonia watched him shouldering his way through the crowd congregated in front of the bar. Again she was conscious of eyes riveted on her. She hunched her shoulders and gave them a quick shake, as if to shrug off the stare. The temptation to turn round was becoming irresistible. The crowd around her began to thin.

A man carrying four glasses in two hands slowed as he passed. "Hi, Tonia. Long time, no see. How's Luke?"

"Bearing up nicely, thank you."

"Lucky dog. Who wouldn't? See you in church!"

She smiled after him, then looked back to watch Roger's progress, and saw that he had reached the bar and was frantically signaling to her. His eyebrows were lifting up and down, and he was making ridiculous facial contortions. What on earth was he trying to convey? She began making signals back, but he couldn't understand and pulled such a lugubrious face that she burst out laughing. "Leave it," she mouthed and motioned him to come back.

Then she could no longer resist the hypnotic pull of the unseen stare, and with the laugh still on her mouth, she deliberately turned round.

She saw him standing alone at the other end of the room—a man with hair the color of ripe corn—and the laughter was hustled off her face by the solemnity in his. For a long moment their eyes held, and she felt the sweep of an emotion she was powerless to contain. A tremendous thrust upward exploded into an exultant: "But this is it!" It was the bells ringing and the music playing and something slapping her violently into life. And just as a newborn infant responds with a cry, so she too wanted to shout aloud. Except that this was not the birth of a girlchild. It was the birth of a woman.

The party, with its noise and banality, suddenly jarred and sickened. It had something to do with the expression in the steadily watching eyes. Abruptly she turned and walked toward the door, vaguely aware that one or two people spoke to her, but not sure whether she answered. Once outside, she stood straight and still, until he came. He was almost as tall as Luke, but big-boned and broader. He put a firm hand round her wrist and guided her down the steps and across the deserted cricket pitch to the far end, where there was a solitary bench.

She sat beside him, shaken and confused. She forgot Luke—forgot him utterly and completely—forgot everything but the clamoring of her heart and the startling response of her body to a stranger's touch, a stranger's clear, calm eyes. She wanted to speak, to say something, anything—but she, who had lived all her years in a gay verbal froth, could find nothing whatever to say.

He saw the ring on her finger. Touched it questioningly. She stared at it stupefied—and quickly and painfully every single thing that had been forgotten was remembered.

"You came into the room alone." He had a quiet beautiful voice. "Was your fiance not able to be with you?"

"No. He was delayed at the hospital. He's a doctor."

"And the man you were talking to?"

"A mutual friend."

She felt heavy and deflated and oddly ashamed. It must have shown because he reached out and, holding her jaw between his thumb and forefinger, gently forced her head round to face him.

"Why did you come with me?"

But surely he knew? Deeply troubled, she looked at him dumbly. A swift smile came, a comforting smile. "Yes. So there need be no apology between us. Or words."

And again she was silent. Understanding, as he so obviously did, that the only worthwhile words were those that could not be spoken. She studied his face. A man of strength, of authority. Distinctive features. Harsh, but the eyes were reassuring and they looked serenely into hers.

"There are other words," he said. "Shall we use them? As a compensation?"

"Yes. Oh, yes! There's so little time . . . so much I want to know . . . soon you'll be gone." The words came tumbling out in panic.

"Steady." The firm touch was on her wrist again. "We have enough time. Now, what do you want to know?"

"Your name. What am I to call you?"

"Stephen. Everyone else calls me Steve."

"Preferential treatment!" She was surprised that she could tease a little.

"Naturally! And what am I to call you?"

"Tonia."

"Antonia?"

"Yes, but that just isn't me." She gave a rueful smile. "Antonia conjures up one of those gracious types, calm, patient, with more wisdom in her little finger than I possess in my whole body. She's all the things I'm not. So I'm Tonia."

"You sound wistful. Does it matter that you're not all these things?"

He saw her suppress a little sigh. "It's been such fun being Tonia, but now it would be better to leave her behind."

"Better for whom?"

"The man I'm going to marry. I'm not exactly the ideal type for a doctor's wife."

"Then why become one?"

"The profession happens to go with the man," she pointed out.

"You misunderstand me. Why become the ideal type? You have your own personality. Start a new fashion in doctors' wives."

She shook her head in smiling protest. "Don't encourage me. You're talking to a nonconformist who's seen the error of her ways. Besides, I'm marrying an old-fashioned man. From now on, someone else can start the new fashions."

"While you watch from the sidelines? You're going to feel very stifled."

Soberly, she said, "Yes."

"I watched you enter the clubhouse, noticed the way you held your head, your superb walk. You're an individualist. It's going to be difficult to become one of the sheep."

She couldn't find anything to say. He was saying it all for her. Somehow he knew all about the continual struggle being waged inwardly. The curbing of the passion, the constant guard against too much exuberance, too much joyousness . . . because Luke became embarrassed so easily.

She turned her head, and the perceptive eyes held hers. "You loathe any kind of pretence, don't you?" she asked.

"Especially when it's unnecessary."

"I put on such an act at times, and then I feel a hypocrite . . . "

"Which you are—at times."

"Please understand!" It seemed so important to gain his approval. "This is the way it has to be. If I'm to make Luke happy, we must live his way, not mine."

"Why? Who in his right mind would want the shadow when the substance is there for the taking? A man marries a woman because of all the things she is, and there's something wrong with a setup that demands otherwise."

"He doesn't demand it. I'm trying to give it voluntarily."

"You fool," he said quietly. "Will you also try to stop the singing of the lark and the shining of the sun? That which is inside you has been placed there by the same joyous hand. Will you fling it back into His face?"

She was startled to feel tears stinging the back of her eyes—she, who rarely cried. But no young man had ever spoken to her thus. Then she discerned that Stephen was not a young man, although the outward trappings of the tanned face and blonde hair created a splendid illusion.

Through her lashes she stole another look at him and yearned to say his name. To touch him. But she, who touched so naturally, forced her hands to stay still. It was a discipline that had never been demanded of her before, and she thought it was just as well, for it was not easy.

He was speaking again. "Some poor creatures never experience the full joy of living because it is not in them to do so. They journey wearily through life without one redeeming moment of ecstasy, and one can only pity them. Others suppress it in the misguided notion that it is good for their souls. But to be abundantly blessed with it, and deliberately renounce it, there's not a man or woman in this world worthy of such a sacrifice."

The last word was not stressed in any way yet it hung between them. And because she sensed that the sacrifice had been great, to put hardness in his face and pain in his voice, she said to herself, "Discipline be damned," and reached out and slipped her hand in his. It was cool and firm, and she could have hung on to it forever.

With an expressionless face Stephen regarded the clasped hands. "You won't change," he said. "The world can do its best—you can try your best—but you'll be wasting your time." He smiled and added quietly. "Thank God."

In the silence that followed, a curious, almost challenging look passed between them, and then he rose. "Come. You must go back to your friends."

"I rather think someone else is coming to say the same thing," she said.

Through the dusky half-light, they watched the approaching figure.

"Your fiancee, or another mutual friend?"

"Neither. He's a doctor at the same hospital as Luke."

Julian reached them, his face dark and cold with disapproval. "Luke has just telephoned. He wanted to speak to you. It seems he can't make it after all, and he's asked me to take you home."

Hastily she stood up. "This is Dr. Julian Goldberg."

Stephen extended his hand. "Steve Marais."

Julian touched it briefly. "Your crowd's flapping," he told him. "They want to move on, and they're wondering whether to go without you."

The mute appeal in Tonia's eyes was transmitted to Stephen, but he simply proffered his hand in a conventional courtesy. "I must go. Good night."

"Good night, Stephen."

She felt the pressure of his fingers. Then he was gone.

"Up to your old tricks, Princess? Habit obviously dies hard. Your conspicuous tête-a-tête with that man has certainly given the gossips something to sink their teeth into."

Julian was coldly furious, but she didn't even notice. On the way home, she only spoke once. "Wasn't Roger supposed to take me home?"

"I happened to be going your way, so I saved him the chore."

"Oh. You needn't have bothered."

"Obviously not," he said.

# ❧ 9 ❧

They were driving back from Rivingham. Every Sunday afternoon, duty permitting, Luke took her to have tea with his mother, a tedious ritual, which Tonia endured with as good a grace as she could muster. She neither liked nor disliked Ann Howard. She was Luke's mother, and she suffered her as such, but apart from Luke they had no common interest, and Tonia was too disinterested to attempt to manufacture one.

During the first few visits, she had been her natural effervescent self, but Mrs. Howard's lips tightened at some of her remarks, and afterwards Luke begged her to tone them down a little whenever they came to Rivingham. She was indignant and retorted hotly that it wouldn't do his mother any harm to modernize her ideas. She calmed down, of course, and subsequently made it her business to be studiously polite and very restrained.

Luke was gratefully conscious of the effort being made, but week after week Ann Howard conversed with the lovely, bored face and trembled inwardly for her son. Both women were usually relieved when Luke looked at his watch and stood up, thus ending the farce for another seven days.

As she stood at the door watching them drive away, Luke's mother thought despondently that the girl had been even more remote than usual and wished for the umpteenth time that her son had chosen a plain, uncomplicated girl for his bride. She shut the door and leaned against it for a moment before slowly climbing the stairs.

Luke was also feeling a little despondent. He flicked an apprehensive look at a strangely quiet Tonia and decided it was time to clear the air.

"You're still mad with me, aren't you? Honestly, Tonia, I did intend to pick you up last night, but that child I told you about, the one undergoing such drastic treatment . . . "

Guiltily, she cut him short. "I'm tired."

"Tired? You! I think you're sulking," he said coldly. "It's been a most disappointing day. Even Mother remarked how odd you were."

"She would!" muttered Tonia.

"What is that supposed to mean?"

She gave an expressive shrug.

"I asked you to explain that remark," he said doggedly.

"Well, first she disapproved because I was too noisy, and now she moans because I'm too quiet. I can't win, can I?"

Luke was decidedly annoyed. "There are times, Tonia, when you are definitely not nice to know . . . "

" . . . and this is one of them," she agreed listlessly. "Luke, I'm sorry if I've spoilt your day. Can we leave it at that?"

"It seems we'll have to," he said.

They drove along in silence for a little while, and then she turned to him, her lovely eyes shadowed, "Luke, do you love me? Really love me? Desperately—with all your heart?"

Her intensity caught him by surprise and made him uncomfortable. Cautiously, he sought for the right words. "Tonia, you know I do. I'm going to marry you. Very shortly, you'll become my wife."

"But that's not the answer I want! A marriage ceremony is no automatic guarantee that we'll live happily ever after. Luke, will we? Am I going to make you happy? Will I be happy with you?"

He slowed the car down and patted her arm. "We're going to be very happy," he said firmly. "We'll have our ups and downs in the beginning like all newlyweds, but once we've settled down and grown used to each other, we'll get along fine." He turned his head to smile at her. "Is that why you've been so quiet? Have you been worrying about us?"

"Yes," she said.

"Silly girl." He felt relieved and rather touched to know that she was thinking deeply of their future together. He caught his breath. Their future together! If she only knew how his blood kindled at the thought, but he could never put this kind of thinking into words. Strange that in the lecture theater he never had any difficulty expressing himself, but with Tonia he was inarticulate. Still, once they were married, words would be superfluous . . .

He glanced again at her profile and saw that she still looked troubled, and a wave of tenderness coupled with desire swept through him, so that he wished he'd avoided the fast motorway to St. Michael's and taken the winding country road. Then he could have stopped the car and reassured her with actions instead of inadequate words. Now that the wedding was close, he could relax the self-imposed restraint a little; and because the wedding *was* so close, he could now acknowledge how difficult that restraint had been. Not a living soul, not even Julian, knew that he was capable of a passion to match Tonia's. But his upbringing had taught him that passion was shameful and not to be allied with the purity of love. So he had suppressed it and buried it deeply, denying its very existence. That is, until he met Tonia, and her warmth had almost proved his undoing. Thank God that he'd been strong-minded enough for the two of them, because if they had become lovers, afterwards he would not have been able to stomach himself—or her. Sex belonged in the marriage bed, not out of it.

But it had been a near thing. She was so generous with

her affection, and so very lovable. He frowned as he recalled her admission that it had been a near thing with
others . . .

Determinedly he forced his thoughts to other things as
they approached her home.

"I'm looking forward to the concert on Wednesday
night," he said. "And I'm glad there'll only be the two of
us, I'm tired of sharing you with all and sundry." He pulled
up outside the house. "I'll pick you up about 7:30. Sorry I
can't stay for supper tonight."

As he kissed her goodbye, he said softly, "No more
worrying now. Only one and a half weeks to go, darling . . . and Tonia, I do love you."

She was shivering as she got out of the car, but then
the weather had turned so damp and cold. As she walked
up the garden path she could see her father's head and
shoulders through the lounge window. He appeared to be
holding forth animatedly to an unseen audience. Disinterestedly she went upstairs to her room, threw her coat on the
bed and walked to the window, pressing her forehead
against the pane.

Where was he? The bright-haired stranger with the
clear, calm eyes. What was he doing at this moment?
Stephen. Stephen. All day long his face had been in front of
her. Superimposed over Luke's, over Mrs. Howard's, in
front of the windscreen on the drive home.

Stephen, she whispered, did I imagine it? Did something magical leap between us? Did you feel it, too? Or was
it a flight of fancy—my imagination running wild? Her
breath misted the windowpane, and as a child would do,
she traced his name, but with a sad unchildlike concentration, as though painfully signing away some precious deed
or gift—to someone unknown. She inspected her handiwork, added her own name underneath, and then, with an
angry brush of her sleeve, obliterated both names.

She walked to the bathroom, scowled at herself in the

mirror, washed her hands, and went downstairs to find her mother in the dining room, setting the table for supper. Tonia noticed that an extra place had been laid.

"Who's coming?" she asked.

Her mother gave a resigned smile. "Your father got a bee in his bonnet and went dashing off to the Savoy Hotel to see if he could find any of the South African visitors and bring them home. He's never forgotten his stay in Durban . . . the good time he enjoyed . . . said it was another chance to reciprocate. Other people must have had the same idea, however, because they were all out except one."

Her heart slammed against her ribs. All except one. Please, please, let it be him!

"And Daddy brought this man back with him? Are they talking in the lounge?"

Mrs. Marshall stood back to survey the table. "Yes. Oh, salt and pepper . . . on the sideboard . . . please pass them, dear. Thank you."

"Mummy." Her mouth was stiff, but she had to ask. "What's he like? Nice?" Let it be a man with yellow hair, she willed.

Her mother creased her forehead. "No, not nice, that's quite the wrong word. His face is arresting enough, but so hard and unsmiling. And yet, there's something reassuring about the eyes . . . "

" . . . and he has yellow hair," said Tonia.

"Yes, he has. Obviously you saw him last night. Did you speak to him?"

"For a little while." She could see her reflection in the mirror over the fireplace; a girl with shining eyes and flushed cheeks, the mouth already curved in eager anticipation.

"Oh, I've just remembered . . . " She rushed from the room and flew upstairs. She stood in the middle of her bedroom, exultant. She'd conjured him up! The clear oval patch on the damp window pane became a conspiratorial face laughing with her. All the time she was writing his name he was here, unbeknown to her, sitting in the room below. She wondered if he knew that this was her home. She was halfway down the stairs when the door of the lounge opened, and the two men emerged, deep in conversation. As they saw her, they paused.

"My daughter, Tonia." Her father motioned towards her. "Did you meet her last night? Unfortunately, I wasn't able to stay as long . . . Damn, that's the phone, excuse me." He disappeared into his study.

She remained where she was, transfixed by the sight of the sun-streaked hair and the full realization of what this man meant to her. It was so clear and simple that she ceased to be astonished.

Stephen looked up at her. "You have a very expressive face," he said.

"So my mother tells me." She began to move down the stairs, trailing her hand along the bannister, her eyes never leaving his. "But you haven't! You don't even look surprised to find me here."

"Why should I be?" he said calmly. "After what happened to us last night, you had to be waiting for me somewhere along the line."

She caught her breath. "You said 'us'."

A smile warmed the gray eyes. "Come, Tonia! I had a head start on you—a full twenty minutes. And you know it!"

A great gladness took hold of her, and she stood smiling. Again, there was no need of words.

Her father reappeared. "Sorry to leave you. Ah, I see you two've met. I think my wife has the supper ready, Steve, so let's go in." He led the way into the dining room, rubbing his hands briskly. "Brrr. I'm cold. The barometer's fallen. Summer to winter in one short night. Couldn't happen in Durban, eh?"

It was Mr. Marshall's evening, and he made the most

of it. Using Stephen as a captive audience, he relived to the full his three-week stay in Durban.

"... Never forget it as long as I live. Do y'know, Steve, when our ship docked there was a great queue of cars lined up on the quayside, each waiting to take a soldier or two out for the day. Within fifteen minutes of walking down the gangway, my pal and I were sitting in a lovely home on the Berea. And what do you think the first thing was that the lady of the house said to us?" He slapped his knee in delighted anticipation. "You'll never believe it! Go on, take a guess!"

Stephen was very accommodating. "I haven't the slightest idea."

"She said, 'Would either of you two boys like a bath?' And what did my gormless pal say? He looked a bit blank, and then out it came! 'Why, do we look dirty?' he said. Oh dear, oh dear!" He gave a mock groan and chuckled again at the memory.

"And did you have the bath?" asked Stephen.

"I certainly did, and only a man who's bathed in salt-water for days on end can appreciate the luxury of a fresh-water bath. It was grand. But then, everything in Durban was grand. No wonder so many of our lads emigrated there after the war. Like me, they never forgot the hospitality. Which reminds me, are they looking after you all right at the Savoy?"

"Very well, indeed."

"That's good." Then he was off again. "Is the Playhouse still there? By the way, what's that peculiar word you use for a picture place? You don't say *cinema*. You say something else."

"*Bioscope?*"

"Aah, that's it!" Mr. Marshall nodded his satisfaction. "Been trying to remember that for ages. You don't still use it? Well, I never! Bit old-fashioned, isn't it?"

"Positively archaic," said Stephen gravely.

He looked across the table at Tonia, and she caught the amusement in his eyes. He closed an eyelid at her briefly, and she put her head down and let her hair form a screen lest the leaping exhilaration betray itself in her face.

Mummy was wrong, she thought. He *is* nice. As her father went rambling on, engrossed in his reminiscences, Stephen exhibited neither impatience nor boredom. He made the required responses at the right times, interposed places and names, and kept the older man's enjoyment simmering throughout.

" . . . But the highlight of our stay came when we left, and the Lady in White came down and sang to us. You must have heard of her, Steve."

"Everyone in Durban has heard of her. She's become a living legend."

"I'm not surprised. I can still see her, a big woman in a large white hat, carrying a megaphone. She sang all the old, familiar songs to us—sang us out of sight. There wasn't a peek out of the lads during her songs, but you should've heard the cheers that went up in between. We were told that every troopship leaving Durban had the same sendoff. What a woman!"

Mrs. Marshall looked at the clock and decided that enough was enough! Very firmly she changed the subject. "Tell me, Steve," she said, smiling at him, "have you a wife and family waiting for you back in Durban?"

His face closed, and Tonia stiffened. "No one awaits me," he said curtly.

Tonia's eyes sought him, startled, but the impassive face was difficult to read and told her nothing.

And that was the end of the evening. The sparkle went out of the conversation, and Stephen left shortly afterwards. Her father drove him back to the hotel.

Later, Tonia sat on the edge of her mother's bed, chatting. As casually as she could, she asked, "Do you think that Stephen was once married? He shut up like a clam when you asked him about a wife."

"I would say so, dear. He must be in the mid-thirties, and very few men of that age are still single. Maybe his wife died young; he did look rather grim when I questioned him, so much so that I was sorry I'd been personal. It just goes to show that one should never judge on outward appearance alone. For all we know, that formidable face may hide a deep personal tragedy." She settled back amongst the pillows. "I'm falling asleep, Tonia, but I enjoyed the evening. Good night, darling, sleep well."

For all we know . . . It suddenly became imperative for her to know.

The symphony concert was held in the opera house. Luke and Tonia had barely taken their seats when a small group arrived and were shown to their places two rows in front of them. Tonia was instantly and intolerably aware of Stephen's bright head between her and the stage. She recognized the woman next to him as the wife of the president of the chamber of commerce and she, who had never known jealousy, was knifed with it every time the woman claimed his attention.

It seemed an age to the interval. They came face to face in the foyer. Stephen nodded at her briefly, gave Luke a hard penetrating stare, and passed on.

"Tough-looking customer," murmured Luke. "Who is he?"

"One of the visiting South Africans." She fought down the urge to look over her shoulder.

"His face matches his country's politics," said Luke. "I'd hate to live in a place like that."

"Like what?"

"You know, *apartheid* and such. I believe that medical

services for the blacks are practically nonexistent, while schooling . . . "

"Let's go back to our seats," said Tonia.

All through the second half of the concert, she watched the back of Stephen's head. When the program finished, he and his party seemed in no hurry to leave. The president's wife was talking animatedly with him.

"Come on," said Luke. "If we hurry, we'll have time to have coffee somewhere."

# ❧ **10** ❧

Friday morning, and the turning of the tide brought a wind that shrieked and moaned and whipped itself into a hysterical frenzy, causing the black cone that signaled a gale warning to be hoisted on the end of the pier.

Tonia, a lone figure on the deserted promenade, saw it as she passed by. "For those in peril on the sea." She remembered singing that once in school. And those in peril on the land? Was the black cone a somber coincidence, a warning against the sudden storm that threatened to blow her off a safe, well-charted course? If so, it had come too late. She belonged with Stephen. Stephen of the closed face and calm eyes. She didn't know how, or why, or where. Or if it would ever come to pass. But in one quiet moment of simplicity, she had recognized in him all that she ever desired.

And Luke? Luke, her darling scarecrow?

Made miserable by her thoughts, she ventured to the edge of the promenade and leaned heavily against the railings. The sea was angry, its frothing surface whipped into a thousand white horses, a never-ending army that surged forward, line by line, hurling itself against the sea wall. She shivered as the wind cut through her. Unpredictable English summer. She wondered what the summers were like in Durban. Her father had been there in winter.

Hands suddenly gripped the railings on either side of her. Muscular hands burnt by the sun. Her heart leapt and she said joyously, "Stephen!"

The gale buffeted them and tugged at their clothing, loosening her kerchief from her hair. It went sailing over the water, twisting and dancing like a thing bewitched, a splendid flash of emerald green between the somber grays of sea and sky. Tonia made an involuntary move to try to catch it, but Stephen crossed his hands in front of her, to hold her arms and keep her steady.

"No," he said. "You can't fly away, too. You're wanted here."

Wanted. What a warm word, she thought.

She let her body lean back against his and felt the hard, encircling strength. They stood like that for a few moments, careless of the spray and the turbulence, each quieted in the refuge of the other. The heaviness went out of her, and she looked out to sea and smiled.

"How did you know I'd be here?" she asked.

"Easy," he said. "I saw you from my bedroom window."

"What!" She twisted round to see the familiar blue and gold facade of the Savoy Hotel. "I'd no idea I'd walked so far." She colored faintly. "I didn't stop here on purpose, Stephen."

"No? I rather hoped that you had."

A quick smile lit his face and fascinated her. "You should do that more often," she said. "You have such a lovely smile."

Her hair blew against his face and he wound a handful round his fingers and gave her head a gentle tug. "Forward minx, aren't you?"

She laughed. "I embarrass Luke when I say things like that."

"You don't embarrass me. But then, I'm not Luke."

Instantly she sobered. "No, you're not."

"You'd forgotten again," he said.

"Yes." Her head dropped against his chest for a moment, then she straightened and tried to push herself away from him, but he kept her firmly imprisoned against the railings.

"You're very confused, aren't you?" he asked gently.

"Yes. My mother said this only happened in films."

"Your mother was wrong."

"She isn't usually."

"What has happened to us isn't usual. When are you going to tell Luke?"

Her eyes were frightened. "I can't tell Luke anything. I'm going to marry him."

"I think not," he said.

Her shoulders sagged, and she stared at him. He smoothed her cheek gently with the back of his hand. " 'The time has come, the walrus said, to talk of many things.' Many things, Tonia. Now we need the words." Taking her by the arm, he said simply, "Come."


The hotel room was quiet and warm. Outside, the wind still assaulted the windows in great, tearing gusts, but now it was remote, and the two of them were sheltered from the storm without—but not from the one within.

It was the first time they had been together in private, and it should have been welcomed by them both. Instead, they sat uneasily in an air of uncertainty and restraint.

"This thing between us," he said. "You can't accept it?"

She made a gesture of defeat with her hands. "I'm not free to accept it."

"You can make yourself free."

His stern face made her resentful. "It's so easy for you to talk. Tell Luke. Just like that! *What* do I tell Luke? 'A few nights ago, a stranger looked at me, and because of that I'm about to shatter your life, and please forgive me?' "

"You'd rather condemn him to a life of mediocrity?"

"Luke isn't mediocre," she defended him hotly.

"He will be. You'll either reduce him to that level or

destroy him. Because you'll only be capable of giving him second best. You'll be a hypocrite for a little while, and then the pretence will wear thin, because hypocrisy is not for you, and second best is not for him."

He came to her and caught her by the shoulders. "Look into the years. Watch Luke becoming bewildered as he gropes for that which is lacking. Blaming himself, wondering how he's failed you. Watch yourself, dragging out the years, *knowing* what is lacking, turning for temporary reckless consolation to others." He felt her shiver, and his voice became inexorable. "As you most certainly would. And when the realization dawns that he's been cheated— and that you are the cheat, how is he going to feel? How are you going to feel? Well, Tonia?"

She refused to look at him. "It's not going to be like that. I'm going to try . . . to try my very best . . . "

"Try? Try to love?" he asked softly. "Come, you know better than that! Besides, neither the martyr's crown nor the halo were meant for you." His hands tightened their grip. "Look at me," he said.

Unwillingly, she raised her head. Studied his cold, clear eyes and grave face. "I don't believe in compromise," he said, "nor in self-sacrifice. It's highly overrated, often destroys others, and then becomes a selfish luxury. Well, Tonia? When are you going to tell Luke?"

Her teeth chattered, and it was difficult for her to speak. "I can't. It's too late. Everything's ready. I couldn't face it, Stephen. My parents, Luke . . . " Her voice trailed away, and the room was very still.

Stephen finally said, "I think we've both made a mistake. You are not the girl for me, and I'm obviously not the man for you. I'll call a taxi to take you home."

She watched despondently as he picked up the telephone and made his request to the porter. She didn't want to go. Didn't want to leave him. "Stephen . . . " She had to say something more, something to justify herself.

"Shall we go downstairs?" He picked up the room-key tag and stood waiting for her to rise.

She did so reluctantly, her face wistful. "Stephen . . . I'm sorry. Sorry that you've come too late. If only you'd come a year ago—even six months ago—how wonderful it would have been. I'd have married you on the turn."

"That wouldn't have been possible. I already have a wife."

Tonia put a hand out blindly and caught at the chair to support her trembling legs. "You have a wife?"

"Yes." His face was like granite.

The telephone rang. "That will be the taxi," he said.

"Send . . . it . . . away." She spoke between clenched teeth. "We're not . . . going . . . anywhere." She took a long, shuddering breath. "The time has come for me to talk. And, boy, do you need the words!"

"Just a moment," he said. He picked up the telephone, cancelled the taxi, and replaced the receiver.

"Right," he said. "The floor is yours."

She was seething. "How dare you . . . *you* . . . lecture me, on cheating, hypocrisy, compromise! You actually had me feeling guilty. Guilty! Me! That's pretty rich! Tell me, Stephen—Mister Married-Man—just what did you want of me? I had to be waiting for you, you said. Waiting for what? A hectic two-week affair before you go back to Durban and I walk down the aisle? Don't look at me like that, blast you! Keep your pity for yourself. You need it more than I do."

Her knuckles showed white as she clutched the back of her chair to steady herself. She tried to speak more calmly.

"You must be a very callous man. I've been an awful fool, but did you have to tell me you were married? Another five minutes, and I'd have been out of here. Was it necessary to shatter my illusion?"

"It was very necessary. I don't want our life together to

start with an illusion. Neither will there be room for cheating, hypocrisy, and what was the other? Oh, yes, compromise."

There was actually a hint of a smile in his eyes.

"Our life together," she repeated in a whisper. "Are you making fun of me?"

"No, Tonia," he said quietly. "I'm asking you to come and live with me."

She gave one incredulous stare and then collapsed in a chair, shaking with silent, helpless laughter.

"Oh, no! This is pure comic opera," she gasped. "You've no idea how funny it is. This is a case of the biter being bit, the tables turned with a vengeance. If Julian Goldberg was a fly on the wall listening to this little lot, he'd be in his seventh heaven!"

"Why Julian Goldberg and not Luke?"

She pushed a hand distractedly through her hair. "I don't know. I just thought of him first. He and I have a hate thing about one another, that's all."

"Please explain—about the tables being turned."

"I didn't want to marry Luke in the first place. I didn't think we were ready for it. So I offered to . . . well, not live with him . . . but to be with him whenever he wanted . . . "

Her voice faded before his intimidating expression.

"Whenever *you* wanted would be more accurate, I think. You are a minx," he said slowly. "I'd have tanned your backside for you."

The crudity of the words made her blink and caused a flood of color to rise under the fair skin, but she quickly rallied. "The pot calling the kettle black? At least I was free to make the offer. And I didn't need to lie about someone waiting at home for me."

"Neither did I, and morally I'm as free as the wind. There was a child. It wasn't mine but I couldn't prove it. I married just before my twentieth birthday, and it lasted one distasteful year. I haven't set eyes on my wife for fourteen years, neither do I know her present address. I communicate with her once a year through her lawyers, requesting my freedom. The answer has always been negative."

"Oh." She didn't know what else to say. The anger and the ridiculous sense of betrayal were no more. All she cared about was the bleakness in his face. "To say 'I'm sorry' doesn't seem enough," she said. "I want to put my arms around you. It would appear that I am a minx, Stephen."

A half-smile tugged at the corners of his mouth. "Of course you are! An endearing, unique, little minx. If I'd met someone like you when I was nineteen, my life might have taken a vastly different course."

She scoffed at the thought. "You'd have wanted to change me, once we were married. Just as Luke does, deep down inside."

"No. As I've already stated, I'm not Luke."

"Then you'd have spent the best part of your time tanning me," she retorted. "And for your information, girls don't have backsides. They're strictly for men. Girls have bottoms."

"You must pardon my ignorance," he said, keeping a straight face. "I've been literally out of touch. Well, whatever you choose to call it, it wiggles!"

"It does not!"

"It most certainly does!"

She gave a little gurgle. "You know something? Once I've learnt to read that poker face of yours, life will be . . . " Both hands flew up to cover her mouth, and the eyes above were shocked and enormous. The silence stretched between them, and because Tonia was incapable of ending it, it was left to Stephen to do so.

"You realize that you've arrived at a decision?"

Mutely, she nodded.

"There are tears streaming down your face." He

touched her wet cheeks. "For Luke—and he will never know. You're a nice minx," he said. "Now you'd better come here."

He reached out and drew her close, and the feel of his arms soothed and comforted her as she sobbed unrestrainedly, the tension broken.

Presently he said, "Now that's enough. You're half drowning me. Don't you possess a handkerchief apart from that ridiculous little tissue?"

She shook her head. Stephen felt in his pocket. "Use this, it's quite clean. Now blow. Feeling better?"

She managed a shaky smile. "Talk about burning one's boats! I seem to have flooded mine. I feel as if I've washed away all my old life."

"Not quite. Your confrontation with Luke is still ahead. Are you seeing him today?"

"This afternoon. Stephen, will you come with me?"

"No," he said.

"It will be very hard for me—alone."

"Very hard. It must be, Tonia. You know why."

"Yes," she said.

A watery shaft of sunlight made a faint line across the carpet, and she absently traced up and down its path with the toe of her shoe. He wants me to be sure, she thought. She remembered telling Luke that she was quite sure. Why was it so different with this man?

She looked up from the pattern of the carpet to see Stephen watching her intently. Something in his expression was different, and she struggled to see what it was. The eyes were still calm; the face austere. Nothing changed there. But the mouth? Tight, compressed, a thin straight line. A contemptuous mouth? A stranger would certainly interpret it thus.

But she was not a stranger, and she discerned the tautness of a bowstring in a waiting that had dragged into weariness, a controlled anticipation of disappointment experienced all too often, a mouth molded into a thin scar of resignation.

Stephen saw the face of the tearful girl become calm and strong, as if a measure of his own strength had passed into it.

"I'm sure," she said clearly. "I don't know the first thing about you, whether you're a rich man, poor man, beggarman, or thief. And it doesn't matter. That's how sure I am. I just want to be with you, in whatever you do, wherever you go. I belong to you, Stephen. Without reservation. Here, if you like, or in South Africa, or in Timbuktu."

It was as if the initiative had passed from the man to the girl, he was so silent.

Then he asked, "Do you believe in miracles?"

"Of course," she said promptly. "Don't you?"

"I do now," he said.

He looked at her for a long time, and eventually the waiting frightened her. "Oh, I do wish I could read your face," she burst out passionately. "I want to so much. Stephen, what is it? What are you thinking?"

"I am thinking," said he, "that it is the time of the year to go and ask my question, because I should like this thing between us to be done decently and in order."

"And if the answer is still the same?" she asked, suddenly cold and fearful.

He smiled, because he knew what she was thinking. "No," he said. "No more sacrifice. But this miracle of ours will then become an offence to many. It will hurt your family, outrage your friends, and create a magnificient Roman holiday for those who whisper behind their hands. We shall be derided, and attract harshness and ugliness. Nevertheless, so long as we give no offence one to the other, none of it should matter. If there is integrity between us, there can be no disorder. So, my Tonia, because it is rare for a man and a woman to have a perfect understanding from the beginning, we shall reach out and grasp our miracle tightly. It shall not pass us by."

There was a sudden mist before her eyes. "You are making love to me with words," she whispered, "and I can hardly bear it because you fill me with such sweetness that it is terrible, for now I want to say beautiful things and I can't begin to match you."

He placed his hands on either side of her temples and held her face. "But you have! Those brave words you spoke, another woman translated them into great beauty." He quoted softly, " 'Entreat me not to leave thee, nor to return from following after thee; for whither thou goest, I will go; and where thou lodgest, I will lodge; and thy people shall be my people . . . ' "

The ancient words made her throat constrict and she shook her head at him, half laughing, half crying. "This is so unfair! You're such a fraud. Tough as nails on the outside, and all this . . . *this* . . . inside you! Stephen, I'm so thankful you looked at me. I'm going to love you very much."

The words stilled him momentarily, then he ran his finger lightly down the centre of her nose "Cheeky, lovely nose. Perfect for a minx."

She sensed that he said so little because he wanted to say so much, and the sweetness moved her to say, "The woman who used my words, I hope she felt as I do now."

Stephen quirked an eyebrow. "She didn't! Those words weren't spoken to a man. Her husband was dead. She was addressing her mother-in-law."

"Her mother-in-law!"

Her vehement astonishment made his lips twitch. "It's obvious that you didn't win any gold stars in Sunday school. A virtuous woman named Ruth said that to Naomi, her mother-in-law."

"Crikey," mourned Tonia. "What a waste! Imagine my saying something like that to Mrs. Howard." She froze.

*"Mrs. Howard!* Oh, poor Luke! He'll get 'I told you so' with a vengeance." She walked to the window, and there was complete silence while he studied the straight taut back. She turned. "Stephen, I'm going now. I want to be ready when he comes." She added, "I'm not afraid any more," but his quick eye caught the suppressed shiver. She pretended it was the weather and tried to be flippant. "Baby, it's cold outside!"

He looked at his watch. "I think you need some piping hot coffee to warm you on your way. Shall I order some?"

"Oh, lovely. Yes, Please."

She sat on the bed, watching as he dialled room service, marveling that she was able to sit so calmly. She'd entered the room engaged to one man; she was about to leave promised to another. She'd committed herself to go halfway across the world to a man who hadn't even kissed her. And ahead lay an afternoon the mere thought of which made her shudder. And afterwards? Stephen had said nothing about afterwards. Would he take her with him? Could he? He was with an official party, on a business trip. What business? Whatever it was, she must concoct a marvelous story for Mummy. Dear God, please make her understand and don't let her be ill. . . .

Stephen replaced the receiver and, keeping his hand on it, turned his head to her. "However difficult or unpleasant the confrontation may be, hold fast to this thought. I shan't move away from here. I'll be waiting for this phone to ring, to hear that it's all behind you. Once I know that, I'll come to your home and talk to your parents."

A flush spread over her cheeks. "I thought . . . "

"You thought I'd leave you to do that alone, too."

"You refused to come with me to Luke . . . "

"Because Luke is not my responsibility. He's yours. The events that prompted you to become engaged—the things that will be said this afternoon—are strictly between

the two of you. Afterwards, you become my responsibility."
He took his hand away from the receiver and stood looking
down at her. "One I intend to take very seriously."

He pulled her slowly to her feet, and they stood linked
in a loose embrace, each a little spent, a little awed.

"We almost missed each other," she said, panicky at
the thought. "I didn't really want to go to the Cricket Club
party."

A knock came at the door. "That was quick," said
Stephen. "Come in," he called.

The door crashed open. "Thanks for the invite," said
Julian harshly. "I was coming in anyway. I think you've
been up here long enough. Even had time to make the
bed, I see."

He looked at Tonia and his lip curled. "You little tart,"
he said. His glittering eyes moved to Stephen. "And you're
a bastard of the first order. You and she should have met
much sooner. You deserve each other."

Unhurriedly Stephen detached himself from the suddenly immobilized girl. "We've decided to take each
other," he said.

Julian's sallow face took on an almost dirty tinge. His
eyes, incredulous, sought Tonia's, and the confirmation
stared back at him out of gray defiant depths. "Why,
you . . . " Without warning, he lunged for Stephen. His fist
aimed straight for the jaw, but Stephen swiftly sidestepped
and parried the blow with his elbow. The two of them scuf-
fled briefly for a few seconds, but Julian was no match for
the taller, heavier man and found himself forced against the
wall and held there.

"Take your hands off me," he panted furiously.

"Steady," cautioned Stephen. "I don't want to have to
hurt you, and karate will." He released him and stepped
back keeping a wary eye on him.

Julian, breathing heavily, adjusted his jacket and tie,
and ran a hand through his hair. He shot a venomous

glance at the rigid girl and seemed about to say something, but changed his mind and turned on his heel.

"Just a moment," said Stephen. "Telling Luke is Tonia's responsibility. Don't anticipate it."

Julian looked back from the doorway. "I wouldn't dream of it. She can do her own dirty work. I only hope he breaks her neck. And yours, too, while he's about it."

Stephen looked thoughtfully after him. "Interesting. Why are you and he so abrasive to each other? Is there a story there?"

Sheer scorching anger quickened her. "Abrasive is putting it mildly. He's rubbed me up the wrong way from the first moment we met. You heard what he called me. Why didn't you hit him?"

His voice was calm. "Why should I? You don't strike a man for being loyal to his friend, and his assumption was perfectly natural. He must have seen us enter the hotel, and we've been up here for quite some time. Pretty compromising from any angle." He saw that she had become very pale. "*Tart. Bastard*," he repeated. "Ugly words. No wonder you're shivering. Rather a contrast to 'Whither thou goest'."

"I'll bet Ruth never felt like this," she choked. "It wasn't the words. It was the expression on his face. I hate him."

He shook his head. "No. You hate what you saw in his eyes. The image of you that he's taken away with him. The little cheat who wouldn't scruple to go to bed with one man on the eve of her wedding to another. He not only called you a tart, he made you feel like one. That's what you hate."

She frowned. "How odd," she said slowly. "You've only met him briefly, and yet you've put your finger on it—the thing which bothered me and which I never could explain." She recalled vividly her first meeting with Julian when his eyes practically undressed her. "He assumed I *was* a little tart."

"So, of course, you—being you—lived up to your supposed reputation whenever he was near?"

"Yes." It was true. She had always been her most audacious self whenever Julian was around.

Her eyes met Stephen's ruefully. "That nonsense I told you about sometimes putting on an act—it seems it wasn't only confined to Luke's mother."

"There'll be no such nonsense with me," he told her equably. "Putting on an act won't get you far. I understand you too well." He walked across to the bed. Sitting on the edge, he drew her down beside him. "Let us use all the words now, Tonia, and blend them together, the delicate with the ugly, to end your confusion. There's potentially a little of the tart in every woman, and any man can be a bastard if he puts his mind to it. A given set of circumstances, the wrong combination of man and woman, can produce astonishing reactions."

"Like Julian and me." She looked at Stephen with a shyness that was foreign to her. "You're different. I could never feel like that with you."

"You're wrong," he said. "When you arrive in South Africa, shall I install you discreetly in a little flat and furtively sneak in and out at all hours? With a bit of luck, we could fool the neighbours. The idea doesn't appeal to you? No, I can see that it doesn't. Well then, suppose I make you my secretary? We'll invent mythical trips to take together, and I can always arrange urgent, last-minute work to keep us late in the office after everyone else has left . . . "

She jerked away from him violently. "No! No, Stephen! Not like that. Not even for you. Stephen, don't do that to me. Please don't!"

"Let me finish," he said. "We wouldn't fool people for

long. But if we remember to look guilty and ashamed and half apologise for one another occasionally, we'll be accepted. People love feeling righteous, you see. They like to be able to forgive others. It magnifies them in their own eyes. Enables them to play god." His voice was quietly contemptuous, and it seemed to her that the contempt was for things which had gone before rather than those which lay ahead.

"Don't look like that," he said. "That is not for us. We shall live openly and joyously together, seeking approval from none. And that will be our cardinal sin. Not that we live together but that we deny others the right to grant absolution; and for this we shall be condemned. But neither tart nor bastard shall we feel. There, I've finished. What have you to say now?"

She stood up and he loved the set of her head. "I'm so glad you're not going to hide me away, because I'm afraid it would be rather a waste of time. I haven't got your poker face, and all the world will know that Stephen Marais is my own personal miracle." She picked up her coat from the chair. "Will you hold this for me?" He took it from her and helped her to put it on, and as he turned her round to face him, he sat that she was smiling to herself.

"You know how Julian made me react. Shall I tell you how I feel when I'm with you? Don't you dare laugh at me," she warned. He waited patiently as she hesitated, and then the words came out, shyly, "You make me feel like Ruth."

He looked down at her, his face expressionless. Then gently, so gently, he said, "O, worker of miracles, you've just wiped out fourteen hollow years."

They smiled at each other, and he asked "No more confusion?"

"Oh, no," she said. "You've made things so simple. There is you, and there is me. You will go, and I shall follow. And we shall live happily ever after. That's what it all boils down to, doesn't it?"

"That's all," he said.

She began drawing her gloves on. "I won't wait for coffee, Stephen. But I do think, as a substitute, you could kiss me to warm me on my way." And she turned her face up to him.

When he took his mouth from hers, she mocked softly, "And what are you thinking now, O, impassive one?"

"How unobservant you are," he said. "I am thinking that life with you will be exhausting. Without you, unendurable."

Then he kissed her again, and let her go.

# 11

"However difficult or unpleasant the confrontation may be,"
Stephen had said. It proved to be both, which was only to
be expected. Plus a great deal which was not expected. To
begin with, her mother was not in the house when Tonia
arrived home, which was in itself most unusual; she was
seldom out for lunch. Utterly dismayed, the girl wandered
aimlessly downstairs and stopped short on the threshold of
the little morning room. All the wedding presents had been
unpacked and put on display, and the mere thought of her
mother performing this labour of love, serenely unaware of
the drama being unfolded at the other end of town, started
a sickening chill of remorse gnawing through her.

She forced herself to sit down, to review again the implications of what she was about to do. She began to shiver.
It seemed to her that she sat shivering a very long time before she heard the unmistakable sound of Luke's footsteps
in the hall. Quick, eager strides, approaching the door. She
braced herself to face him.

He came in, his face lighting up as always when he saw
her. "Hello, sorry I'm a bit late." His mouth brushed hers,
and then he looked around the room in pleased surprise.
"My, what an impressive collection! I'd no idea we knew so
many people. Oh, I like this!" He reached out carefully for
an exquisite little seahorse, a windblown fantasy of
gossamer glass. "It's quite beautiful. Who sent it?"

"Angela." Her throat was dry, and it hurt.

Automatically he reacted as a doctor to the little

croaking sound. "You sound peculiar." He turned his head. "You look peculiar. Don't tell me you're getting an attack of premarital nerves. Not you, Tonia!"

Then he saw her face—really saw it—and the teasing smile slipped a little. "Darling, what is it?" he asked urgently, and the concern in his voice knifed through her.

She moistened her lips. She thought: Say it now. *Now.* It only has to be said once.

"Luke, I'm not going to marry you."

The hand holding the seahorse was arrested in midair. The remainder of the smile hung for an instant, making a lopsided caricature of his face. He thought of asking if she was joking, but her tormented face told him that to ask would be ridiculous.

"Why not?"

"Why not?"

She swallowed painfully. This, too, need only be said once. "I've met someone else."

The seahorse was returned jerkily to the table. He straightened up, and the struggle for control taking place inside him was such that Tonia could almost hear it. She was alarmed to see how white he became. Always pale, he now looked ill.

"Who is he?"

Before she could answer, the door opened and her mother came in with two women in tow. " . . . yes, they're a very lucky young couple . . . such lovely things they've received. Hello, Luke, I must have followed you in. I don't think you've met these particular friends before. Mrs. Kirby. Mrs. Shaw. My future son-in-law, Dr. Howard."

Luke said mechanically, "How do you do," and shook hands with both of them before turning to Mrs. Marshall. "You've arrived at a most interesting moment. Tonia has something to tell you."

"Oh?" She looked inquiringly at her daughter. Only then was she aware of the tension between them. Startled, she took in Luke's white, thinned face and Tonia's flushed, uncomfortable one. The two women onlookers exchanged bewildered glances. Even they were aware that something was wrong.

"Darling, what is it?" The question came now in her mother's gentle voice, and the remorse bit even deeper. And then Stephen's face rose up before her, and no one else mattered, and she said simply, "Mummy, it's Stephen."

"Stephen?" Her mother and Luke spoke simultaneously. A babble of words broke over her head. She heard Luke's puzzled voice questioning and her mother's placating voice answering and the opening and closing of the door as the two friends hurriedly withdrew. She waited until the voices paused. Looking again at her mother, beseeching her to understand, she said pleadingly, "I'm sorry, but it's Stephen."

Again the words beat into the air with a great clamoring. And now she was weary and wanted to be done with it, to lay down the burden of hypocrisy she should never have shouldered. Wanted it behind her, leaving her free to go to Stephen. To be possessed again of the sweetness.

The room was unnaturally quiet. The two shocked faces stared at her, each mutely questioning.

She said shakily, "Darling Mummy, I think you should leave us. I'm not going to marry Luke, and I have to tell him why, and it will be easier for both of us if you're not here. I'll explain to you and Daddy later."

Her mother changed color. Luke saw her sway a little and asked quickly, "Are you all right?"

Mrs. Marshall looked up into his face and wept inwardly for what she saw. "Yes . . . yes, I'll be all right." Keeping her own shock under control, she placed her hand on his arm, "My dear, I'm sorry. So sorry."

She looked at Tonia. "Darling, before you do anything

irrevocable, will you try to remember that you're very precious to us?"

She saw the girl's eyes go suspiciously bright, and then she turned and left her.

"I don't believe it!" Luke found his voice, his face incredulous. "Not even you could be so irresponsible. You stand there and tell me that our marriage is off because of a man you met a week ago . . . a man of whom you know nothing . . . a complete stranger!" He shook his head dazedly. "You must be out of your mind."

"I'm not. The madness was in thinking that I could make you happy. I wouldn't, Luke, not in a thousand years. I think I've known for quite some time, and I should have faced up to it sooner. If it's any consolation I'm feeling very ashamed . . . for tantalizing you in the first place. If I'd left you alone, none of this would have happened."

He stared at her stupidly. "Are you trying to tell me you never loved me? You did, Tonia. You know you did." He looked around at the gifts. "Look, our wedding presents, darling, from our relatives and friends. You can't back out now. This other man, whoever he is, will soon be gone . . . let's not talk about him anymore . . . it was just infatuation because you were disappointed in me. I won't disappoint you again."

"Oh, don't. Please don't . . . " Self-reproach from Luke was something she hadn't bargained for. "You haven't disappointed. It's me. It's all my fault." Wearily she dragged her hair back from her forehead. "If only I'd never started all this."

"Why did you?" he asked slowly. "I've often wondered."

She managed a strained smile. "You were nice. And different. I don't quite know how to put it."

"Try. How different?"

She twisted her hands. "Well, you know . . . "

"No, I don't."

"Well, you were nicely different. In so many ways. You were shy, and I'd only known bold types. You worked hard and actually enjoyed it; I ran around with spoilt little boys who pretended to work and loathed every moment . . . "

"I was a novelty," he said flatly.

"No! Yes . . . I suppose so, in the beginning. But I liked it. I liked *you*, Luke. I grew to like all the differences. Even the fact that you stayed at arm's length . . . had to be coaxed nearer. The others needed no coaxing, they couldn't get close enough."

"This Stephen—has he been close enough?"

"No. Not in that way."

"How many ways are there? Let's talk about this man of mystery. I haven't fully absorbed all the facts yet. You met him at the cricket party last Saturday. You went with your father and came home with Julian, so you couldn't have spent much time with him there. On Sunday your father invited him home for supper. Were you alone with him then?"

"No." She shifted uneasily. The look on his face disturbed her. "Luke, you don't have to conduct a cross-examination. It's not going to alter anything."

"We'll see. Wednesday night we attended the concert. He was with his own party. So when did you see enough of him to decide that you wanted to marry him instead of me?"

Marry? The nervousness jolted up into her throat. A little voice whispered: Let him find out about that later, and she gladly agreed. Stephen, that gay courage, it's slipping away fast.

"Well, when *did* you see him again. And where?"

"This morning. We met by accident."

"What a coincidence. Where?"

"On the promenade."

"What kind of gullible fool do you think I am?" His face was now as hard as Stephen's, but there were no reassuring eyes here to compensate. "There was a howling gale blowing this morning. Hardly conducive to standing around chatting. We had an old man brought into Casualty who'd actually been blown over and hurt. That's how strong the wind was on the beachfront. And somehow I can't see you roughing it in a promenade shelter. That's not your style. Especially when there's a more comfortable place close at hand."

She looked at him helplessly, knowing what was coming.

"You went into the Savoy with him, didn't you?"

"Yes. We had a lot to talk about."

"I'll bet you had." His voice was hard and flat as she had heard it only once before. "You did your talking in the lounge, I take it?"

She felt cornered. Trapped. Somehow the initiative had passed out of her hands, and with painful clarity, she saw where the questions were leading. Stephen, this I didn't expect . . .

"Or did you go to his room?"

"Luke, please, what's the point?"

"Did you?" He was inexorable.

"Stop it," she snapped. "What is this—an inquisition? I know what you're getting at but must you automatically think the worst? Couldn't you possibly give me the benefit of the doubt for once? What's the next question, Luke? Or have you already answered it?"

His hand fastened over her wrist. "I'm waiting for you to answer this one. Did you go with this man to his room?"

She tried to wrench herself free, but he tightened his fingers until she gasped with pain. "I'm still waiting, Tonia . . ."

"Yes! Yes! Yes!" His fingers went slack and she broke

away from him rubbing her wrist, seething with an incredulous anger because Luke had actually hurt her. "Satisfied? Now go ahead and think the worst, which you will anyhow no matter what I say. But you'll be wrong. Do you know why?" Her voice rose. "Because I'm going to live with Stephen for ever and ever, and with all those lovely years in front of us, neither of us were interested in a thirty minute effort in a hotel bedroom. When I go to bed with him, I want all the time in the world so that it can be beautiful and magical, the way I once wanted it with you."

She saw his eyes blaze but the momentum of her temper was such that she lost all caution. "But that's nothing! I haven't come to the worst yet, Luke. Oh, this is much worse. To you, this will be the absolute rock bottom. I can't marry Stephen because he's already married and his wife won't divorce him. Yes, I thought that would shake you. It will shake Rivingham too, won't it? Now the old fogies will really have something to gossip about." She mimicked the broad accent, "Ee, 'ave y'eard t'latest? That fast little Marshall girl's jilted our Luke and gone off with a married man . . ."

She stopped for breath, and the pendulum of her temper, its furthest point reached, began to swing lower and lower. The impetus died, and as Luke stood staring, it seemed to her that something in him died a little, too.

"You little slut," he said slowly.

She bowed her head. Hearing, accepting, sick with disgust at herself. From Ruth to this! Oh, Stephen, will I ever learn?

She forced herself to meet his eyes. They were not pleasant. "I'm sorry, Luke. That was terribly cruel. I didn't intend to come out with it that way. I planned to tell you quietly and nicely . . . "

"*Nicely!* You thought that such news could be broken nicely? To fit in with my image of a nice man, I suppose!" He moved toward her, and she shrank from the white fury in his face. "I suddenly find that I'm not a nice man at all. I
120

come from rough working-class stock, and I should have remembered it earlier. However, it's not too late." He dragged a chair forward and pushed her into it. "Sit down. It's time you heard a few home truths." He pulled another chair out for himself and straddled it, resting his elbows on the back.

"I'm seeing you clearly for the first time. You never really wanted marriage, did you? Other things appealed more. An occasional dirty weekend, an affair with a married man, any kind of spicy excitement, so long as it was sexy."

"That's terribly unfair . . . "

"Shut up," he said. "You've had your say. Now I'm having mine."

He looked at her sitting bolt upright, her hands clenched tightly, the lovely, curved mouth straightened in a stiff, unnatural line.

"I notice that for once you're not laughing. But you must have had plenty of giggles over me in the past. Luke Howard, the not-with-it man, clinging to an old, worn-out code of conduct. When decency and integrity really meant something, when promises were binding, and a man's word was his bond, and every bride was expected to be a virgin on her wedding night, and God help her if she wasn't. Because according to those old standards—which happen to be my standards—any other kind of girl was a slut. Which brings us back to you."

He took a deep breath, and she closed her eyes, despairingly, against the scathing contempt in his face. Stephen, this has become a nightmare . . . he's taken it far worse than I thought.

"Open your eyes," said Luke. "You can do your dreaming later on when you're with your lover." A muscle jerked beside his set mouth. "Princess Tonia! Nothing but a common little slut who had the good fortune to be born into a respectable home. In another environment you'd have been on the streets by now. A moment ago you mocked my background and sneered at my mother . . . oh, yes, you
121

did . . . but I wish you'd known my grandfather. He'd have been a match for you. He wouldn't have given you house room. He'd have taken a strap to your back—your bare back, Tonia—if he'd been in my place today. Come to think of it, I'm told there's a lot of my grandfather in me . . . "

He stopped, and for one black moment, Luke Howard, the quiet man of healing, was filled with a vicious desire to wound and destroy. He was possessed of every base passion. He yearned to crash the back of his hand against the ashen cheeks, to strip and rape and laugh in the act, to place his fingers around the soft throat and squeeze them tight, tighter, to feel her grow cold and know with certainty that no other man would ever be kindled by the precious warmth . . .

Sanity returned. The black mist slowly cleared, and her face came again into focus. He stared in disbelief, and then buried his head in anguish because of what he could see. Gone was the laughing girl. In her place was the woman for whom he'd been waiting. Her expression tender-eyed, compassionate, the grave comprehension telling him that the depth of his torment was understood and shared.

The laughing girl had entranced and delighted him. He'd found her adorable, but she had never really been his. How could she have been, when underneath the laughter, this quiet woman patiently waited. The girl he'd loved lightly. The woman he would have worshipped.

He heard the creak of her chair, as she stood up. Her arms cradled his head, and blindly he let himself slump against her. She laid her cheek against his hair, and his hands crept round her waist.

She said, incredibly, "Darling scarecrow, how ironic that I'm closer to you now than I've ever been. Remember my saying that we'd both been born out of our time? Brought together in another era, we could have loved each other deeply."

He raised his head. "It isn't too late, Tonia. I'd meet you halfway."

She watched the lips form the words but heard the voice of another man say: I don't believe in compromise.

She said, "No. Please go, Luke. I can't bear to hurt you any more."

Clumsily he got up from the chair and returned it to its place by the table. He did the same with the chair used by her. He looked at the wedding presents and motioned toward them. "Will you return all these?"

"Yes."

"You must do it, Tonia. Don't leave it to your mother."

"I won't. Luke . . . don't hate me for too long."

From the doorway his eyes lingered. "I shall always hate you because I shall always love you. Does that make sense?"

She was unable to answer, for she had no voice.

He said, "Don't cry, Tonia. It's too late for tears." His footsteps receded down the hall. Faintly she heard the click of the garden gate. She reached the bathroom just in time to be painfully, agonizingly sick.

Stephen came—and went. Her father's fury coupled with her mother's sick anxiety all but annihilated her.

Angela also came and went—Angela, who had once been her friend.

The local newspaper reported:

> Dr. Luke Howard left yesterday for America, in order to take up a research fellowship at the Johns Hopkins Medical School. The sincere good wishes of all his colleagues go with him.

Tonia sat at home and waited. The waiting was very bad. Ten days later the cable arrived. It began: "The answer is still the same."

The next evening she boarded a South African Airways flight to Johannesburg. To Stephen.

# 12

In the fair province of Natal, in South Africa, about three hours drive from Durban, there is a range of mountains, majestic, purple, serene to the eye, and uplifting to the heart. These are the Drakensberg—the Dragon Mountains—legendary home of dragons and court of the mountain kings, whose dwelling places have been clawed by the fingers of erosion into wildly beautiful shapes, spectacular, fantastic, reaching for the sky, and disappearing into great, white clouds.

The names of these abodes are equally fanciful. Champagne Castle, Cathedral Peak, the gaunt Monk's Cowl, Devil's Tooth, Dragon's Back and Giant's Castle. The Sentinel guards the Amphitheater of Mont-aux-Sources and mighty Cathkin, exposed and aloof, which Zulus call *Mdedelele*, meaning "Make room for him"—the name given to a bully.

The little people lived here, too. The pale-skinned Bushmen, with deadly dart and clicking speech, who left their mark for all time in the paintings covering the walls of their caves.

Dragons, mountain kings, giants, and little people. They all wove their special brand of magic into the Berg.

Today the Bushmen are gone; the dragons' fire is quenched; their forked tails are stilled. The kings have abdicated. The giants sleep. The mountains are quiet. But the magic of the Berg lingers on.

Stephen Marais had a cottage in the Berg, and it was

to this cottage that he brought Tonia immediately following her arrival in Johannesburg.

The flight was traumatic, an eighteen-hour marathon of a postmortem. All through the night, as she huddled against the window of the darkened cabin, and throughout the long haul down the African continent, thoughts whirled round and round in her mind like a continuous carousel.

The incredible hurt in Luke's eyes. The white scorn in Angela's. Her mother's anguish, and her father's wrath. His curt ultimatum that, if she went to Stephen, she need never return. Her mother defiantly climbing into the taxi to accompany her to the station . . . the garden gate clicking with finality.

London in the rain. The bustle of the departure lounge at Heathrow. Looking down on the English Channel and the moment of panic as the pattern of a lifetime gradually receded.

Then another day and the desperate impatience to be finished with the aircraft and the smoke-filled air on which the queasy smell of a hundred-odd breakfasts still lingered. The touchdown at Johannesburg and the sheer bliss as the clear, brilliant air tore into her stale lungs. The unbelievable welcome of the sun upon her head.

Through the immigration and customs, and then, standing out from the waiting crowd, a man with yellow hair . . . He caught her to him, and she thought: Not here, either, do we need the words. They were all there, fully stated, in the feel of her legs jerked against his, in the tense hardness of his body, in the proprietary hands moving slowly across her back. And because the waiting had been hard and the night overlong and the relief was great, she sagged limply against him. The hands moved swiftly down to grip her elbows and steady her, and then she was all right, and she whispered, "I'm sorry," for she had intended to be very gay.

He shook his head at her. "Tonia." It was both an endearment and a reproach, and she realized she was forgetting again. No act was needed, and there was nothing to hide and never would be, and the knowledge made it right and natural for her to be gay.

She picked up her overnight bag, held out her hand, and said, sweetly mocking, "Come!" He laced his fingers with hers and that, for both of them, was the end of the waiting.

The sun was blazing through the windows of his car, and as she climbed in and sat down the contact with the hot leather seat burnt her legs momentarily. Most of the cars in the car park had sun visors, she noticed, and a rash of predominantly TJ numbers.

"Province first, and then the town," explained Stephen. "Transvaal, Johannesburg."

His car had an ND number. "Natal, Durban."

"Are we going there now?" she wanted to know.

"Natal, yes. Durban, no."

She turned her head enquiringly.

"We're not going to Durban. I'm taking you somewhere else." He slanted a look at her. "Now I've made you inquisitive!"

"Naturally!"

"Can you contain the questions?"

"For how long?"

"About ten days."

"Ten days! It would be the waiting all over again, and she felt a little dismayed. She thought about it until they were clear of the airport traffic, and then she said, "No personal questions at all? I know nothing about you and want to know everything? I must!"

"I intend that you shall, but no questions about our future, not until later. Let's get to know one another first. Agreed?"

"Agreed," she made herself say. It took a bit of an effort, though. By nature, she was most inquisitive.

Without taking his eyes off the road, he reached for her hand. She felt his lips against her wrist, and then her hand was lowered and placed firmly on his thigh. "Keep it there," he said.

She looked down with the same sense of wonder that Luke Howard had worn when observing these fingers linked with his. Then, looking at the hands on the wheel, she fought a sudden, violent longing to lean forward and brush her mouth against them. She was conscious of shock. Now what is this, she thought. But the answer was clear. She, who had been adored by many, was about to do the adoring.

She sat strangely still. So this was to be the way of it, then. Well, she'd never been one to do things by halves, and as she looked through the windscreen at the mirror of his image, a smile tilted the corners of her mouth. Stephen—you with the sun trapped in your hair—you're going to be smothered by an avalanche of loving, and I do hope you'll be able to cope!

Her eyes flew to the strong profile, and Stephen turned his head at exactly the same moment and lifted an eyebrow. "All right?"

The understatement of the year. But she nodded. It would do for the moment. She settled back in her seat, delighting in the comfort of the big car, the sun upon her arm, and the taut feel of the hard thigh under her hand.

The scenery was disappointingly dull. The gray ribbon along which they traveled uncoiled in monotonously straight lengths through brown, parched veld. "Wrong time of the year for color," said Stephen. "Easter is the best time, when there's a border of pink and white and purple cosmos on both sides of the road stretching as far as the eye can see. Wait until we come into Natal, though, you'll find plenty of green there."

Some of the towns through which the ribbon drew

them bore names which seemed oddly at variance in an African setting. Heidelberg was one. Signposts pointed the way to Bethlehem, Glencoe, Dundee, and even more familiar, Newcastle. They left the Transvaal and crossed into the Orange Free State. The heat, coupled with the effects of a sleepless night, caught up with Tonia, reducing her animated chatter to desultory snatches, and Stephen, catching the end of a wide, prolonged yawn, said, "What about a little zizz?"

"A little *what?*"

"Zizz. Three fat men snoring in unison. Forty winks. Haven't you heard it described like that before?"

She was laughing. "No, but it's very expressive. Is it a South African word?"

"I don't know where it originated, but it's widely used out here."

"It's perfect. Any more like it?"

"Yes. One that's tailor-made for you." He sounded amused, and she looked at him suspiciously.

"Well?"

"Now-now-now."

"Now-now-now? Is that supposed to mean something?"

"Very much so, as any South African will tell you. Ask for something to be done *now*, and you'll get it in half an hour. Say you would like it *now-now*, and you'll get it a little quicker, say, ten minutes. Ah, but if you stipulate that you want it *now-now-now*, you'll get it immediately if not sooner. Get it?"

"Got it. Stephen, please, will you kiss me now-now-now?"

"With pleasure," said he, braking hard, and bringing the car to rest well off the road.

"Oh, I do like you," she said involuntarily. The more she looked at him, the more she was glad that this was to be the way of it.

"A most encouraging statement," said Stephen, reaching for her. Presently he said, "Now, that's enough."

"It's never enough," she murmured, and delighted in the quick flash of his teeth as he threw his head back and laughed.

The wind caught the car as they came through Van Reenen's Pass, causing it to sway a little, and then they coasted down into the green grassiness of Natal, and Stephen said, "Well, here it is. The garden province."

Later, as they came off the tarred road, the ribbon changed color, from gray to brown, and began to wind through gently undulating landscape that could have been hacked out of the misty isle itself, past neat Zulu *kraals* dotted with *rondavels* and *piccanins*, who waved to the passing car just like the children who sat on the milkchurn platforms in the country lanes outside Rivingham. But Rivingham was already a light year away.

It grew dark, and a rare dry cold penetrated the car. Amazingly, she began to shiver. Stephen took a hand off the wheel and reached behind him for a rug. "It's our winter, remember. Tonight will be freezing, especially in the mountains where we're heading."

Now here is something else, she thought. Many of the waiting hours had been spent studying her atlas, concentrating on Durban and the adjacent coastline, and now there was this talk of mountains. But mountains conjured up appealing pictures of log cabins with cosy, intimate interiors, and these in turn started a train of thought which was interrupted by Stephen saying, "You won't be cold, though. That I promise!"

She searched his deadpan face until she found that which she sought, the tiny smile loitering at the back of his eyes. They looked at each other easily and happily, and she said, "What a tremendous relief, not having to pretend . . . " but the rest of her words were swallowed in an enormous yawn, followed by another and yet another.

"Didn't you sleep at all on the plane?"

"Not a wink." She yawned again as fatigue overcame her, but the more she fought it, the wearier she became, and so it was that when they reached the cottage she was asleep.

Stephen left her in the warmth of the car, snugly wrapped in the rug, and went inside, lit the lamps, put a match to the fire and another under the kettle on the tiny gas stove. He made two journeys to and from the car. The first, to fetch her two cases; and the second time he lifted the sleeping girl high in his arms and carried her through to the bedroom.

She stirred and opened heavy eyes to see Stephen looking down at her. It was an effort to keep her eyelids open. "Where are we?"

"Home," he said.

She smiled drowsily. "Home. Sounds nice . . . the way you say it. What time is it?"

"Time to eat. Hungry?"

"Ravenous." She yawned and stretched luxuriously.

"Good. There's soup simmering on the stove and a roaring fire awaiting you next door. Bathroom on the left."

"Gracious! Five-star service, no less!"

"Preferential treatment, as promised. Come through when you're ready."

Her eyes smiled after him as he walked away, and then they traveled curiously, eagerly, round the room. A moment later she struggled upright, bewildered. It was not possible! This was his home? Stephen's home? But . . . it was ghastly! She wrinkled her nose. It smelt ghastly, too, as if fresh air had not entered it for some time. Shocked into wakefulness, still cocooned in the rug, she slid off the bed to make a closer inspection. Not that there was anything worth inspecting. Dreary was the operative word. For everything. For the gray walls and the even greyer postage stamp of a carpet, the old-fashioned dressing table, and not much else.

The memory of her own luxurious bedroom rose up before her, and swiftly she strangled the traitorous thought. None of that, she told herself. She turned back to the bed. Apprehensively she lifted a corner of the bedcover and was relieved to see an obviously new mattress. Then, hearing Stephen's tread, she reddened and hastily smoothed the cover neatly into place.

He came in holding a pile of sheets and blankets. Quickly, she moved to take them from him and heard him say, "Leave these for now. I want to see you down some food."

"I'm suddenly not all that hungry . . ."

"You'll still take a little soup. Come, I want you by the fire."

Her dismay deepened as she stood in the middle of the lounge. Rich man, poor man? She'd landed herself with a beggar if this miserable place was anything to go by. The simple cottages in Rivingham were luxury homes compared to this hovel. That's the only word to describe this little lot, she thought. Five-star service, my foot! This may be Home Sweet Home to you, Stephen, but from where I'm standing it looks decidedly sour.

He brought the soup to her as she crouched by the fire. It was a clear soup and smelt good, and he served it to her in a cup to retain the heat, but she sat warming her hands round the cup feeling that if she drank it she'd be sick.

What's the matter, *Princess?* she asked herself scathingly. So he didn't bring you to a palace! So this place is an awful letdown. But he's here. You wanted the man, and you've got him. Isn't it enough? She pondered a little and then wondered what she was pondering about. It was enough.

She could almost hear her father's voice growling: You've made your bed, my girl, now lie on it. She reflected that some of the old proverbs were very sensible, and she intended doing exactly this and the sooner the better.

Stephen reached down to place his empty cup on the floor and then lay back in his chair. The firelight played tricks with his face, especially the eyes. A man could control his face, she thought, but the eyes were always a giveaway.

She pondered, then, over him. If this bleak little shack had been the way of it, then it was a pretty rotten way, and tomorrow she'd do something about it. But not tonight. First things first and the look in his eyes had priority.

His quiet voice broke into her musing. "The moment of truth, Tonia?"

She drained the last of the soup and set the cup down decisively. Two pairs of gray eyes exchanged a level look. "Of course not," she said. "Now who's forgetting? I've burnt my boats, remember?"

"Not yet, you haven't. But take your time. There's no hurry."

And then she was angry.

"Oh, for heaven's sake! You dear, sweet, *stupid* man, haven't you waited long enough?"

He rose abruptly, and so did she. His face changed, and she exulted in the blaze of hunger that leapt toward her. She said, "If I haven't already burnt my boats, Stephen, then it's high time that I did. Now-now-now, in fact."

Still he stood, and now she was close to tears, and she whispered fiercely, "Oh, say it, *say it!*"

The swift, brilliant smile transfigured him. "Come, then," he said.

She came. And the manner of her coming was such that Stephen never forgot it, for only Tonia could have presented herself so.

Naked she stood before him, with the pride of a woman who knows that she is beautiful, but it was with the candor of a child that she asked, "Do I please you?"

"Oh, yes," he said slowly. "You please me. You please me very much."

"I'm glad." Then in her clear direct fashion, she said, "Stephen, I'm a virgin. More by accident than design, but I'm so thankful now. Because you'll teach me what it's all about, won't you?"

In the end, it was she who taught him, for it was as her mother had foretold. There was great beauty in her giving, so much so that Stephen, at the height of his knowledge of her, was constrained to cry out, "My love. O, my love." Then as his body left hers, he looked down at her, at the amazing tears in the radiant face. And he, who could only recall greedy shameful couplings, selfish and quick and cold, suddenly hid his face on her breast, and she held him and said never a word.

Still entwined, they fell asleep, and then there was the sun slanting across the bed, caressing their bodies, and wishing them the first of all the good mornings that were to come.

# ❀ 13 ❀

Stephen Marais, at the age of thirty-four, was a loner.

At the age of nineteen, with a fine sporting record behind him, he matriculated with five distinctions and the solitary problem of whether to read law at university or architecture. While making up his mind he spent his days on the beach. Success went to his head, and the young Stephen, all too conscious of his flamboyant good looks, strode the Durban sands like a blond-helmeted sun god, his roving eye selecting the cream of the worshiping girls.

On the day that the matriculation results were published, he met Kathy, graceful and slender-limbed, with crisp chestnut curls and a delicate wildrose coloring. Standing tall in an old-fashioned bathing suit, which immediately separated her from her friends, she had in her eyes a remote look which Stephen identified immediately. The cool type who looked as if butter wouldn't melt in her mouth. But with a little careful strategy, the butter usually did melt, and it warmed and spluttered and sizzled until it ran hot, searing hot, and the taste of it was like honey.

He managed to repress a grin. Throughout the afternoon, he was courteous and very solicitous. Later, at the *braaivleis*, when the eating was done and the fire glowed red, a portable record player throbbed its way through a dreamy LP, and the youngsters paired off. And Stephen made sure that he got Kathy.

He was utterly and completely wrong about her eyes. Kathy was just out of convent boarding school, and

Stephen's practised love-making both frightened and repelled her. She fled, to seek the protective cover of a neighboring group, and Stephen Marais was left high and dry, publicly humiliated and rejected.

Infuriated by the snide remarks and sniggers of some of his cronies, the boy retreated from the camp fire circle and wandered down to the water's edge. He counted the number of ships waiting outside the anchorage. To his left, the stabbing point of the Umhlanga Rocks lighthouse made its regular rhythmic sweep. Disconsolately he slouched his feet through the swirling vicious backwash, and the roar of the surf was a fitting complement to the storm raging within him. The moments with Kathy had inflamed his young manhood to a dangerous degree, and now, his hunger sharpened and left unassuaged, with every nerve end irritated, he cursed himself for a blundering precipitate fool.

Retracing his steps, keeping well outside the glowing perimeter of the fire, he moodily flung himself down on the sand, wondering whether to move on or go home. Preoccupied with self-pity, he only gradually became aware that someone was lying next to him. The face was a pale blur, and he peered into the indistinct features. "Where the devil did you spring from? Who is it?"

A girl's smooth shoulder brushed against his. A girl's voice answered. "One of the crowd. I've been watching you. Are you still mooning over her? She'd have been a dead loss. Her type always are."

"What type are you, then?"

"Your type, Stevie." Deliberately she leaned over him, and the warm weight of her breast pushed against his arm.

It was all over in a matter of seconds. He rolled away from her, his lust slaked. He should have felt triumphant; in some strange way, he felt vanquished. The girl was making movements, sitting up, and adjusting her dark shorts against the dull gleam of her body. He was suddenly glad

135

that he hadn't seen her face and as suddenly terrified he would have to. He stood up and mumbled an unconvincing explanation that he would have to go, and without demur, she accepted it. He stayed only long enough to see her merge with the anonymous shadows round the fire, then he was running, running, his feet hampered by the soft, dragging sand, his heart thudding as never before.

By the time he reached home, he had calmed down and was able to face his reflection sheepishly in the mirror. But he didn't think he would ever forget the matric celebrations of his year.

Nor did he. He was to remember them to the end of his days. Three months later he was ordered out of Cape Town University and home to Durban to face a strange, pregnant girl—whose face he disliked on sight—and her irate father.

His own father, an Anglican clergyman, looked at him steadily and asked but one question. "Did you go with her, son?"

It never occurred to him to lie. "Yes, Dad. Just that once."

"Once too many, Stephen. She holds you responsible for her condition."

The acid vomit of fear surged up in his throat. "And if I'm not?"

"Can you be positive? Did you take any precautions?"

A tide of color ran under the boy's fair skin, and he felt as uncomfortable as he looked. "No. It wasn't premeditated," he muttered.

A quick gleam of triumph lit the two hostile faces, and his father sighed. The boy hadn't a leg to stand on. He looked sadly at his only son—this brilliant bird of plumage whose wings were so shortly to be clipped—and wondered when and how he'd failed him.

Gently, he had the final word. "It's a matter of conscience. Turning dishonor into honor. This coming child must have a name. It will have to be your name, Stephen."

Stephen looked at her. At the eyes like shiny black pebbles, the coarse complexion, the hefty arms and legs.

"I can't, Dad. I can *not!*"

"Go down on your knees and pray about it. It's not too late."

It was, as far as Stephen was concerned. He thought the Almighty had allowed a dirty trick to be played on him, and he wasn't prepared to kneel and ask favors from someone who wasn't on his side. He preferred to stand and fight.

The girl's father had the same idea. He insisted on seeing the boy for a few minutes in private. He came straight to the point. The boy could either marry his daughter or fight a paternity case in court. The boy would do well to remember that, whatever the outcome, the attendant dirty publicity would tarnish the name of a respectable man of God. The boy had exactly twenty-four hours to make up his mind . . .

Stephen Marais and Trilly Malherbe were quietly married in the church of Christ the Redeemer by the Reverend Paul Marais, and afterwards the young couple went to live on Kranskloof, the farm of the bride's father. He was a widower with no sons, and he appraised the splendid physique of his new son-in-law and reckoned it a just compensation for his daughter's fall from grace.

The young husband was bitter and resentful and spent as much time as possible on the land, dragging his feet toward the homestead only when the light faded. He rarely touched his new bride. When he did, he used her as a vessel to ease his physical needs, and Trilly came both to hate and fear him. When the child was born, prematurely, Stephen was as indifferent to the baby boy as he was to its mother. Relations worsened, until one day in the heat of a blazing row Trilly let slip an unguarded remark. Terrified, she tried to retract it, but Stephen choked the truth out of her. It was as he always suspected. He was not the father of the child—merely the scapegoat.

Before the sun went down that day, he left the farm. The one good thing he carried with him was a healthy respect for land, and when on his twenty-first birthday he inherited £4,000 from his grandmother's estate, he purchased two tracts of land, one on the Natal North Coast, the other in the Berg. Then he deliberately forgot about them.

He hitched his way to Cape Town and found a job as deckhand on board a Norwegian whaler. The crew were a tough callous lot; Stephen went away a boy and came back a man. When the whaler docked again in Cape Town, a weather expedition ship was making up its crew, and for three consecutive years, Stephen Marais went down into the loneliness of Antarctica. Gradually, amidst the dazzling ice and silent wastes, he lost his emnity. But in the process something of that glacial world entered into him, and it was a chilled man who emerged, to remain emotionally frozen through many a long, cold year until one evening, in a distant country, he saw a girl standing in the doorway of a room. In that moment the thaw began.

Now that same girl lay sleeping in the crook of his arm, a stranger who was not a stranger, destined with laughter and love and incredible warmth to melt the last remnants of the ice, to call back the lost years of his youth.

There was never anything to equal the beauty of that first awakening in the Berg. Tonia took one look through the window and quietly, stealthily, so as not to disturb Stephen, crept from the cottage to stand entranced, a rapt worshiper in a vast outdoor cathedral.

All around were mountains, vast brooding shapes tipped with gold—now deep purple, now pearly lilac—as the clouds moved across the early morning sun, trailing drifting shadows behind. The light was unearthly in its golden brilliance, tinting the dry veld with a blaze of orange, and the silence was the sound of a world at peace. The sharp air caught at her and made her shiver, but it was sweet and good and exhilarating—all the things last night had been. Then she remembered there were things to be done and turned and put the glory behind her.

Stephen woke an hour later and went in search of her, but as he reached the kitchen his face became grim. From within came the sound of sobbing. He pushed open the door. The floor had been scrubbed clean to reveal colors bright and clear, but he was only interested in the girl on her knees beside the pail of gray, scummy water. There were dirty splash marks up to her elbows and her forehead was steaked where the hair had been pushed back with a wet hand. But she was laughing! Laughing so helplessly that, when she saw him, she tried to stop and couldn't.

"I've got such a stitch,," she gasped. "Sorry, did I frighten you?"

"What's so funny?"

"Oh, goodness . . . " She wiped her eyes with the back of her hand. "I suddenly visualized the faces of my old crowd if they could only see me now. Princess Tonia on her knees scrubbing a filthy kitchen floor. Do you know something? I've never scrubbed a floor in my life, but I'm making a jolly good job of it, aren't I?"

"Yes," he said.

"So it just goes to show what you can do when you set yourself. Shall I tell you something else? I'd rather be scrubbing a floor in your funny little cottage than living with a prince in a palace. Oh, Stephen . . . darling Stephen . . . Stephen, mind the bucket!"

Eventually he released her and studied the blissful, dirty face. "Scrubbing floors suits you," he remarked.

"You suit me, too." She rubbed her cheek against the rough sleeve of his pullover. "Now look, don't get all uppity but I've brought a little money with me, so how about using it to give this place a face-lift? We'd have it looking like Home Sweet Home in no time! A few tins of paint . . . curtains with brilliant colours . . . I'm the world's worst sewer, but even a dud like me should be able to manage a dead straight hem. Marais, you're wearing your poker face. Are you listening?"

"Most intently. I was prepared for an energetic minx, but I hadn't bargained on such a literally-minded one! Did you really think I intended this funny little cottage to be your home? Or that it was ever mine? It's been many things, my Tonia, but never that. An oasis rather, somewhere to come when the way seemed rough. I would absorb the peace, drink in the beauty, decide that things were not nearly so bad as I thought—and go on my way refreshed."

Tenderly he smoothed her cheek. "I can imagine what the waiting was like, that was why I had to bring you here; no other place would do. There's also a more practical reason. My house in Durban was rather monastic. It needed a few changes before a minx could be introduced to it, and the workmen are still there."

He looked down at the newly scrubbed floor with a smile. "One of the Zulu women was supposed to have done that yesterday, but obviously my message didn't get through. I'm rather glad. I thought that this would be an ideal getting-to-know-you place, and I've learned more about you in an hour than I could have done in a week had I taken you to a luxury hotel."

"You said no questions, but I'm beginning to feel a bit of a fool. Could you have afforded a luxury hotel?"

"Yes," said Stephen.

"Well, that will teach me not to jump to conclusions," she said slowly, and then saw the funny side of it. "While we're on the subject, you wouldn't happen to *own* a luxury hotel, now would you?" Her voice invited him to share her laughter at such a preposterous thought.

"I did happen to own the land on which a couple of them now stand."

Her jaw dropped. In her mind's eye she was back in her father's study, stiffling a yawn of boredom while he read from the itinerary: "Let's have a look who's coming . . . manager of a building society . . . head of a real estate firm . . ."

She said, "You're the real estate man."

"That's right," said Stephen.

"Oh, crikey!" she said faintly. "I don't know whether to laugh or cry. You see, I'd practically written you off as a pauper. Darling Marais, I *am* a fool, aren't I?"

He said quietly, "Would that there were more fools like you, my dearest."

My dearest. Oh, the sweetness of the man! If he kept this up she'd be sniffling continually . . .

"I suppose you want to borrow my handkerchief again? Is this to become a habit?"

"I know of a better one. You could kiss me again."

"Insatiable, too," he sighed.

There was a satisfying pause; after which Tonia said, "Now that I know you're not counting pennies, what about that face-lift? Stephen, let's! Because even if you take me to the loveliest home imaginable, this will always be our very special place, won't it? What I mean is . . ."

"I know what you mean," he said.

"Then can we? Please, Stephen, we'll have such fun."

He looked at her eager face. "I suppose you want to rush out and buy the paint and curtains now-now-now?"

She said, most demurely, "I think that should be our code word for something else."

"Something else?"

"Yes, something else. Get it?" Her arms slid round his neck, and her eyes shone softly. "Stephen . . ."

"You don't think we should have breakfast first?"

"Only if you insist."

"No wonder I had the feeling that life with you would be exhausting . . ."

"Oh, get on with it," she said.
So he did.

They lost all track of time. Ten days passed, and another ten. Golden days, with the mountains forming a splendid backcloth to a happiness so acute that at times it almost hurt. Moments of ecstasy and intimate moments of peace, and Tonia caught each one as it flew and threaded it into a necklace of remembrance. She placed it carefully in the storehouse of her memory, and later, when it was all that was left, all that remained of the brightness and the beauty, she was to use it as a rosary and tell each shining moment, not for remembrance but for sanity and strength.

But not the smallest cloud appeared to dull the brilliance of these days. Always there was the strong, eternal sunshine and the laughter. The cottage resounded with it as Tonia labored diligently—if somewhat messily—with paint and furnishing material bought from a nearby trading store.

Freed from the inhibiting restraints, which she had imposed upon herself to please Luke, she was vital and joyous and blooming with love. A dozen times a day she paused in her labors and rushed to wherever Stephen might be, to stand behind him, to lay her cheek against his broad back, to reassure herself of his presence. Always there was the desire to give and go on giving, and an ever-present sense of wonder that giving could be such a glory in itself.

In turn, Stephen watched her—the lovely long legs as she turned exuberant cartwheels across the veld, the ingenuous transparency of her face as it reflected each lightning change of mood. Even as he watched she came to grief and collapsed on the grass hooting with laughter like a three-year-old. She turned her head and saw him watching. She went quiet and still. All she said was, "Hi!" with the shadow of a smile, but the tenderness which came up in her face tightened his throat. His young love. His infinitely dear young love.

One afternoon, when the painting was completed and the vivid curtains hung—slightly lopsided, the ragged stitches resembling shark's teeth—they climbed the slopes of Cathkin. There was not a breath of wind, and the only sound was the dislodging of an occasional stone under their feet. They halted on a wide platform and stood hand in hand for some time, looking down on the shrunken cottage, and there was no other habitation to be seen. Neither was there any sign of human life. Nor was the silence broken until Stephen turned toward her and she saw his face. Immediately she sensed his need of her and moved to meet him.

"Yes," she whispered. "Oh, yes, my darling," and they came together with such aching tenderness, such shared rapture, that she was to remember it always.

Afterward, as they lay quietly together, she asked, "What was it, Stephen?"

And he replied, "I'm happy."

A simple enough statement, but the girl who had always regarded happiness as a right, thought it the most moving she had ever heard.

The *umfana*—a young African boy—brought the message the next morning. Tonia saw him coming and went to call Stephen.

"A stranger in the camp," she reported. "Very small, very black, and riding on a pony. Where's he sprung from?"

Stephen went outside and spoke to the boy in Zulu. When he returned, Tonia scanned his face, but as usual his expression told her little. "Marais, you're holding out on me again," she complained. "What does he want?"

He gave the long blonde hair a tug. "It's time you

143

learned to read my face. Go and pack your things, and let's see what Durban has to offer."

Durban had many things, but only two that mattered, so far as Tonia was concerned—a house, and the woman she found inside it.

Stephen's home stood high on the ridge called the Berea. It was built in old Colonial style, with shutters at the windows, bougainvillea entwining the pillars of a long cool *stoep*, and a swimming pool that shimmered in the center of an immaculate garden. Inside, the house was now anything but monastic, and the girl entered with awe, passing a massive carved *imbuia kist* in the entrance hall and glimpsing to her left a typical masculine study with silver trophies crowded behind glass doors and a comfortably-dented, olive-green leather armchair. To her right was the dining room, elegantly striped in gold and amber. Then she stood bemused at the entrance to a high-ceilinged, beautifully-proportioned lounge, with deep purple drapes emphasizing pale coffee-colored walls, a carpet that looked like velvet moss on a gleaming parquet floor, and the whole complemented by a magnificent seascape of wild green waves and a tossing silver ship.

She stood so long that Stephen's hands went round her waist, to turn her gently and guide her up the wrought-iron staircase to a spacious bedroom of coolest aquamarine and white, where a half-open door revealed an apricot-tiled bathroom and huge sliding panels of glass led onto a balcony giving a panoramic view of the city and sea.

It was suddenly too much, and to her disgust she burst into tears. "Only because it's all so beautiful," she sobbed.

But her tears quickly changed to giggles as Stephen said, "Oh, crikey! Not *another* handkerchief? Now talking about beauty . . ."

He walked away, leaving her mystified, to return with a definite smile in his clear, gray eyes. "You remember

Scarlett O'Hara's Mammy? We can only offer a mini-Mammy, but she's quite formidable, so brace yourself. Come!"

"Darling Mummy," Tonia wrote later that week. "If you could only see her, this Zulu housekeeper of Stephen's. She's the size of a house, her name is Beauty, she is anything but, and she calls me Madam! She also keeps me firmly in my place, condescends to let me cook the occasional meal, and we're getting on like a house on fire . . ."

It was true. Mainly because the young English girl and the elderly Zulu woman had one focal point of existence—Stephen Marais.

To the girl he became all things: the mother she had left behind and the friend she had lost, the brother she had always wanted and the lover she so ardently desired. There was also a touch of the heavy father in the discipline to which he subjected her at times—discipline which outwardly she pretended to resent. Secretly, however, she rejoiced that at last she'd found a man who was strong enough to handle her.

He was also the stronger when it came to a clash of wills. Toward the end of the first year, a British postal strike brought a temporary halt to the blue airmail letters that arrived regularly twice a week and were so eagerly awaited. The result was that Tonia displayed the first signs of homesickness in her wistful watching for the postman and the letters that never came, and although she tried valiantly to conceal it, Stephen was not deceived. He passed no comment but came home from town one day and placed a form in front of her. It was an application for enrollment in a secretarial course offered by a private business college.

Her first reaction was one of outrage. She opened her mouth to say something rude and then closed it again. One simply did not say rude things to Stephen Marais. Instead she swallowed hard and said gaily, "Become a potty little typist? Me! No thanks, darling."

"Yes, please," he said. "Sign."

"But darling Stephen, *why?*"

"A precaution against boredom. Besides, it may come in useful should I be careless enough to walk in front of a bus. Now come, Tonia, stop arguing and sign."

She made one last plea, with her most beguiling smile. "Now, look . . . if you're really serious, then I don't mind taking a course on beauty culture, or flower arranging, or even cookery! Not plain stodgy cooking, naturally, but . . . "

"Sign," he said.

To her astonishment, she thoroughly enjoyed the course and—for Tonia did not believe in half measures—surprised everyone but herself by gaining top marks when it ended. She came home waving her diploma like a triumphant banner, and Stephen insisted that it be framed and hung on the wall of his study. They put it up with great ceremony and toasted it with champagne. And neither had the slightest premonition that during two vital periods of Tonia's life, the knowledge represented by this piece of paper would become what Luke Howard's mother would term a godsend.

# 14

Tonia Marshall's sensational departure from St. Michael's provided a juicy scandal which was hotly debated among the town's younger set, and long after the initial excitement subsided, two years after, three people in particular still thought of her and wondered how she was faring in South Africa. Luke Howard, over in America, wondered. Angela Morris wondered. A third person did more than wonder. He went to find out.

Tonia was working on the rockery below the swimming pool when Beauty came down to her. "There's a man to see Madam. From England, he says."

"England!" Dropping her trowel she scrambled to her feet, stripping off her garden gloves and tossing them behind her as she ran. She flew across the stoep, into the lounge, and stopped short as the slim, dark-haired man moved toward her.

"Salaams, Princess," he said.

Julian . . . Luke . . . St. Michael's . . . Mummy. A lump came up in her throat. Involuntarily she stretched out her hands and then remembered who this man was and the circumstances of their last meeting. She placed them firmly behind her back and there was no warmth in her breathless voice.

"Hello, Julian. What brings you out here?"

"Curiosity," he said.

"Then satisfy it and go."

He looked round admiringly. "Nice place you've got

here." Through the picture window, he could see the swimming pool, invitingly blue and sparkling, and the lemon fringed umbrella over the white garden chairs and table. Beyond lay the beautifully-kept lawn and colorful bank of the rockery, and in the distance the sharp line of the navy blue sea.

"You've certainly hit the jackpot, Princess. Did you know of all these mod cons before you came?"

"Stephen didn't need to bribe me, if that's what you're suggesting."

"Dear, dear!" He pursed his lips reprovingly. "As touchy as ever, I see."

"And you're as impossible as ever. Please go."

In a gentle non-Julian voice, he said: "I'm here on behalf of your mother."

"*Mummy?*" Her imagination ran riot. Something was wrong. It must be. This is what she'd been afraid of—Mummy terribly ill and all because of her.

Yet Julian was smiling and explaining, "When I was asked to attend a symposium in Johannesburg, I got in touch with her, told her I was coming to South Africa. You have a nice mother. She misses you."

Relief flooded in. Such blessed relief. But memory flared, of that forlorn little figure, with tortured eyes and hands that communicated what the voice could not, waving goodbye so bravely and never a word of recrimination. Dearest Mummy. The girl's lip trembled. "I miss her, too. How is she? I'm never really sure from her letters. Julian, did you actually see her?"

He asked abruptly, "Is he at home?"

"Stephen? No, he's in Maritzburg. I don't expect him back until evening."

"May I spend the day with you, then?"

She stared. "The whole day? Surely you have business to attend to?"

"I'm making you my business."

"You've flown down to Durban just to see me?" she said slowly. "What a strange, unpredictable person you are."

"That makes two of us, then. Because I find you a strange, unpredictable girl." Ignoring her frown he looked longingly through the window. "Hot day . . . thick English suit . . . tempting pool! Unfortunately, I didn't think to bring my bathing togs, but I am sporting a natty line in tartan underwear, and I'd love a swim." His gay smile was very disarming. "How about it? Will Her Royal Highness most graciously give her consent?"

Tonia refused to be sidetracked. She said bluntly, "I'm suspicious. I don't equate kindness with Julian Goldberg. Underneath that smarm of yours, I'm willing to bet you have some ulterior motive for coming here today."

Julian didn't reply at once. Instead he began a slow careful scrutiny of the room. His keen eyes missed nothing, taking in every object and memorizing each tiny detail, until finally they came to rest again on one lovely but very hostile face.

"Mission accomplished," he said briskly. "I came; I saw; I haven't conquered, but I didn't come here in a conquering mood. I came to assuage the sadness and loneliness in your mother's eyes. I shall now report back that her daughter is living like a queen, let alone a princess, that she looks the picture of health, and is lovelier than ever. That last bit will please you." He thrust his hand into the inner pocket of his suit. "Here, I promised to deliver this letter personally. I've kept my promise. Now I'm off."

He was almost at the door when she was galvanized into action. "Julian! Julian, don't go. Please . . ."

He slowed down, but his voice was disinterested. "There's really nothing more to add."

"But there is! I want to hear about Mummy . . . ask so many questions . . . oh, don't go . . . " She caught up with him. "Please, I'm begging you to stay."

He halted. "Say that again!"

She colored hotly but her chin came up determinedly. "I'm begging, Julian. B-e-g-g-i-n-g." She spelt the letters out. "Also I apologize for that ulterior motive crack. I withdraw it unreservedly."

The coldness began to leave his face. "I think I shall have to add a P.S. to my report."

She blinked with relief. "What will it say?"

The old mocking smile was back. "That, I'm afraid, is confidential. Now, Princess, are my tartan briefs going to be christened in your pool or not?"

He emerged from the water grinning happily, and reached for a towel. "I haven't enjoyed myself so much in years. What a heavenly climate you have here. Does it ever get really cold?"

"Not compared to England. The so-called winter here is a joke. Did you notice that we have no fireplace in the lounge? It was the first thing I missed; nothing to group the furniture around. We've made a lovely fireplace up at the cottage, though."

"The cottage?"

A secretive little smile played round the corners of her mouth as she stretched out in a long reclining chair.

"Stephen has a cottage in the mountains, and it's heavenly up there in the winter in front of a roaring fire."

Julian stood toweling his thick hair, looking down at the golden, near-naked body in the tiny white bikini. She was lying with eyes closed but they flew open unexpectedly, and she sat up abruptly. With disconcerting suddenness she asked, "Why do you always look at me in that beastly way?"

"It wasn't meant to be beastly. I was thinking how fortunate you are to possess a beautiful, healthy body. My trade lies mainly in sick ones."

She lay back again with an exasperated sigh. "You

sound just like Stephen. He always manages to take the wind out of my sails."

Julian dragged a chair alongside hers and sat on the edge. "Are you happy with him? Really happy?"

There was astonishment in her face that he should even ask. "Utterly and completely."

"No regrets at all?"

"Not where he's concerned." Her eyes held his. "It's inevitable that we talk about Luke. Have you kept in touch?"

"Of course!" It was his turn to show surprise. "He's still in America, though. The original two-year fellowship was extended by mutual agreement."

"How is he? Did he . . . did he find someone else, another girl, I mean?"

"After what you did to him? That's expecting rather a lot, isn't it?"

"Distance lends perspective. By now I should imagine Luke Howard would be the first to admit I could never have made him an ideal wife."

"He didn't want an ideal wife. He wanted you."

"Out of your own mouth, Julian." She said it with a wry twist to her mouth.

"Meaning?"

"Oh, leave it! Don't open it all up again! I'm deeply sorry for the heartache I caused, yet at the time my feelings seemed genuine enough. After meeting Stephen and realizing they weren't, I went at once to Luke and told him. At least I was perfectly honest."

"Were you?" There was a definite edge to his voice. "After the episode in the hotel bedroom, I would say that's the last thing you could claim."

With a flurry of long, graceful limbs she came off the chair, her eyes blazing. "Let's get this straight, Julian. You probably won't believe it—any more than Luke did—but Stephen touched me for the first time in the cottage in the

Berg. You called me a tart. Luke called me a slut. And both of you meant it in the physical sense and blamed Stephen. Well, you were wrong. Give my love to Mummy, thank you for delivering her letter, and now take yourself and your ghastly tartan briefs out of my pool."

She raced up to the house, seething. Curiously, however, she felt a tremendous relief at having put the record straight for Julian. Although why she'd bothered—why she should care—she didn't know. Detestable man.

Calming down she showered leisurely, put on slacks and a shirt, and lingered a while to enable him to get out of the way. When she went into the kitchen, Beauty was making a salad, and Tonia said, "Lovely. I'm ready for that. I'll take it onto the stoep, Beauty."

"Doesn't Madam want it by the pool? With the gentleman?"

"You mean he hasn't gone!"

The black face was indignant. "Madam isn't going to send him away without lunch? When he's come all the way from England?"

"He didn't come all the way from England just to see me," Tonia snapped. She marched down to the pool. Julian lay face down, his head resting on folded arms. He looked so relaxed and peaceful that she had an overwhelming impulse to take her toe to his lean, flat, decidedly masculine backside.

"You do," he murmured, "and I'll retaliate by tossing you fully clothed into your own pool."

"I asked you to go. Why are you still here?"

He squinted up at her with one eye. "Have a heart! What do you suggest I do about my ghastly tartan briefs? Put my suit over them while they're still sopping wet? Sorry, Princess, but you're stuck with me until they're dry. And I do not intend to borrow a pair of Stephen's, thank you very much!"

Tonia was nonplussed. She looked up at the brilliant sky, willing the sun to shine a little brighter.

"At least an hour," he said cheerfully. "Half an hour on my front and another half on my back should do the trick." He watched her turn toward the house.

"Tonia."

She paused. "I'd like to say something," he said. "I'm glad to hear that you didn't sleep with Marais in the Savoy Hotel. That puts rather a different complexion on things. Thanks for telling me."

When she found her voice, she said, "I didn't expect you to believe me."

"Well, I do."

"You didn't at the time."

"Do you blame me? Be fair! You must admit the circumstantial evidence was pretty strong."

He saw that she still looked resentful. "Come on, Princess," he coaxed. "Another armistice? Until the four o'clock plane?"

It was no good. She couldn't maintain the hostility. Sulking had never been the way of it with her.

Beauty carried lunch down to the pool, and afterwards Julian plied her with news. "Do you know that Angel is doing her training at the Q.E.?"

Tonia knew, but only through her mother. Angela had even refused to exchange Christmas cards with her.

"She's an excellent nurse. Incidentally she has to call me sir," he said gleefully. "One afternoon just for the hell of it I got all stern and bolshie with her, and the poor girl stood there with a flaming red face and didn't dare say a word because a consultant was present." He chuckled reminiscently. "I had a heavy date with her that night. I must say she took her revenge."

Tonia was conscious of a sharp shock. Gay, amoral Julian with Angela? Whatever had happened to Roger?

"That's a very censorious glance you're aiming at me, Princess."

"Angela used to be so . . . "

"She still is. She lives up to her nickname one hundred percent, and every doctor in the Q.E. knows it and behaves accordingly."

"Even you?" The words shot out.

He grinned. "Now that would be telling, wouldn't it?"

She asked hesitantly, "Would you consider marrying a non-Jewish girl?"

"I wouldn't consider marrying anyone—Jewish or non-Jewish."

"What a drastic statement! Do you have to be so dogmatic?"

"Yes." He bit the word off crisply and with a finality that brooked no discussion.

Tonia was puzzled but reluctant to pry, so she merely said lightly, "Oh, I expect you'll change your mind. You'll have to get married one day."

"Why?"

"Well . . . most people do!"

"You haven't."

"Maybe I'm different."

"Rubbish. You've met a man who's different, become tied up in circumstances that are different, but that doesn't make you different! If Marais were free to marry you, you'd be as eager as the rest to get that plain gold band on your finger."

"Yes, of course, I would." Her voice was soft and tender. "It's Stephen, you see. He frets inwardly about it, and I can't bear to see him distressed or unhappy in any way."

It was like watching the sun break through, he thought. This glow that emanates from her each time she says his name.

"You love him—that much?"

"That much, Julian."

"He's a lucky man. I only hope you get back as much as you give."

He sounded so grim that she shook her head at him. "You've never loved deeply, have you? Don't you know it's the giving that counts? If no one gave, then who could take? Work it out for yourself."

"I already have. What happens if you want to give and the person concerned refuses to take?"

A little of the glow faded. "Are we back to Luke again?"

"Not necessarily. Answer the question."

A little shiver passed through her. "I couldn't imagine anything more soul-destroying. However, I was talking about giving and taking between two people who love. I wasn't referring to unrequited love."

"But I was," said Julian. He said it quietly, with a sudden air of weariness, which hovered like an incongruous shadow between his gay mocking face and the sun.

Equally quietly, she said, "I'm sorry. What happened? Would you care to tell me?"

"Nothing," he said. "Absolutely nothing. It didn't even get off the ground." He stood up. "My briefs feel quite dry. I'd better go and dress."

"Julian . . ."

He smiled, and it was the old derisive smile. "You're looking at your enemy in a very unhostile way, Princess. Careful, now! The armistice is running out."

"I never really wanted to fight," she said. "We got off on the wrong foot, didn't we? I wonder why."

He bent down, picked up his towel and slung it over his shoulder. "Not to worry. You couldn't help it. That's the way the cookie crumbles." He sauntered off, whistling, leaving her staring after him.

Strange, strange man.

She drove him out to Louis Botha Airport. When his flight was called, she put out her hand, "Goodbye, Julian," but he said, "To hell with that," and grabbed hold of her. "That's to take back to your mother. This is the mouth that kissed the mouth . . . Good lord, I've made you blush. What's the local equivalent for *Au revoir?*"

"*Tot siens.*"

"*Tot siens* then, Princess."

The next day was Sunday, and Stephen walked into the bedroom balancing a tray on one hand. "Room service," he said. On the tray was orange juice, a boiled egg, toast and honey, and lying across the cloth an exquisite double pink hibiscus. He laughed down at her. "What big eyes you've got. Come on, minx, sit up."

She couldn't. The tears of joy that Stephen tapped so easily threatened to spill over.

"Why am I living with such an emotional woman?" he queried, and she said, as she had said so many times, "Why do you spoil me so?"

"Oh, I'm not spoiling you! Don't get any ideas! I'm spoiling myself, I'm nineteen all over again, didn't you know?"

She sat up, and he placed the tray across her knees. With the tip of his finger he absorbedly removed one stray tear from her cheek. "I'm nineteen again," he repeated softly. "It's wonderful. Now why do you spoil me so?"

"Because you are Stephen, and I adore you."

"Such an intense woman, I'm living with," he teased. "Move over."

She picked up the flower and turned it this way and that, saw how the beauty of the bloom was completed by the shimmering drops of dew. And for all that she desired the plain gold band on her finger, she thought with pity of those who were legally joined in body, but not in spirit, who had never known completion and never would know, and thus could never understand that love boasts no pride of ownership, nor can it ever be owned.

Stephen, troubled by her silence, said, "Dearest?" She leaned on her elbow and searched the face of this man who had completed her; and there was no hardness left in it, neither was there any bitterness to be found in his mouth.

She clung to him suddenly. She said, "I'm frightened. This perfection . . . it can't last, can it?"

He removed the tray, the food untouched, and drew her down beside him. "The learned and the scholarly will tell us that it cannot, that all things fade. But the wise are often confounded by the foolish, and so the answer, my Tonia, I know not. Nor do I seek to know. This perfect thing, we have it now. Is that not enough?"

And she answered, as she had done that first night, "It is enough."

It was enough for another two years, two years of glorious discovery, of exploration of a man and his country. They swam in a warm sea at Christmas and drove up from the beach under canopies of scarlet flamboyant tress. And Tonia thought only fleetingly of bare branches on a winter's day.

They went to Pretoria at Jacaranda time and walked delicately on pavements carpeted with mauve petals. They meandered along the Garden Route to the Cape and drank the wine of sun-drenched vineyards. They trembled to the earth-shaking stamp of Zulus performing their Ngoma dances. They walked through the Wilderness Trail to Umfolozi, stood rooted in fascinated horror as a rhino suddenly charged and the ranger shouted, "Scatter!"—and Tonia laughing teased Stephen because he became so breathless. And there was one never-to-be-forgotten evening that they watched the pink flamingoes come slowly to rest on the lake at St. Lucia. Time and again they were drawn back to the Berg—but the moment always came when they looked one to the other, and with silent acquiescence turned for home.

It was more than enough. Then abruptly it was not enough any more.

"Darling?" Tonia put her head around the bedroom door, and her eager expression changed to an anxious frown. She hurried over to the bed. Stephen was lying fully clothed, except for his shoes, and he was sound asleep. It was only seven in the evening, and they were expecting a guest for dinner. She stooped to kiss him, but it took another two to persuade his eyelids to open. He smiled when he saw her but looked so weary that she said, "Sorry, my darling. I hate to waken you, but Dirk will be here at any moment."

Stephen looked at his watch and gave a low whistle of dismay. "Is that the time? I've slept for over an hour!" Lazily he reached out and pulled her to him. "Mmm. Nice . . . Let's have a few more minutes. Thank goodness, it's only Dirk who's coming. He won't stay late, and if he does we'll throw him out, shall we?"

"Shame on you! You're becoming very antisocial, Marais. Dirk is so fond of you, and it's been weeks since we asked him over. Heavens, that sounds like his car now. I'll go and hold the fort while you splash some cold water on those bleary eyes, and don't rush! Take it easy!"

Dirk Muller was intrigued to see his hostess place a finger across her lips and motion him through the lounge onto the stoep. Once outside she took his arm and drew him well out of earshot of the house.

"Bless you for coming at such short notice," she whispered.

This genial bespectacled man with the fast-receding hairline was Stephen's only real friend. He had matriculated with him, accompanied him to the *braaivleis* on that fateful night at the beach, and doggedly made it his business to maintain a correspondence during Stephen's wandering years. Whenever Tonia saw them together, she was strongly reminded of the rapport that existed between Luke and Julian. By coincidence, Dirk was also a doctor. But instead of the antagonism which Luke's friend usually provoked, she had developed a warm appreciation of this tubby little man and had come to recognize his deep integrity and steadfast loyalty.

He listened attentively now as she talked, without betraying any sign of his inner misgivings.

"You say that this pattern of fatigue has become very pronounced over the last six months?"

"Yes. At first I teased him about it, told him it was the first sign of advancing years, and he laughed and agreed. At the age of not-quite forty, I ask you! But it's gone beyond teasing now. He can't go through the day without a sleep in the afternoon. What began as a few minutes zizz after lunch has stretched to half an hour, sometimes more . . . "

"Which in our enervating climate is not a bad idea," Dirk interrupted. "I do it myself without fail every Saturday and Sunday."

"Not each and every day in the winter, though! Also, if we go out at night—which we rarely do—another rest after his bath is a must. Otherwise halfway through the evening he goes a ghastly color and looks as if he's about to pass out. We went down to the drive-in cinema last night, the first time in ages, and only because it was a film he wanted to see. Yet he slept solidly through the best part and all the way home. Just as well I was driving!"

She hesitated and looked back at the open French windows. Dropping her voice even lower, she went on hurriedly, "Look, one other thing. I only mention it in case it's relevant from a medical point of view. Stephen and I are closer than ever, but we haven't made love in over a month." She gave him a strained smile. "Something terribly wrong, wouldn't you say?"

Definitely, thought Dirk. He knew what this English girl meant to Stephen. What is more, he wholeheartedly approved. Admittedly his approval was partisan, for Dirk had been Stephen's best man, and Dirk remembered Trilly. His was the voice that had pleaded with Stephen not to embark on what could only be a travesty of marriage. At the same time, he silently admired him for doing so. Also, he happened to know of the handsome allowance that found its way into Trilly's bank every month. It was none of his business, as Stephen quietly pointed out, but it was Dirk's contention that this was a far more cogent factor in Trilly's refusal to grant a divorce, than her so-called religious scruples. Strange that the scruples had only surfaces when she discovered that Steve Marais had come into a bit of money—scruples that had hardened with hate and vindictiveness through the years. Oh yes, Dirk remembered Trilly! Small wonder that Stephen just about worshiped this enchanting young woman.

"Has any of this been discussed between you?" he asked.

Tonia shook her head. "He refuses point-blank to come and see you, shrugs off any suggestion that something may be wrong. All I've managed to do is persuade him to take some multivitamin tablets, but he pooh-poohed a second bottle, and they're a bit too large and the wrong color to slip into his breakfast cereal." She tried to laugh, but he could tell that she was desperately worried. "Coax him in for a checkup, Dirk," she pleaded. "You're my only hope, and he might listen to you."

They both turned as Stephen came towards them.

"Dirk? Good to see you. All well?"

"Fine. And you?" He tried to look at Stephen with a professional eye, but the orange light of the stoep lantern precluded more than a cursory examination. "What am I drinking? Brandy, thanks."

"Cinzano for me, please," said Tonia. "Shall we have

our drinks out here?" It was a warmish night, and the moon rode high over the ocean, making a wide luminous pathway across the water.

"Why not? No, Dirk . . . " Stephen waved away the offer of help. "You sit and talk to Tonia. It's ages since she's had a visitor."

She watched him go inside. "He's lost weight, too. Did you notice?"

Dirk had, but he wasn't going to say so. "I'll haul him in for a check-up somehow," he promised. "Now let's talk about you. What's the latest news of your mother?"

"I don't know, to be honest. I can only tell you what she tells me—that she's fine. Whether it's the truth, however . . . "

They both jumped. From the house there came simultaneously the sound of splintering glass and the thud of something heavy falling.

They reached the window together. Through it they could see the inert figure of Stephen as he lay stretched out on the floor.

# ❊ **15** ❊

In the lush subtropical climate of Durban, there flourishes an unusual flowering bush. Unusual, in that the blossoms it bears pass through three color phases. Initially they open as deep purple, later become pale mauve, and finally fade into fragile, paperwhite. Its name? Yesterday, today, and tomorrow.

Such a bush grew in the sunny courtyard of a Berea nursing home, and from the window of Stephen's room, Tonia looked at it and saw portrayed in the delicate colors a symbolic cycle of life. Perhaps she was oversensitive, but today the touches of white seemed to be significantly in the minority.

Dirk had been blunt. She had asked him to be, with a new maturity which tensed her lovely features and shadowed her eyes. His tongue had stumbled over the cumbersome word. *Myelomatosis.* A malignant process involving the bone marrow. The primary stage, through which Stephen had passed, was symptomatic of anaemia, with increasing lassitude, bone pain, and weariness. Blood tests had been taken, Dirk explained, together with urine tests and a whole skeletal X-ray. It was not anaemia, and the prognosis was chilling—approximately twelve months, with the aid of repeated blood transfusions, which would prolong life but could not cure.

"Does he know?" she had asked.

Dirk took off his glasses and polished them vigorously.

"Yes, he knows."

At home she broke down and gave way to a paroxysm of grief. After which she took herself firmly in hand. This was not to be the way of it. The weeping could come later. Please God, *much* later.

She prayed that they might have a year; she was granted eight months. They retreated to the cottage, with Beauty in dogged attendance and Dirk their only visitor. The proximity of mind, which Luke had once desired, was never more evident. Their spoken words were few, but each discerned the other's heart and the pain of their silent understanding grew daily. The golden winter faded. The spring rains came, and the girl sensed the sap rising in the trees and draining from the man. Inevitably the day came when the journey for the life-boosting blood transfusion so exhausted Stephen that he spent the night in a hospital bed, while Tonia drove back to the Berg alone, to close the cottage and fetch Beauty. The elderly Zulu saw her coming and ran to meet her; the tears of the black woman and the white girl mingled and the force of their weeping was terrible.

She turned from the window and sat down beside the bed. Stephen opened his eyes, and they smiled at each other. His hands were very brown against the white of the sheet, and she lifted one and held it to her cheek.

"I love you," he said.

Her mouth curved tenderly. "And I you. But why say it?" You've never said it before."

"I never needed to. We were together. I'm saying it now for all the tomorrows we'll be apart."

Her throat worked. "There's an Afrikaans proverb about tomorrow . . . "

"*Môre is nog 'ng dag.*"

"Tomorrow is another day. How true! So let's concentrate on today, shall we?"

"Yes, let's. Tonia . . . no regrets?"

"Oh, darling, darling . . ."

"I have," he said. "Just one. That I was never able to say, 'Good morning, Mrs. Marais. Did you sleep well, Mrs. Marais. You're very lovely, Mrs. Marais.'"

She gave a troubled cry of protest. "For heaven's sake! Bothering about that *now!* It's never really mattered."

"It has to me," he said, "but He who ordained all things must have intended it this way. Otherwise I would now be faced with a whole lot of backchat about promises which cannot be broken."

"Whatever are you talking about?" she whispered.

"For richer, for poorer; for better, for worse . . ."

"In sickness and in health; to love and to cherish until . . ." Her teeth were chattering. "I may not have said them out loud, but I honor them every day in my heart."

"And the bit about obeying?" The clear, calm eyes held hers.

She said slowly, frightened, "At last I've learned to read your face. You're about to ask me to do something which you know I'll hate. What is it?"

"I want you to leave me and go back to your parents."

There was a silence, which seemed to endure for hours. At last Tonia said, "You know, for one terrible moment, I could have sworn you asked me to leave you."

The continuing silence shocked her into speechlessness, until an anger composed of agony ripped through her and she let fly.

"What a contemptible suggestion, and you know what you can do with it! I've never heard of anything so . . . so . . . What kind of woman would that make me? To stay while the going's good, then scuttle at the first sign of trouble. Up to now I've taken everything and given nothing . . ."

"You gave the only thing that counts. Yourself. Unquestioningly, unstintingly."

"Well, I'm questioning now. You're stuck with me, Marais, whether you like it or not. You can argue till you're blue in the face, but I won't go. What is more . . . oh, my darling, my darling, don't look at me like that!"

She went limp, the anger extinguished by the torment in his eyes and the weariness, which overlay him like an early shroud.

He said, "Dearest, listen . . . " and because his voice told her that it was harder for him to speak than for her to listen, she listened.

"Don't fight me on this. You and I have been blessed with such perfection that to watch it die would destroy me. I refuse to subject it to the monotony of a slow terminal illness, to watch that spontaneous smile of yours grow fixed, to wait for relief to appear in your face as the days grow short. Walk away, my Tonia. Walk away before the brightness dims. For my sake. For my most selfish sake. Leave me with the perfect memory."

"Desert you, you mean. Abandon you to the monotony and the loneliness."

"Loneliness is a state of mind. I was lonely in that crowded cricket pavilion in St. Michael's. Then you turned and looked at me. 'You will go, and I shall follow,' you said. 'And we shall live happily ever after.' " He ran his finger down the center of her nose. "We did, too. Our time together was altogether lovely."

"Don't talk as if it was finished! There's plenty of time left yet . . . there *must* be . . . " An undertone of hysteria was building up. "Darling Stephen, don't send me away . . . please don't send me away . . . " She kissed his hand passionately again and again. "I won't go . . . I won't." In one quick movement that took him by surprise, she flung herself across him and laid her face against his. She felt his breath on her cheek. Felt something else too. An imperceptible shudder, as if he repressed a groan. She turned her head, and what she saw brought her up slowly off the pillow. "I'm only making things more difficult, aren't I?"

He didn't answer. He didn't have to. She rose awkwardly and walked to the window. Her own eyes were probably just as revealing. "When do you want me to leave?" Her voice seemed disembodied, as if it didn't belong to her at all.

"Dirk says I'll be able to go home at the end of the week."

"Which means you want me away by then. All right. I'll go. I'll obey you—up to a point. How I'll survive without you, I don't know. But I will." She swung around. "I've jolly well got to, because you haven't seen the last of me, my darling. And don't think that you have. You're wiser than I am in every single way, except this one. So, my dear, sweet, stupid Marais, *tot siens*. God bless . . . God bless . . . "

She almost suffocated him with her kiss. Then there was only the fading sound of frantic footsteps.

Before leaving Durban, she had a long talk with Beauty. Dirk attended to the travel arrangements and saw her off at the airport on the day of departure. The flight path of the Boeing lay over the Berea, and a man with yellow hair stood at a window and watched it out of sight.

Immediately following her arrival in Johannesburg, Tonia went to the international departure counter, canceled her flight to London, and then booked herself on the next available plane back to Durban.

She took a room in a small boardinghouse. She found a job in the office of one of the big stores in West Street. Every day she telephoned Beauty at the same time. Once she was unavoidably delayed. Stephen answered, and when the tired voice came over the line, she leaned against the wall and the scalding tears blinded her.

"Hello? Hello?" His usual patient manner. No irritation. Unseeing, gently, she replaced the receiver.

For the first time, she shunned people. One of the

166

young managers tried to date her, but she stared at him with such perplexity that he turned away, hot-faced and furious. The word got around, and the other girls thought that she was stuck-up.

The days were long, the nights more so. She tried to lose herself in reading. Her life revolved around the daily telephone call.

Then one day Beauty telephoned her.

Tonia walked out of the store. She went to the nearest taxi rank and was driven to the nursing home. Stephen was being given a blood transfusion, and she waited in the corridor. Dirk came out of the room and stopped dead when he saw her.

"Don't scold," she said.

"I wasn't going to. I'm glad you're here."

"How long has he got?"

He spread his hands, palms up.

"May I stay with him?"

"For as long as you like."

She sat by his bed. His hands were no longer brown; they were as white as the cover. Dear, familiar hands. She took hold of one. For as long as I like . . . that would be forever, my darling.

He opened his eyes, and deep down behind the dull facade, it was as if a light switched on.

She smiled at him. He looked as though he had seen the Holy Grail. He asked, "Do you believe in miracles?"

"Of course. Haven't I always?"

"You've just flown in?"

"Yes," she lied.

"Your parents . . . there was no trouble with your father?"

"None at all."

"You're thinner."

"Yes."

"But lovelier."

His hand tightened on hers. His eyes never left her

167

face, but the short exchange left him exhausted.

Dirk pushed the door ajar and made a sign to her.

She said, "Sleep, my dearest. I'll still be here when you awake."

He smiled. He slept. She never let go of his hand. She didn't return to her job; she never gave it another thought. Dirk must have given instructions to the nursing staff, for no difficulties were ever placed in her way. Stephen became noticeably weaker. The day came when Dirk said, "I've arranged for you to sleep here from tonight."

He was surprised at her calm face.

There were occasional lucid moments. Moments of definite recognition. Once he tried to say something, and she leaned forward to try and catch what it was, but the struggle was too much. To soothe the agitation in his eyes, she gently placed her mouth on his. When she raised her head, she saw his mouth curve slightly and felt a slight pressure on her hand.

She whispered, "Again?" and caught the imperceptible nod. She kissed him lightly three, four times. "Now, that's enough," she said, and distinctly heard him say, "It's never enough." She laughed.

A few hours afterwards, while in a half-doze, she realized that the hand she was holding was cold.


She sat next to Dirk, only half-aware of the words being recited.

"Man that is born of a woman hath but a short time to live." Pitifully short, my darling, like our time together. "He that believeth on me shall not perish . . . " Stephen perish? He lived in every fibre of her being. "But have everlasting life." Was he sleeping peacefully? Or had he passed through a doorway to conscious eternity? You will go, and I shall follow . . .

" . . . and I look for the resurrection of the dead and the life of the world to come. Amen."

# ❄ **16** ❄

Luke Howard arrived back in England one hot afternoon in June, when the gardens of suburban London were crammed with roses and strawberries lay in mouth-watering heaps on the carts of the barrow boys in the city. He had all but forgotten the scent of English flowers, the taste of English fruit—forgotten almost everything but the one thing he could never forget.

The years in America—besides being a palliative—had been busy and rewarding. He achieved satisfaction in his work and recognition in his field. He was in constant demand as a speaker, and on the eve of his departure, it was the height of irony to receive an invitation to address the Annual British Medical Congress, only to discover that the venue was to be St. Michael's-on-the-Sea.

He promptly accepted; he refused to believe that this was mere coincidence. Clearly the season of his exile was over. It was time to go home.

Julian was waiting for him at the air terminal. An older, anxious-looking Julian, whose jaw dropped as the erect, smiling man strode confidently toward him, hand outstretched.

"Hello, old son," said Luke.

Julian gripped his hand wordlessly. Well, I'll be damned, he thought in wonder. He's over her!

They dined in a little restaurant in Soho—at Luke's suggestion—and it was he who did most of the talking. Julian couldn't take his eyes off him. A startling metamorphosis had taken place, and this eloquent assured man bore no resemblance to the dejected creature who had stumbled silently out of town four years ago.

"Uncle Sam's done wonders for you," he said at last, when he could get a word in.

"Their hospitals are good, Julian."

"To hell with their hospitals. What about their women—are they any good?"

Luke grinned. He'd sorely missed this banter of Julian's. "A tough lot in the main. They eat Englishmen like me for breakfast. But I made a few worthwhile friends."

"Only friends?"

"Only friends."

Julian said, "Luke . . . " He hesitated. Tonia's name had not yet been mentioned between them.

Luke promptly helped him out. "Am I still carrying a torch for Tonia Marshall? I don't think so. She left a pretty big scar, but looking back I shudder to think how naïve I was. If I'd known as much about women then as I do now, I wouldn't have made such a fool of myself. The original country boy, was I, green as they come!" He lifted his glass. "Let's drink to his passing. Cheers!"

"The country boy was nice," said Julian.

Luke groaned. "Oh, lord, don't you start! Little old ladies think I'm nice. Children think I'm nice. Tonia Marshall thought that I was very nice, but it didn't stop her from going off with someone who appeared to be anything but nice! Don't look so grave, Julian. A postmortem on the past is an exercise in futility. Let's abandon it. Tell me about that practice of yours. How's it going?"

An exercise in futility. Nevertheless, back at the hotel and unable to sleep, listening to the muted heartbeat of the city outside, Luke found himself once again going through the exercise.

Could he have relaxed his rigid code of behavior and

met her halfway? *Could he?* He doubted it, but moments of desolation produced subversive nagging doubts. Need he have appeared quite so priggish at times? That warmth of hers, which made ever other woman seem cold by comparison, need he have rebuffed it quite so often? If—and ah, wasn't this the crux of the matter—if he hadn't sublimated his own powerful sex urge and refused to become her lover, would he then have held her? Or would she have gone on seeking the challenge of things forbidden?

He would never know. Just occasionally, when he had time on his hands, he thought on these things.

There was plenty of time the following morning.

Julian flew to Spain on holiday, and Luke boarded the Euston–St. Michael's express and sat alone in a first-class compartment. He watched the steady rise and fall of the telegraph wires against the summer sky. He looked at the cattle in the summer fields. He saw a pond and a young boy fishing; and in the cloud of dust trailing a swiftly moving car, he saw again the laughing face that had haunted his alien summers. Usually he brushed it aside impatiently, but today he allowed it to ride with him all the way to St. Michael's.

The familiar surroundings revived memories with startling clarity, especially when the taxi took him past the Savoy Hotel. And when the town hall came in view, Luke found himself wondering if the usual civic hospitality would be forthcoming and whether the present mayor had as obliging a daughter. Then, as they began the climb up the hill toward the hospital, another face sprang to mind.

The day porter looked over his glasses at the tall man who paused in front of his office. "Why, Dr. Howard! A pleasure to see you again, sir. I heard you were coming— Sister Morris told me—and she's been at me this last hour, wanting to know if you'd arrived. Waiting for you in the staff dining room, she is, sir."

She was. An astonishingly mature Angela, cool and

poised in her crisp white uniform—at least, until she saw Luke. Then an enchanting color flared in her cheeks, to make a delicious mockery of the self-possessed Sister Morris. Luke had all but forgotten this, too, her delicate features and sensitive smile, and was surprised by the warmth that crept into him as he reached for her hand. He held it a little longer than was strictly necessary.

"It's been a long time, Angela."

"Too long, Luke."

"A lot of water has flowed . . . "

"Yes. My thoughts have often been across the water. Welcome home."

Luke Howard looked at her, this charming soft-spoken English girl who was a refreshing personification of home. Her steady eyes never left his, and he felt a sharp sense of shock at what they were saying. Then he was not shocked at all, except at his own obtuseness that he should have stayed away when he could have come home to someone like this.

"I've only just realized I *am* home," he said, and a quiet sympathy flowed between them, which was only interrupted by the waitress clearing her throat apologetically.

During lunch they plied each other with questions. While Julian was still at the Queen Elizabeth, he regularly passed on news from one to the other, but now that he was in Manchester they were both a little out of touch.

Luke waved a hand at her uniform. "You suit that as if you were born to it, but I was staggered when Julian wrote that you were nursing. I imagined you married to Roger and the proud mother of a couple of babies."

"No. He was transferred down south, and we gradually drifted apart. No regrets on either side, Luke. He's happily married to a girl in Kent, and she's got the couple of babies."

"For which I am most grateful," said Luke. "His loss is certainly my gain. That is, if you have no objections."

Angela could scarcely speak. She was too busy sending up a *Te Deum* of thanksgiving. Her expressive eyes gave him his answer, and it was another moment of warmth. Then without warning, it chilled, as a little ghost gaily joined them at the table, and it was Luke who pushed aside the plate of half-finished food and suggested quietly, "Shall we talk about her? We'll have to, sooner or later. I take it she's still in South Africa?"

The *Te Deum* ended abruptly with a jarring discord. Angela's lips parted but no sound came.

"So she isn't" said Luke slowly. "Where is she then?"

"She's here." The words came out reluctantly.

"Here? In St. Michael's, do you mean? When, Angela? And why? Did the great romance fizzle out? Is that why she's back?"

Angela shut her eyes briefly against the mounting elation in his face. "Her mother's health might have brought her home. Mrs. Marshall was admitted to the hospital a few weeks ago . . . renal failure. She's not in my ward, so I've only exchanged a few words with her."

"You've spoken with Tonia?"

"No." Her voice was sharp and determined.

"Which ward is her mother in?"

"B-sixteen. The private rooms on the second floor."

Luke pushed back his chair, but Angela laid a restraining hand on his arm. "Must you?" she pleaded. "Is it wise? Time has obviously healed. Don't lay yourself open to further hurt."

He stood up. "Curiosity, Angela, nothing more. I was in at the beginning of the drama. I merely want Mrs. Marshall to fill in the middle and the end. If it *has* ended!"

"Luke," Angela said, in the most desolate of voices. "Tonia's here . . . here in the hospital. I saw her waiting for the lift as I came down the stairs. You're going to walk right into her."

Tonia heard the approaching footsteps and patted her mother's hand. "This sounds like the doctor. Now let me do the talking, and we'll see how soon we can get you out of here."

The door opened, and she turned, to find herself staring straight into Luke's penetrating blue eyes. Apart from a gasp from her mother, there was dead silence. Tonia's face mirrored her shock, while Luke successfully concealed his. For he knew at once that the days and weeks and months of telling himself that it was finished were an illusion, that it was not finished, never had been finished, had even grown, so that his need of her was stronger than ever.

"Oh, God," he thought in bitter anguish. "Am I always to feel this way? Is there to be no end to it?"

"Luke?"

He found both his hands in hers. She was still a toucher, then.

"Luke . . . I'm not seeing things? It really is you?"

He saw that she was very moved. Then she smiled— that remembered, longed-for, unforgettable, wide smile— and he thought what a beautiful woman she had become. And it was at this precise moment that Luke Howard made up his mind that, come what may, this time he was going to have her.

So he smiled back and said the last thing he had intended to say. He said, "Will you have dinner with me tonight?"

# 17

"You're staring," she said.

He couldn't help it. When a dream has hovered tantalizingly for years, then materializes into warm, scented flesh sitting opposite you, of course you stared. He had eyes for nothing beyond the circle of candlelight and the girl contained within it. She was dressed in a shimmering gown of palest amber, which left her shoulders and back bare. Her skin gleamed golden in the soft glow of the candle. And the polished hair was coiled into the nape of her neck like whorls of rich smooth honey.

She was everything he wanted—and more. For this was not the extrovert girl he remembered. Here was a woman beautiful in a quieter way, with a sadness in her eyes and a stillness that was new. A stillness born of waiting, of enduring; and Luke liked the thought of that. That she'd had to endure. It fitted in with his tidy world of morality, for you simply could not sin and expect to get away with it. There had to be a reckoning. He was shocked to hear of the man's death, which was a fearful reckoning in itself. At the same time he wished it hadn't been so perfect for them while he lived. If Marais had turned out to be a brute, a drunkard—anything, so long as it was rotten—and she'd crept home disillusioned, and more important, repentant, how much easier it would be to forgive her. Such a girl would be a humble girl, a pliable girl, and although there would still be a formidable barrier of prejudice to overcome, he might—just might—feel hopeful enough to consider presenting her again to his mother.

He had spent the afternoon in Rivingham.

After registering for the congress, he took a taxi home. His mother was ready for him, wearing her best coat and hat, and Luke dumped his suitcase on the bed without even unlocking it, knowing what was expected of him.

He could not have chosen a better day for his return. It was market day. Rivingham was out in force, and not even a returning Nobel Prize winner could have been accorded a finer reception. Every few yards, a hand was clapped on his back or thrust at him in greeting. There were nudges for his mother and quick asides, "Lovely to see your Luke back," and always the same question for him, "Are you home for good?" The butcher gave him a cheery wave as though he'd seen him only yesterday; the chemist left his shop to come outside and talk to him on the pavement. Later, as they reached the bottom of the hill, Luke had to show himself inside the post office as well as the crowded coop where his mother had shopped all her life.

She was quietly relishing every moment. Now all Rivingham could see for themselves what she'd been saying all along. That her son had more sense than to fret over what was good riddance. She'd never seen him look so well and it was obvious that he was enjoying himself.

Luke was experiencing more than enjoyment. The warmth of his welcome engendered a reaction that was quite revealing. In America he had tried to lose his identity, to rid himself of his village background, as a snake sloughs off its skin, to clothe himself with a pseudo-worldly facade modeled on Julian, whom he'd always envied. Now he wondered why he'd bothered. Here, in this simple little community, it all seemed so pointless. Deep down he was still "our Luke," and with a quick flash of insight he knew he would always remain so. He could no more deny his roots than deny his mother. Here was his home. Here he belonged. Here he would settle and raise his family—and at this point the laughing face intruded once again and brought his plans for the future to a troubled halt.

The flower stall in the market was the last port of call. Luke bought a dozen roses, took his mother's arm, and a look of quiet understanding passed between them as their steps turned toward the parish church and the iron gates of the flower-filled cemetery.

Ann Howard watched her son as he arranged the roses on his father's grave. He's a grand lad, she thought. Always this same ritual whenever he comes home. Aloud she said, "We may as well have five minutes inside now that we've come."

Luke knelt beside his mother, knowing that she was giving thanks for his safe return. His own eyes were open, fixed on the deep blue carpet flowing down the aisle. In this church he had been baptized, sung as a choir-boy, later been confirmed. And before this altar he had hoped to stand, watching a girl move slowly toward him, dressed as his mother would expect his bride to be, in virginal white. It was too late for the white dress. But could he—could his mother—could Rivingham—stomach her without it? He buried his face in his hands, but his prayer lacked conviction. Luke Howard did not believe in miracles. Like a tidal wave, the joy of his homecoming came and went. The tug-of-war began all over again. It would be madness to return to St. Michael's tonight. He would not go. In the same moment, he knew that he would.

He was forced to lie to his mother. There was an eve-of-congress cocktail party, and as one of the invited guests his presence was more or less obligatory. It made him feel guilty, and thus resentful. Hardly a good start to the evening.

"You're still staring," Tonia said, smiling. "I'm also doing my share. Maturity becomes you, Luke. You've grown more handsome with the years. Silver wings at your temples, a scholarly air of disdain—you still look down your nose!—and a very arrogant walk. Now having lived in America, why didn't you cultivate an interesting drawl? It's all you lack to make you completely irresistible!"

"My accent always did irritate you, didn't it?"

The undercurrent in his voice made her look thoughtfully at him. "No. Never," she said gently. "You were far too sensitive about your background. As a matter of fact, I find your accent refreshing. Some of the South African accents are not nearly so pleasing."

"Weren't you tempted to stay out there?"

"No. It was Stephen's wish that I leave. He didn't want me to stay on alone."

"Did you always respect his wishes?"

"Always. I respected him, you see," she said simply.

Respect. The word jarred. She hadn't the foggiest notion of what it implied. As if there could be any talk of respect in an adulterous relationship. He stood up abruptly. "Let's dance," he said.

"I thought you hated dancing."

"Not with you."

As they stepped onto the floor Luke drew her into his arms and held her close. Her back was warm and satin-smooth under his hand, and the warmth evoked in him an arousal that he strove to quell. The music was soft and haunting, and a black girl vocalist got up to sing. Her song was sad, of a love that had gone, and her velvet voice was husky and emotive of all the melancholia in her race. When the last notes died away, Tonia's eyes were filled with tears.

"I'm sorry," she said. "I'm a little low emotionally. Don't take any notice. Let's go back to the table. I see the waiter has brought our food."

The circle of candlelight became a pool of silence. They ate mechanically, one engrossed in the past, the other in the present. Luke didn't ask her to dance again. He toyed with his meal, watching the other couples, feeling a pressure build up inside him. Then Tonia's serviette slipped off her lap and he bent to retrieve it. As he handed it to her their glances met and held. The years fell away, and immediately her hand closed over his.

"Dear scarecrow," she said, and the tenderness in her voice turned his heart over.

What a nice person he is, she thought. To have asked me here tonight. Obviously he bears no grudge. If only there could be someone marvelous waiting round the corner for him. Had there been no one in America?

The band swung unexpectedly into a noisy, stamping jive session. "Oh, no!" She wrinkled her nose, and Luke did the same. They both laughed, and impulsively, she said, "Let's get out of here. You never liked such places, and I've outgrown them. I have a much better suggestion. My father's gone to Wales for three days, so let's go home and talk. Really talk, like we used to do. There's so much I want to say. Would you mind?"

Luke's face was expressionless as he called for the bill. But his heart began to pound. *My father's gone to Wales for three days.* She shouldn't have told him that.

Outside it was a lovely, clear night. There was a halo round the moon, and Tonia said, "Let's walk home along the promenade."

But Luke said, "No. I've asked for a taxi, it should be along in a minute."

Inside the dark interior of the cab, he let his arm go casually around her and was surprised to feel her stiffen. "Hey, remember me?" he chided, and Tonia bit her lip fiercely. This man was being incredibly nice. Whether it was the comfort of a masculine arm again, or the strain of the last twelve months, or merely because it was the first gesture of kindness that anyone had shown apart from her mother—whatever it was, it made her turn her face convulsively into his shoulder. Immediately she felt ashamed and tried to sit up, but Luke tightened his arm and said quietly, "Stay there."

A fierce hope, coupled with the reborn longing—no, not reborn, for it had never died—began churning inside him.

As soon as they entered the house she said. "Look, I'm sorry about that exhibition just now. I thought I'd come to terms with life—or rather, death—but every so often I get a reminder that I'm not as strong as I thought. Especially when someone is kind." She walked into the lounge and switched on the electric fire. "It's chilly in here. I miss the Durban warmth."

He stood watching her kick off her shoes and make herself comfortable. She smiled up at him. "Isn't this better? Now we can catch up with each other. Do sit down, Luke."

"Wasn't it a facing coming back?" he asked.

Her face clouded. "Yes. It's funny how you think you know a person through and through. I would never have imagined my father to be so unforgiving. Do you know he rarely talks to me? Usually after the evening visiting hour, I go on the cliffs and walk and walk. Rather than come back here. He's never forgiven me for bringing his year of office to an embarrassing end." She looked at him levelly. "I can't be sorry, you see. How can I say I'm sorry for having been blessed with those wonderful years?"

"You could be sorry for the worry you caused him."

"Worry? Inconvenience and civic loss of face would be more apt. He resents my being here—a constant reminder of his embarrassment—but Mummy pleaded with me to look after him, so I'm the housekeeper and general factotum. Anything but his daughter."

"What about the unhappiness you caused your mother?"

"Oh, Luke . . . I agonized over her. But it was the

separation, more than the situation, which distressed her so terribly. If we'd lived in England, she'd have accepted Stephen."

"And the unhappiness you caused me?" The words were out before he could stop them.

"Do you want complete honesty? I'm not sorry that I walked out on you. I mean . . . I would only have brought you more unhappiness if I'd stayed, as I told you at the time. I just wasn't ready for you, Luke, and when I look back at that empty-headed little brat, I wince! Thanks to Stephen, I've learned since then that my tiny ego is very unimportant. Complete honesty did I say? Ironically, my dear, dear scarecrow, the woman I am now would have been ready for you. But unfortunately, it's too late. And that I am genuinely sorry about."

"Is it too late, Tonia? *Is it?*"

She answered his question with another. "How did you react to Rivingham again? After America?"

"It was good to be back."

"Are you going to settle there?"

"Yes."

"Can you see your mother accepting me?"

"Under certain conditions . . . I think so."

"What conditions?"

"Tonia, if she could only see you as a contrite girl, full of remorse and shame for what you did . . . "

"Shame! For loving Stephen!"

"For living with a married man and defying the norm of decent behavior as she sees it. Tonia . . . it's the only way she *would* receive you. Can't you see that?"

"Oh yes, only too well. If I pretend to be ashamed and guilty, I'll be accepted. People love feeling righteous. They like to be able to forgive others; it magnifies them in their own sight, enables them to play God." She recited the words with a sudden weariness. "Stephen said all that. Right here in St. Michael's, he said it, and now his words have come home to roost. But our time together was lovely beyond belief, and if I repudiated it, I would never be able to face myself in the mirror. Everything Stephen taught me was good, and if I ever love again, then the man, whoever he is, will reap . . . "

"*If* you ever love again!"

He sounded so aghast, so dismayed, that she looked at him in surprise. "What's wrong with saying that? I hope that one day I will love again. Not yet, obviously. But at my age . . . "

"*Not yet*. But I thought . . . I thought . . . "

Her mouth went dry and her heart gave a sickening lurch at the torment in his face. "Oh, my dear," she whispered. "Surely you didn't . . . you couldn't imagine . . . "

"That you were ready for me? Of course, I did! You've just said so. Only two minutes ago, you said so."

"But I didn't mean it literally!"

"You asked all those questions . . . particularly about my mother . . . "

"Hypothetical questions, Luke. To make you see how impossible it would be."

He bent down and yanked her to her feet, and the bitter hunger in his face shocked her. "It isn't impossible. You loved me once—you could again. That moment in the taxi proved it." The brilliant blue eyes were pleading, begging. "Tonia, Tonia, be sensible . . . "

"Sensible is what I'm trying to be! Maybe in a year or two . . . in a different part of the country . . . Oh, I don't know. How can I? It's too soon. But not now. Not now."

Her head began to throb. Since Stephen's death, the slightest emotional stress tended to produce a migraine. "Luke, I'm sorry, but I'm going to ask you to go. I've gone very tired. I think we should call it a day."

He couldn't credit it! He simply couldn't! He'd offered her marriage. And by God, how many men did she think would be willing to marry her? But instead of being grateful, she'd told him to go. She was tired! In a lesser degree it was the jilting all over again. Almost ill with anger—with himself as much as her—he thrust her from him and walked into the hall.

Tonia stared after him in consternation. She seemed fated to do nothing but hurt him, and it had all flared up so quickly. Yet to part like this was unthinkable. The front door was already open by the time she reached him. "Luke, don't go like that. Please! Not in anger. At least allow me to thank you for the evening."

She held out her hand, and he looked at it in disgust. A polite handshake, as if he were a stranger. "Is that the best you can offer? Didn't it rate any higher than that?"

Tonia wavered, aching to comfort him, torn between guilt at his misery and a warning voice that cautioned her not to make things worse. She was not to know that Luke had remained celibate because of her, and that the last few years of continence had been harder than any before, or that the scourge that this fastidious man had used to keep his body under subjection was the remembrance of the very warmth she was about to offer. If she had known, she would never have done what she did.

With a smothered sigh, she reached up to him, and because she couldn't be half-hearted if she tried, she gave him her mouth as sweetly and generously as she knew how.

It was fatal for Luke. It set him on fire; a catalyst releasing the years of continence. His arms closed round her like steel bands, pinioning her to him while he pressed his body into hers. He kissed her cheeks, her eyes, her hair; his hand slid down her smooth throat into the opening of her dress. The scent of her and the warmth—ah, the warmth and softness of the curve under his hand— transported him. He wanted this woman more than he had ever wanted the girl. But underneath the passion, he was weeping. This was the end of his dream. The final fadeout. And tonight it had come so close to reality.

Tonia spun out of his grasp with a shudder.

"Damn you," she gasped. "Did you have to end the evening on such a sour note? Pawing me like a . . . like a . . . " She straightened her dress, shaking like a young girl who'd never been touched, thought Luke bitterly.

"My apologies. You once invited—and welcomed—such pawing."

"Not any more. I've progressed beyond greedy fumblings. Evidently you haven't."

"You certainly did progress. Straight into the bed of a married man."

Her shoulders lifted tiredly. "You see? It would always be between us. Always! Always! Yet a little earlier you were actually talking of marriage."

"A pipe dream, if ever there was one. I can't think what got into me. After all, Marais didn't have to marry you to get you, did he?"

Tonia counted up to ten before she said, "Go home, Luke. Before you say any more. I think you'll be sorry in the morning for the little you have said."

He slammed the door shut. "No. Having said so much, I might as well continue. I've just remembered one of your pearls of wisdom. 'Wanting me and wanting marriage,' you said, 'are two different things. Don't confuse them.' I was confusing them. I want you, but I don't really want to marry you. And as you're still so averse to marriage, why don't we compromise and reach a mutual understanding? I've always wondered how a man felt when he took a mistress. Would you care to enlighten me?"

How dreadfully unhappy he must be, she thought sadly.

"My dear," she said. "Please go home. You're becoming nasty, and I prefer to remember you as I always have—and always will. My dear scarecrow, the nicest of men."

He threw back his head and laughed, the ugliest sound

she had ever heard. "What a wonderful epitaph that would make. 'Here lieth Luke Howard—the nicest of men.'"

"It is an epitaph," said Tonia quietly. "Goodbye, Luke."

His face puckered. Then it contorted into a smile, and if the sound had seemed ugly, the visual expression was worse. As he moved toward her, she backed away. She would never have believed she could tremble simply because a man with a smiling face walked toward her.

"Luke . . . what . . ."

The small of her back came up against the wall. He was very close to her now. Still smiling. She put out both her hands to ward him off.

"Luke . . . please, please, listen . . . this isn't you. Not you, Luke . . . not you . . . you're much too *nice* . . ."

She never knew what triggered off the fury or caused the grotesque smile to crack. Never knew exactly what pushed him over the hairline between love and hate. All she was conscious of was the revulsion and horror at the monstrous face that loomed up and blotted out the light.

In the spew of words that accompanied the nightmare, only one phrase made sense. "All these years the dream . . . at last the reality."

Luke Howard exorcised his ghost, the one with the laughing face. It never troubled him again. But in the guilt-ridden years to come, he was to go down on his knees repeatedly and pray that it would. And to plead for the voice to be removed from his ears, that tired, toneless voice, which predicted so accurately: "You should have kept to your dream. The reality will be harder to forget."

Not harder. Impossible.

# ❧ **18** ❧

Tonia was also trying to forget. She told herself that one forgot the bad by remembering the good, and saturated her memory with thoughts of Stephen in an attempt to blot out that unspeakable hour with Luke. She shrank from seeing him again, while recognizing that seeing him was inevitable. Knowing him as she did, she felt that conscience would drive him back, and every time the doorbell rang, she steeled herself for the encounter. Thankfully, however, he kept away, and the nightmare gradually began to recede. But not for long. Not for long.

Six weeks later, it returned agonizingly with the fear that she was pregnant. She sat on the edge of the bath gasping and shivering after the first bout of retching. She prayed desperately: Please, God, don't let this be what I think it is. She bargained desperately: Please . . . I'll accept anything else. Anything! But take this from me. Let me find I'm mistaken!

There was no mistake, and in the days that followed, a black despair settled upon her, a sickness of the soul. Luke would marry her. Of that there was no doubt. His Rivingham morality would compel him to, and they would neither be the first nor the last to produce a baby seven months after the ceremony. But her whole being revolted against a marriage based on the cornerstone of compulsion. Not only compulsion, but contempt. Stephen had tried it: 'My marriage lasted one distasteful year.' Would she and Luke fare any better? At least a genuine affection had once

186

existed between them, and with a lot of forgiving and forgetting, it might be possible to rekindle a little warmth from the seemingly cold ashes. They would jolly well have to try, she decided grimly. For the sake of the baby. *But please, O Lord, there's still time to take it from me!*

The the nightmare assumed more hideous proportions. Where was Luke? Now he must come. Why didn't he come? After all, this was not just any man—this was Luke. Luke Howard. The very name symbolized a code of conduct that surely not even one ugly lapse could alter. But where was he? Feverishly she counted back the squares on the calendar. She became frantic. Then early one morning, almost crying with relief, she scrambled out of bed and flung her clothes on. What an idiot she'd been! What a stupid idiot! Of course, he wouldn't come. She could wait until Doomsday, and he wouldn't come. By now Luke would have reverted to the nice shy scarecrow that she knew he still was and be abject with shame. So much so that his conscience would work the other way, and remembering her final look of loathing, he would keep out of her sight and think he was doing her a favor. But once he knew about the baby, he would come . . . he had to come.

Her father was using the phone, and too impatient to wait, she ran the length of the street to the nearest call box. Her fingers shook so much that she had difficulty inserting the coins. Poor scarecrow. Sitting at home despising himself. Believing that she despised him. I'll do my best to make him a good wife, and please let his mother accept me.

The woman who answered was not Luke's mother. She volunteered that she was looking after the shop while Mrs. Howard was away on holiday. No, Dr. Howard was not at home, he'd gone with his mother. How long would they be away? Well, she didn't rightly know, but Dr. Howard's young lady had to be back for . . . What was that? Yes, the line was a bit noisy, wasn't it? She knew he had a young lady? Oh yes, and everyone in Rivingham was delighted, especially after that last dreadful business. He seemed to have done well for himself this time, a perfect lady this one was, and Mrs. Howard had taken a real fancy to her.

The telephone slipped from Tonia's hand and performed a crazy jig at the end of the cord. Dr. Howard's young lady? She had difficulty in breathing and thought she would faint. Mrs. Howard had taken a real fancy to her? Dear God. Not even in the darkest moment of the nightmare had she envisaged a development such as this. Luke, what has happened? To you—to us? What is *going* to happen?

She had to wait another eighteen days to find out. Eighteen more ominous squares on the calendar. Eighteen dragging days of resorting to her old act of gaiety. For her mother, although improving, was still in hospital and low in spirit, and the only time she brightened was at the sight of her daughter's smiling face.

It was on a sunny Monday morning, shortly after her arrival at the hospital, that the sun finally fell out of the sky for Tonia Marshall.

She was too preoccupied to notice the silence that greeted her entry through the reception area, or to wonder why the porter looked at her more searchingly than usual when she gave him an absentminded wave. True, there was an incident that needled when she stepped out of the lift on the second floor, but not until later did she attach any significance to it. Two nurses were coming towards her talking animatedly, but when they saw her, their conversation immediately ceased. They nudged each other meaningly and stared boldly as they passed. Tonia kept her head high—the old story doing yet another round, she thought—and wondered wearily how much longer she would be required to visit this building, with its constant reminder of the past.

On reaching her mother's room she paused, to take a

deep breath and fix the smile on her face, but it was wiped off instantly by the sight that greeted her as she opened the door.

Mrs. Marshall was weeping, her face pressed into the pillow, and the low, smothered sobbing tore at the girl's heart and sent her across the room with a rush.

"Darling, darling, whatever is it? Mummy, don't, this is so bad for you. Oh, don't, it's such a lovely morning to be crying. What on earth has upset you so much?"

The crumpled newspaper lay open across the bed, and the photograph was damp with her mother's tears. Tonia bent forward to read the caption underneath:

The marriage of Dr. Luke Howard and Sister Angela Morris was solemnized at Rivingham Parish Church. The happy couple are here seen toasting each other's health at the small reception which followed. Prominent among the guests . . . well-remembered in St. Michael's . . . Dr. Julian Goldberg, now a consulting gynaecologist and obstetrician in Manchester . . .

"I had such high hopes," her mother wept. "I want so much to see you settled, and when he saw you—that first week—I thought there might be a happy ending."

Tonia was strangely calm, almost cheerful, as she comforted her mother and wiped away her tears. She remembered feeling this unnatural calm with Stephen, when Dirk told her that the end was near. Afterwards she felt it was the end, that nothing could be worse. Nothing could eclipse the stark reality of that moment. She had been wrong. *This* was the end. The desolate heartbreaking bitter end.

She took the newspaper away from her mother and carried it home. She tore the picture out and studied it for a long time. Her eye went once more over the caption, and a sentence leapt out of the print and underlined itself in her mind: "Julian Goldberg . . . consulting gynaecologist and obstetrician . . . "

Later that afternoon she made a telephone call. What she intended to do was ugly, but then something ugly had happened to her, and she failed to see why she should be the sole recipient of misery. In any case, it was seldom that a man was elevated to divine status and invited to take over His role. She was confident he would not refuse.

Mentally she rehearsed her opening words. "Remember me?" she would say gaily. "I won't keep you long. I simply popped in to whisper a little something which I think you should know . . . "

Julian Goldberg looked at the card in front of him. He picked it up and studied the typewritten name for some time before pressing the buzzer to his receptionist. "This next patient . . . Marshall. When was this appointment made?"

"Yesterday afternoon, doctor. She rang up and stressed that it was most urgent, and because of a cancellation, we were able to fit her in."

"I see," he said. But he most certainly did not. He had no idea that Tonia was in England, and if the matter was so pressing then she should have called him at home. Good lord! His thoughts flew to Luke and Angela. Did they know of her return? Obviously not, or they would have told him. Not that the news would cause either of them concern, but he was very relieved the Princess hadn't shown up a week ago.

The minute she came through the door he scented trouble. She wore a clear lemon dress, sleeveless and brief, and during her short passage across the carpet, he registered that her long slim legs were as lovely as ever. The rest of her wasn't, though. Her eyes were hard, and there was a brittle forced gaiety in the way she thrust her hand at him and said, "Hello! Remember me?"

He eyed her warily. He couldn't quite fathom her expression, a curious blend of defiance and . . . and *what?*

"Once seen, never forgotten." He gestured toward a chair. "Salaams. Make yourself comfortable. If I'd known you were coming . . .

"You'd have baked a cake."

She is brittle, he thought. Nervous, too. He smiled disarmingly. "Hardly, but I would have stood you lunch as a belated thanks for that memorable day we spent together. When did you arrive?"

Her hand fluttered upwards. "Just dropped out of the sky. It's these itchy feet of mine."

"Nice to have capitalist friends," he said. "Is Marais with you?"

Marais. She wouldn't tell Julian. She couldn't afford pity; it would cause her to soften. "No," she said, "and I don't want to talk about it. I've something more important to tell you." She settled more comfortably in her chair, and he was puzzled by the sheer malice in her smile. For all her faults, the Princess had never been malicious. What the devil had she been up to?

Bluntly, she told him, "Julian, I've started a baby—not Stephen's—and I don't want it. I thought you might like to help me."

In the ensuing seconds, which seemed like hours, it was his hands which fascinated her. They fell limply on the desk before contorting into hard ugly fists that clenched and unclenched in an anger all their own. Whether the anger was repeated in his face she never knew. But when the fists finally stopped moving it came through forcibly in his voice.

"Get out," he said. "Get out of these rooms before I throw you out bodily."

"Now is that nice," she reproached him. "A girl travels six thousand miles to come a-visiting . . . "

He stood up. "My nurse will show you out," and he reached towards the buzzer but she covered it with her hand.

"Not so fast, Julian. You wouldn't welcome a scene in

191

these dignified rooms of yours, now would you? So why don't you relax and let me answer all those unasked questions, which you're dying to ask. Number one, of course, being the name of the lucky father-to-be."

"I'm not interested," he said.

"Really? Do you know I thought you might be! He's such a nice man but unfortunately he's married, which puts me in rather a fix. I do pick 'em, don't I?"

He sat down heavily. "Once a tart, always a tart," he said. "Only a moron like me could have thought otherwise. But I'm delighted you've dropped in. Overjoyed to hear your glad tidings. Now let me tell you mine. Last Saturday I went over to Rivingham. To attend a ceremony. A wedding ceremony, Princess, between two of my dearest friends. Luke Howard and Angela Morris. You didn't know about that when you walked in here, did you?"

"Well, actually, I did," she replied coolly. "I read all about it in the newspaper, and I was so sorry I didn't know earlier. As an old friend of the bride—and the bridegroom—I would certainly have made it my business to attend. Pity! I think my presence would have caused a sensation."

The mere thought made Julian blanch and launched him into a blistering diatribe. "And wouldn't you have loved it! You'd have been in your element! The sensation-seeking Princess—running true to form. And when I think how close Luke Howard came to marrying *you*, I break out in a cold sweat. When you cleared off to Durban you did him the greatest favour any woman could, and if I'd heard your news a week ago I'd have toasted your baby's health, Princess. At their reception. In their champagne. So that Luke could see what a lucky escape he's had."

"Finished?" she asked.

"Not quite. A postscript just for laughs. I happen to care a hell of a lot for Luke, and before I left Johannesburg, I actually wrote to him in your defence because he was concerned about you. I'd have damned you to all eternity, but not Luke. So I allayed his fears because Marais seemed to be doing such a good job. Heaven knows what his technique consisted of, but it was paying off. Thanks to him you had the makings of a fine woman, loyal, steadfast, unselfish, with a bit of integrity chucked in which was sorely needed. God knows what went wrong between the two of you, but Stephen Marais today must be a bitterly disappointed man . . . "

He broke off to see Tonia lying back with her eyes closed. She didn't look at all hard now. Only weary and vulnerable and disturbingly alone.

He asked abruptly, "Who is this other man?"

She didn't answer. She didn't even hear. She was thinking that Julian should not have done that, should not have evoked Stephen so clearly. Because now she couldn't go through with her plan, and how very silly of her to have thought that she could. For if she were to destroy Luke in his friend's sight, in his mother's sight, in his wife's sight— and let there be no mistake, this was the plan—then surely that good thing she had known with Stephen would also be destroyed. She could almost hear his quiet reproach: "Tonia," and the sound of her own name effectively stilled all further desire to voice the name of the man she had come to denounce.

She felt so tired. She wanted to cry. Without Stephen to guide her, the way was a little hard. But somehow she had to get herself up from this chair and out of these rooms and away from the stern face, which was standing proxy for Stephen's.

She stood up, her eyes brilliant with tears, and Julian wondered why he had thought her less lovely. At the door she stopped and turned. Julian rose and stood behind his desk, and they looked at each other.

"I'm sorry I came," she said. "Please forgive me."

She was looking at him, talking to him, but he had the

odd impression that she wasn't addressing him at all. He leaned forward and slammed his hands flat on the desk. "Damn you," he cried. "Why did you come to me? To me—of all people?"

"Because there was no one else I could turn to. But I regret it. How I regret it! Julian, promise me something. Don't ever tell Luke that I came here today."

"Why?" he asked. "Afraid that he'll gloat? He won't, you know. He's far too nice a person."

"I know he is," she said. "That's why I don't want him told," and she walked quickly from the room.

The receptionist in the outer office looked up as Tonia emerged, and paused in her work in sympathy. Tears were streaming down the fair girl's face, yet there was a proud tilt to her head and around her mouth a tired smile. It was the smile of one who had wrestled with the adversary and emerged limp but victorious, but this the receptionist was not to know. So she sighed, wondering what hidden agony the smile concealed and, being both curious and impatient, decided to retrieve the patient's card, intending to find out. She opened the door to her employer's room, then halted on the threshold, shocked and dismayed, Dr. Goldberg was slumped at his desk, his face buried in his hands, in an attitude of utter defeat.

Tonia sat on a bench in some public gardens. There were children playing and old men chatting, lovers strolling and pigeons asking to be fed. The children eventually all ran away. The old men dispersed. The pigeons strutted off, tired of asking, but when it grew dark the lovers remained.

When she arrived home, her father was at the garden gate watching for her. "You're never at home when you're wanted, are you?" he said. "Your mother's taken a turn for the worse. She's been asking for you."

❀

"Julian?" The call came through late one afternoon as he was preparing to leave his rooms, and the line positively crackled with anger. "We've caught him—320 Gresham Street. Can you get over fast? There's a youngster here in pretty bad shape."

He put his foot down on the accelerator, sick with foreboding. The back street abortion, with its aftermath of hideous consequences, was a mounting cause for anxiety to both police and medical authorities, and recently the work of a particularly clumsy operator had resulted in three deaths in as many months.

*Abortion.* For two weeks now the abominable thought had haunted his days and disturbed his nights. The only reassurance was that bitterly spoken, "There was no one else I could turn to," and Tonia Marshall's particularly close relationship with her mother, who would give her love and support instead of condemnation. But who the hell was the man? And where was his support?

The police surgeon was waiting for him, his face grim. "She's gone—but we've got him. Go and take a look at his handiwork."

The girl lying dead in the upstairs room could not have been more than sixteen. She had once been a pretty schoolgirl with a fresh round face and glossy black hair braided into two sturdy plaits. Her striped school blazer hung on the back of the chair, and as Julian turned the sheet back and saw the bloodsoaked mattress, he wept tears in his heart. Dear Lord above, what kind of society drove a child to this act of desperation? To seek deliverance alone at the hands of a bloody butcher.

A child? He went cold, and even as he stared the white city limbs seemed to take on a golden tan, and the dark hair blurred into blonde. His hand shook as he drew the sheet upwards.

An exclamation of disgust from the detective searching the room forced his attention away, and he turned to see

195

the man staring into an open cashbox. Inside, on top of the notes and coins, was a collection of jewelry, each piece mutely telling a story. The policeman picked out several items and held them up, one by one. A string of beautifully graded pearls; no teenager's bauble this, but evidence of a mature woman, an elegant woman, a frightened woman. A fine gold chain with a crucifix, incongruous in its present context. A silver bracelet . . . "There's two names engraved inside this but unfortunately no surnames."

Julian could have supplied them. After all, was it not he who had suggested the bracelet, personally selected it, watched carefully while the inscription had been done in his presence? He wanted to go outside and vomit. His control snapped suddenly, and before the startled man could stop him, he reached for the bracelet and hurled it with all his force against the nearest wall. It was the only time anyone had seen Julian Goldberg in a murderous rage.

When he left the house he did not vomit. He did something else for the only time in his life. He went into the nearest bar and got stupidly, aggressively drunk.

# ❈ **19** ❈

Five years later, on a bright September afternoon, Tonia Marshall walked up the driveway leading to a mellow house and rang the bell. No one answered. She waited a few seconds and then tried again, but although she clearly heard the ring, no movement was visible through the frosted glass pane of the door.

Wearily she leaned against the wall of the porch. It had been a long walk from the bus stop, and her back was beginning to hurt. She scrutinized the employment agency card again and winced. Goldberg. The last name she would have chosen for her prospective employer. But beggars can't be choosers, and the name was common enough. With an effort she straightened up and ventured round to the rear of the house, where she was immediately spotted by a black poodle who came hurtling across the lawn, barking furiously. The noise brought a woman out of a small summerhouse, and she stood shielding her face from the sun, watching Tonia as she approached. She was a handsome woman, tall, with silver hair cut to a shining cap and a dark imperious face, but the strong hint of hauteur was more than dispelled by glowing eyes and a warm passionate mouth.

Tonia liked her on sight. "Good afternoon."

"Good afternoon." She noticed the card in Tonia's hand. "From the employment agency. Thank heavens, I was getting desperate. Let's go into the house to talk. It's much too warm out here," and then to the dog, "Down,

Maxie, you pest, or we're going to end up with ruined stockings. Sorry, my dear, he's a little boisterous at times. Come along." She shut the door firmly on the poodle and led the way into a pleasant room, seating herself behind a businesslike desk. Her hand motioned an invitation to a chair opposite, and Tonia sat down.

"Did the agency give you any indication of the work?"

"Only that it was fairly straightforward, but temporary. I understand that you have a permanent secretary who was called away unexpectedly."

"Yes. Her husband had a heart attack—not too serious, fortunately—and naturally she wants to be with him during his convalescence. Quite right, too. I do a little social work, and nothing distresses me more than to come across people who are sick and lonely, with no one around to . . ." She stopped. "My dear, whatever's the matter? Have I touched on something painful?"

"No . . . please go on." The girl's face was again a polite blank. "You were about to tell me something of the work."

"Yes, of course. It's purely dictaphone work. No shorthand. I'm compiling a journal of family memoirs, which my own secretary seems to enjoy, but she's been with me a long time and knows the family fairly well. I wonder whether it will appeal to you? We could work together for a few days and see how we get on."

"Thank you. I'd like that." Tonia opened her handbag. "I have only one reference, which is a little out of date. I haven't worked recently." She proffered an envelope but the woman waved it away. "I've always found paper credentials to be most misleading. I would much rather you sat down for half an hour with one of the tapes. After which, if we're both satisfied, we can discuss your salary. By the way, I'm being very remiss. I haven't asked your name."

"Marshall."

"Miss or Mrs.?"

"Miss."

"How do you do, Miss Marshall. I have the feeling we're going to suit each other very well."

She rose and walked over to a smaller desk.

"Do you know how to use a dictaphone? Good, then I'll set it up for you." She stood hesitantly. "I'm trying to remember if I completed that cassette this morning . . . Yes, I did. Have a look if it's on the blotter, will you, please? Then I'll leave you in peace to see what you make of it."

Tonia scanned the surface of the desk. "It doesn't seem to be here . . . "

"Try the top, left-hand drawer."

Obediently she walked round the desk, opened the drawer and found what she was looking for. Then she froze. After a moment she returned the cassette to the drawer, lowering it inch by inch as if it had become a very great weight. Her eyes were not on it. They were riveted to something else.

Mrs. Goldberg, sitting with her back to the door, heard it open and close. She looked round inquiringly and blinked in astonishment. The room was empty. A shadow crossed the window, and she reached the front door in time to see the girl running awkwardly down the driveway, her hand pressed to her side.

Tonia was about twenty yards down the road when the car overtook her. She stood panting in the middle of the pavement watching helplessly as the car stopped a little ahead of her, and the woman climbed out and walked back. "I think you owe me an explanation." The voice was accusing, and the amber eyes had lost their glow.

"I'm sorry. That was abominably rude." The pain in her back was becoming unbearable. "I'm sorry . . . I just can't work for you . . . "

"You agreed to try. Then something happened to make you change your mind. What was it?"

A second longer Tonia hesitated, and then the dragging pain forced her to speak. "Under the plateglass top of your desk there's a photograph of Julian Goldberg. He must be your son."

"He is. Do you know him?"

"I used to. Years ago. Your son strongly disapproves of me, Mrs. Goldberg, and would hate the idea of my being in your home. I'm sorry if I've inconvenienced you, but there's no point in wasting further time."

Julian's mother studied Tonia closely and wondered why she persisted in terming this woman a girl. Possibly because she seemed so lost and in need of mothering. Her suit was worn and faded althought spotlessly clean; she looked peaky and undernourished; and the large gray eyes were marred by violet bruises underneath. Also she was holding herself unnaturally as if in pain.

"You're not well," the older woman said quietly. "I'm going to take you home again and give you tea, or maybe something stronger. After which, I think we should talk about Julian."

"No." The girl's face was white and stony. "I will not discuss Julian nor get involved in any way with his family. Please . . . you must excuse me . . . I can't stand for too long at a time."

Mrs. Goldberg refused to argue further. She opened the passenger door of her car, looked at Tonia, and in the brisk, impersonal voice of a woman who is too busy to play games, said, "Come."

*Come!* Stephen's word. Their word. It unlocked the gate of memory. The first night in the cottage. Her voice whispering fiercely, 'Say it.' His illuminated face as he did.

Desperately she fought back the tears. I will not cry. I must not cry. I will not cry . . .

Somehow she found herself seated in the car, being driven back toward the house. Julian's mother's house. Was such a thing mere coincidence?

She was sitting in a comfortable, chintz-covered chair, her head back, hands rigidly outstretched along the arms.

She was looking at the mocking face on the wall. A larger-than-life face in a gold frame. Julian in cap and gown on graduation day. A young Julian, with an arrogant tilt to his chin and a challenge in his eyes. Julian, with smooth forehead and rounded cheeks and a mouth like his mother's.

Mrs. Goldberg handed her a cup of tea, then poured one for herself. She began sipping it, her eyes thoughtful above the rim. "Why does my son disapprove of you, Miss Marshall?"

"I suggest you ask him that. He'll tell you. He'll be only too delighted."

"Make it one or the other, my dear. Julian disapproving or Julian delighted. Not both."

"Both, in this instance."

"You know, I get the distinct impression that you don't like my son."

The eyes in the photograph awaited her answer, and she gave it with great satisfaction, "I don't."

"I see. Forgive the bluntness, but is this a case of a love affair gone sour?"

"A love affair with Julian? You must be joking!"

The contemptuous denial caused his mother to remark dryly, "Strange though it may seem, you're in the minority. Women fall in love with Julian all the time. Let me put the question another way. Was he ever in love with you?"

"Most definitely not! He couldn't bear the sight of me." She sat up. "I really must apologize. For being so melodramatic. There's really no mystery. Julian never liked me, and it didn't exactly help when I jilted the man who was his closest friend."

There was an odd little silence. Then his mother said, "Princess Tonia. Of course." Her voice was that of a woman who has just solved a hitherto unsoluble problem.

"Of course," said Tonia quietly.

Mrs. Goldberg rose abruptly as if anxious to terminate the interview. "I now understand your reluctance to take the job. Where are you living?"

"Please . . . you mustn't feel obliged to . . . "

"I'll drive you home. Without argument, if you please, because it's obvious that you're far from well. It can't be for another half hour though, because I'm expecting a phone call, and I don't want to miss it. Do you mind waiting?"

Her tone seemed so frostily polite that Tonia winced inwardly. "Not at all. You're being very kind."

The older woman paused on her way out. The girl really was a shocking color. "Lean back and close your eyes. I'll see that you're not disturbed until we're ready to go."

She went straight to her study and picked up the phone. When she got through to her number she simply said, "Julian? Tonia Marshall. She's here—with me."

The seconds ticked away, and when he answered, it was not with his usual voice. "Keep her there. I'll be right over."

His receptionist was appalled. "But Dr. Goldberg! You still have two more appointments!"

"Tell them it's an emergency. Fit them in first thing tomorrow morning." He shrugged into his jacket and raced for the door.

Tonia must have been nodding. She opened her eyes and looked into Julian's. Such a young . . . She jerked upright. This was not a young Julian.

In a low, weary voice, she said, "Your habit of making unexpected appearances is becoming monotonous."

"I've come to take you home, wherever that may be. Are you ready?"

The anger in his voice puzzled her. "No, thank you. I'm quite capable of getting home under my own steam."

202

"I'm taking you. Get your things together and go and say goodbye to my mother."

She struggled to her feet. "Please . . . just leave me alone. No one constituted you my keeper, and who asked you to take me home, anyway?"

"I did," said his mother calmly, standing in the doorway. "I've decided it would be nice to have you here, but as your acceptance seems to be conditional upon Julian's approval, then the logical thing was to get him over as quickly as possible." She smiled at him. "You didn't waste much time. Now don't indulge in low flying while Miss Marshall's in the car, will you? Otherwise I might have to look for yet another secretary and that would be so inconvenient." She addressed Tonia. "*Au revoir,* my dear. Give me a ring when you're ready to start. Hours approximately ten to four. And do make it soon."

Tonia said, "You are just as impossible as your son." Outwardly calm, inwardly shaking, she passed them both without a backward glance.

As she walked into the sunshine, she was aware of Julian following her. His car was parked behind his mother's, and as she drew level with it his arm shot out and detained her."

"Get in," he ordered.

After one look at his face she obeyed. "Where to?" he snapped, as he climbed into the driving seat.

She cast around in her mind quickly, and then pointedly looked at her watch. "You can drop me in the center of town. I have a special date at five, which I'm rather looking forward to keeping."

"Then you're going to be disappointed. Your only date tonight is with me."

She sat very still. "I don't want to go anywhere with you."

"I don't give a damn what you want. You and I have

some unfinished business to attend to and attend to it we will. Now, where do you live?"

She was silent.

"Then we'll go to my place. The venue is no problem."

"*No!* Julian, what's the use . . . we have nothing to say to each other."

"You speak for yourself. There's a hell of a lot I want to say to you, my girl, and you're going to hear it. Every last word of it."

"You're furious! Really furious. But why? I don't understand."

"Don't you? *Don't you?* Have you taken a good look at yourself lately? I barely recognize you! When I think of the stunning girl you were—and look at you now—I could throw up. You went through with it, didn't you? When I refused to do your dirty work, you shopped around for someone who would. *Didn't you?* How did he do it, Princess? How did you feel when your baby's life began to flow out of you? Can you remember?"

He watched every vestige of color drain from her face and felt a savage pleasure at the thought of what he was doing to her.

"Am I turning your stomach? I hope so! I hope so! To think that I spend half my days trying to help women who want babies and can't have them, and irresponsible bitches like you . . . oh, God!" His balled fist came crashing down on the steering wheel. "Well, say something, damn you. Come on! What's happened to those sharp claws of yours?"

She sat as if she'd been frozen in time. He turned the ignition key, and his voice was now tired. "Where do you want me to take you? In your condition you should be in bed. I'll qualify that by saying alone in bed."

Tonia said, "Just for the record, and before we go our separate ways, I want you to know that I dislike you more than any man I've ever met."

The car began to move. "Getting subdued in your old

age, aren't you? Wouldn't *hate* be a more suitable word?"

"Yes, but Stephen said . . . " Steady, she thought. Don't give way now . . . oh, please not now . . . not in front of him.

"Ah, yes. Lover Boy. The great South African romance. I wondered when we'd get around to that. What busted it up, Princess?"

"I think I'd like to go home after all. If your offer to take me still stands."

Her voice was odd, and he glanced sharply at her to see her gritting her teeth. "Certainly," was all he said.

She directed him, and eventually asked him to stop in the middle of a busy shopping thoroughfare. A line of parked cars prevented him from pulling into the curb, and he looked at her, puzzled. "Here?"

Tonia pointed vaguely to the windows above the ground floor shops. "I have rather a nice flat up there."

She climbed out and stood in the roadway, and they looked at each other. A driver behind tooted impatiently, and he drove away without another word.

The small bed-sitter was at the top of four steep flights of stairs. She managed the first two, and then sat on the bottom step for a few minutes before attempting the remainder. By the time she reached her room, the pain was so severe she could scarcely stand.

She collapsed on the bed and lay with closed eyes. Julian had revived once more the nightmare that had started with Luke. Would it ever end? Had Luke found happiness with Angela, she wondered. Or was he was tormented by the past as she was.

She heard footsteps mounting the bare, wooden stairs. A visitor for the girl next door who was forever borrowing things. A smiling, good-hearted girl who made no secret of her trade.

The footsteps stopped. The handle of her door turned, and he came in. He stood by the door studying the room in detail. He walked to the plastic curtain and pulled it back. Noted the tiny cracked washbasin and the gas ring. He asked, "Toilet facilities?"

"One floor down."

"Shared with all and sundry?"

"Yes."

He stood by the bed. "Someone very obligingly moved out of a parking place, so I couldn't resist coming back to see your rather nice flat."

"And now that you've seen it, you must be feeling very pleased with yourself. This is really your day of triumph, isn't it? How are the mighty fallen! Laugh, Julian! Please, Julian! Don't disappoint me, Julian! What are you waiting for, Julian?"

"Have you ever cried, Tonia?"

"Oh, yes. Until the tears ran dry, and I got past it. Odd that you should ask. I almost cried today for the first time in years. Something your mother said. I liked her until I knew she was your mother. You're taking a long time to laugh, Julian. You're keeping me waiting."

"You've kept me waiting for years."

"Waiting for what?"

"You've just analyzed it. My day of triumph."

She closed her eyes. "Enjoy it, Julian. Your cup must be running over."

"It is," he said quietly.

Something in his tone made her open her eyes. Something in his face made her shut them again.

"I want you to listen carefully," he said. "Will you?"

She gave a little nod of assent.

"You're a sick woman. I would say there's some internal damage in need of repair. Has anyone else suggested this?"

Again she nodded.

"I thought so. Now, I can arrange for you to be admitted to a private clinic. The sooner the better. Tomorrow, if possible. Will you allow me to do this?

He saw the first tears begin to squeeze their way through the closed lids. "Why?" she choked.

"Never mind why. The reason wouldn't interest you. May I go ahead with the arrangements?"

"Yes . . . thank you . . . "

Then suddenly she was sobbing as she had never done in the whole of her life, without pride or defence, delivering herself naked to the enemy—as a woman who has finally been broken yet knows not with certainty that which has broken her. The years kaleidoscoped, and in her agony she sobbed for what she had done to Luke and what Luke had done to her. She sobbed for Stephen and the years of promise which now would never be. But most of all she sobbed for the pity she saw in the face of one whom she hated.

He stood silently, not touching her, watching the cleansing water flow, and then, as the final seal of ignominy, she was sick. And it was Julian, the hated one, who ministered unto her with the tenderness of a woman, who supported her straining shoulders and comforted her with low, soothing words, who sponged her face when the retching ended and she sank back exhausted.

And it was Julian who later carried her down the four flights of stairs and took her home to his mother.

# ✿ 20 ✿

Her head hurt and her body was so light that she thought it would float off the bed. The surgeon who performed the operation had just left, after telling her only what she feared. That for her, the days of conception were over.

So this was to be the new way of it. A barren woman. The verdict was harsh, and there was no right of appeal. Nature had her way, too, and she had trespassed against it in deliberate defiance of the consequences. *We have done those things which we ought not to have done, and there is no health in us.*

But she would heal. Bodily and mentally she would heal and learn to walk in the new way. She would learn to laugh again, too. After all, there was always something marvelous waiting round the corner. You'll see, Julian. It'll be a piece of cake. And away I'll go on my magic carpet.

The nurse who hurried into the room found her haemorrhaging and delirious, laughing and crying and trying to sing.

The healing was painfully slow. Julian came once. Or rather, Dr. Goldberg came, his face stern and dark. He stood at the foot of the bed, fired a number of professional questions at her, then left. There was no opportunity to express gratitude, or say anything personal. He didn't come again. She wrote a stilted thank-you note and sent it to him via his mother who, surprisingly, visited her every day. Part of the "little social work," Tonia surmised, but the nurses looked blank when questioned and said they'd never seen her before.

At last the afternoon came when she was allowed to leave. She snapped the catches down on her suitcase and thought of the bed-sitter at the top of the stairs. Then she decided there were better things to think about. Outside the leaves were turning, and the crisp air was going to smell good. She was a lucky woman. She was alive. She'd take those stairs slowly, slowly, and everything would be just fine. It was peculiar, all the same, that neither of the Goldbergs had popped in to say goodbye.

"All set?" Julian stood in the doorway, and the blood rushed to her head, making her dizzy. He lifted her case off the bed and crooked his arm toward her. "Better hang on. Walking is going to be difficult for quite some time."

He measured his step with hers as they made their slow progress toward his waiting car. She was confused and ill at ease. Julian behaved as if there was nothing untoward about chauffering her home—but this was not the way home! They were driving into the country, and she became agitated. "Julian, where are we going? Where are you taking me?"

"To a little weekend place of mine in Cheshire. Charming, peaceful, the ideal place for a convalescence."

"Yes, but . . . " More indebtedness. More charity. The thought stuck in her throat. "Julian, I can't. I *can't* accept anything more from you. Please undersand. I'm grateful . . . but I'll never be able to repay you."

"Relax," he said, "I'm not doing you any favors. In fact, I'm counting on you to do me one. This little place is pleasant in summer but damp in winter. If you'll move in, keep it warm and aired, you'll save me a fortune in repairs. Which is how you can repay me."

She closed her eyes. He was manipulating her like a puppet, and in her weak state she felt like one, wholly dependent on this man who was pulling the strings.

Bluntly he explained the reason for the house as soon as they arrived. "I once kept a woman here. When the association finished, I kept it on for those who came after. It was simpler, and more discreet, than an hotel."

She stopped short in the doorway. "I see. Julian . . . "

"Don't say it," he warned. "I have no desire to make you my mistress. Not now—not ever." Then he saw her eyes and went on a little more kindly. "I just want to make it clear that there are no conditions attached. This place is standing idle, and in your present circumstances, it would be foolish not to make use of it. You won't be fit to work for at least six months, so you might as well regard this as your home in the meantime."

She managed to say, "Thank you."

"Now, let's have a look at the food situation before I go and stock up." He disappeared into the kitchen, and she made a slow, exploratory tour of the house. It was charming. Quite small, with two tiny bedrooms and a living room, it was more like a cottage than a house. An odd duplication of events—another cottage, another winter. But the wrong owner, the wrong place.

The garden was pretty, too, but no duplication here. No bright orange fiddlewood trees, or apple-blossom azaleas. No wattle grove at the bottom of the garden, either, and then she stared.

Julian found her struggling with the bolts on the back door, her pale face showing the first spark of animation.

"I can see a lilac tree! Do you know that lilac is my favorite blossom, my favorite perfume? I used to long for the scent of it in Durban, but it was too hot, it wouldn't grow." The brief sparkle died as she recalled the morning of her twenty-first birthday, and Luke laughing up at her with his heart in his eyes. Her voice became indifferent. "I don't expect I'll be here when it blossoms. Six months did you say? I'll miss it."

"Then we must either order an early spring, or grant you an extension of stay. How are you feeling? Ready to lie down again?"

"I'd like to stay up a little longer."

"Good. Just don't overdo the standing. I want to nip along to the little shop to arrange deliveries of bread and milk, ask them to let you charge things. Then I'll be on my way."

"You're not staying? Not even for an hour or so?"

"I can't. I have a dinner party tonight." He shot her a keen glance. "What's wrong? Not afraid, are you? There are neighbors either side within fifty yards, and a telephone beside one of the beds."

"No, I'm not afraid. I'll be fine. But I think I will get ready for bed while you're shopping."

"Good idea. Take my bedroom, the one where the phone is. I won't be long."

She was in bed when he returned, the light from the shaded lamp softening her gaunt face and creating an illusion of the lovely girl he remembered.

"The larder's full. Unless you develop the appetite of a horse, it should last until I come again."

"When will that be?"

"Next weekend, if I can manage it. Ring me at my rooms on Monday if there's anything else you need."

"I'm sure there won't be. You seem to have thought of everything. Thank you, Julian. Goodnight, I hope you enjoy your party."

He hovered for a moment and then said abruptly, "If it hadn't been something special tonight, I'd have ducked it. I didn't plan on leaving you alone in a strange place on your first night out of hospital."

"That's all right. I'm not your patient. Not your responsibility. Not . . . anything! Good night."

She lay still for a long time. Outside the night grew

dark and cold, but the little house was warm and friendly, a haven of refuge to the weary woman within.

Her thoughts were solely of Julian. Why this astonishing concern for the welfare of a woman he didn't even like? What did he *want*? If she'd still been attractive and he'd tried to exact the usual kind of payment, that would have made sense, but her cheeks burned as she recalled his brutal "Not now—not ever." Chance is a fine thing, my dear doctor, and the answer would be "No" and a prompt return to the bed-sitter. The mere thought of going to bed with Julian made her shiver.

But instead of shivering, she did something else. Something amazing and quite incredible. She began to laugh. For whether she liked it or not the undisputable fact remained that she was firmly ensconced in Julian Goldberg's bed, and very comfortable, it was, too.

Her long-lost sense of humor returned, and she laughed. Hesitantly, shakily, and with difficulty, because it had not happened for so long that she was out of practice. She caught sight of herself in a mirror. Yes, she was actually laughing again! Julian, whatever you want, whatever your price, you shall have it to the uttermost farthing, for proving that marvelous things still lie in wait for me and the age of miracles is not past.

Equally incredible, she was hungry! She padded into the kitchen and devoured sliced after slice of bread thickly spread with jam, and it was a royal banquet. Afterwards, moved by some strong compulsion, she walked through the little house, her fingers lingering on every piece of furniture and passing lightly over the walls, to convince herself by touch that this was not a dream. It was not, and with the realization came another, more important one. The long dark night was over—the nightmare ended.

She went back to bed and lay enfolded in a calm that previously had only been experienced with Stephen. She thought of him now, as always, thankfully and with a deep humility, but this time there were no tears.

She thought of Luke—*forgive us our trespasses as we forgive them*—and saw only the shy smile of the darling scarecrow. And again, no tears came.

The telephone rang, and she picked it up at the first ring. The voice came to her against a buzz of conversation and a woman laughing.

"Why aren't you sleeping?"

"I couldn't. I'm quite comfortable, though. Why did you ring?"

"To remind you to take the pills—the torpedo capsules. I left them on the bedside table."

"I've already taken them. Is it a nice party?"

"Very nice."

"Julian . . . " It was easier to say things to his voice, rather than his face. "Julian, I want to thank you with all my heart . . . "

"Go to sleep. It's late. Good night," he said, and put the phone down.

Then, inexplicably, tears came.

Later she fell asleep and dreamed a ridiculous dream. In it, a bright light swept across her window, followed by quick footsteps crunching the leaves, and an audible sigh of relief from the house as it gladly received the caller. Her door opened, and a man came to the foot of the bed. His face was not stern or dark, but raw and vulnerable like hers, and she smiled at him to ease away the pain. She opened her mouth to tell him that even pain endureth only for a season, but he said roughly, "Go to sleep."

It couldn't have been a dream, however, for in the morning he was still there.

She never forgot that first Sunday morning. Remorselessly, ignoring her growing exhaustion, Julian dragged from her the full sequence of events after his visit to Durban.

Stephen's death . . . her return to England and the shock of her mother's illness. Mrs. Marshall's apparent recovery followed by the fatal relapse. Her father's bitter accusation that her actions had shortened her mother's life. Her flight from St. Michael's in an agony of guilt. Then the abortion, her failing health and inability to keep a job, the dwindling money. The humbling of self as she wrote to her father. The mounting bleakness in the wait for a reply that never came. But most of all, the loneliness—dear God, the total loneliness—of the long, despairing, degrading decline.

By lunchtime he knew it all. All except the thing he wanted to know most. "Who was the man, Tonia?"

"I've told you. I've told you a dozen times."

"You mean you've recited the same pack of lies a dozen times. A casual pickup! Someone you've never met before and never seen since. What tripe!"

"Why should it be? Once a tart, always a tart, to quote your own words."

"Oh, be quiet," he said crossly. "I retracted that some time ago, if you must know. Now don't go all dewy-eyed on me, for Pete's sake!"

"I wish I could understand you," she whispered.

"Well, I understand you perfectly. That's why that story of yours won't hold water. You could no more sleep with a perfect stranger than I could."

"Birds of a feather, obviously." She made an effort to be flippant.

There was a cryptic look in his black eyes. "You're halfway to your wish," he said.

She didn't know what he was talking about. But during the long months ahead she puzzled over him greatly and wished that she did.

Julian's bounty that winter was overwhelming. Each month brought something for her comfort, always without warning. Such as the television set, which arrived one afternoon when she hadn't seen him—or anyone—for two weeks, and the loneliness had become an ache. That evening she sat up till midnight entranced with her new toy, and Julian, at the other end of the phone, smiled on hearing her incoherent thanks. Then, in the middle of November, when the inclement weather had imprisoned her indoors for days, a bright red Mini was driven to her door. "Dr. Goldberg's compliments, and will you do him the favor of running it in. Says it'll save him a lot of time and trouble."

Strange, unpredictable man, this Julian.

But the most precious gift of all—he forced her to go on laughing, with odd conversations that, like the gifts, were plunged on her without warning.

"Tell me, did you and Lover Boy ever laugh when you made love?"

She slammed down her book. "I don't much care for your line of questioning." She tried to push past him but he blocked her way.

"No, don't go all bolshie on me. Hell, I've never known such a woman for evading questions. Look, I'm serious. In bed, out of bed, did you laugh?"

"Of course, we laughed," she said stiffly.

"Really? One would never think so. You're supposed to have had four perfect years—years such as any woman would give her eye-teeth for—yet the mere mention of them makes your mouth pull down like a frustrated old maid who's always craved the weight of a man against her loins, yet never had it."

He gave her a little shake. "But you had it," he said roughly. "In a measure pressed full to overflowing you had it, and if you never have another happy moment, those memories should keep you smiling for the rest of your life. When life kicks you in the teeth you either kick right back or laugh in its face. Then press on, regardless. Get it?"

"Got it," she said, and an immediate remembrance made her throw back her head and laugh out loud, just as Stephen had done on that lovely first day on their way to the Berg.

"That's better," said Julian. "If you keep that up, who knows, you might turn out an even better looker than before."

"Julian . . . why?" she asked abruptly. "I've got to know."

"Know what?"

"The answer to the question which *you* always evade. Why are you doing all this? For me, of all people?"

He regarded her strangely. "For you, of all people," he repeated. "I'll tell you what, Princess. Until you answer my question—the one about the man—then accept that as my answer to yours."

There is none so blind as one who will not see, for she still didn't know what he was talking about.

There was no snow that year, and Spring came early. Like an ardent young girl she came, eager and gay of step, enchanting, infinitely desirable; but the lilac tree was old and stubbornly refused to respond to her charm.

"Oh, get a move on!" Tonia implored. She reached for a branch and anxiously inspected the tight green buds. "I'm as fit as a fiddle. I feel on top of the world. Any moment now Julian will throw me out; and how can I leave without seeing you in all your splendor?" She let the branch spring upwards and walked back to the house smiling.

Julian would do no such thing. But having been here seven months instead of the original six, she could hardly stay much longer. Thrusting aside the twinge of sadness, she reached for the flour and the mixing bowl, for today was Sunday—and Sunday meant Julian.

The telephone rang, and it could only be him.

"Buckingham Palace," she said in a deep voice.

"Her Royal Highness the Princess, please."

"I'm sorry, I don't think the Princess is in."

"She'd better be," he declared. "Otherwise she's in for a right royal thump." He waited for her clear laugh before continuing. "What's the menu? I'm bringing someone with me, a cute little redhead who has the sweetest tooth I know. Can you stick some icing on top of your famous shortcake?"

"Icing on top of shortcake! Oh, well! There has to be a first for everything, I suppose. Usual time?"

"Usual time—on the dot."

She returned to the kitchen and began measuring out the ingredients. A cute little redhead! Julian had always been partial to redheads. Why on earth didn't the man get married? He must be over forty, and if he wasn't careful he'd find himself left on the shelf. She laughed. It occurred to her that laughter and Julian were synonymous.

Promptly at three his car turned into the drive and she stood in the doorway smiling a welcome. The small boy with Julian didn't smile, however. His face fell, and he looked up accusingly at the man.

"You tell lies! You said we were coming to see a princess, but she's no princess, she's an ordinary lady."

"It's her day off," said Julian. "From the palace. It gets very boring living in a palace, so she takes every Sunday off to come and make tea for me."

"What does boring mean?"

"No fun. No fun at all. Long faces all the time like this." He pulled his chin down and crossed his eyes, and both Tonia and the child burst out laughing.

"Uncle Julian's funny," the little boy said.

"Very funny," said Tonia. "Do come in, Uncle Julian."

"Thank you, Princess. In you go," he said to the child, who ran inside. He made straight for the bookshelves, selected a book, then stretched himself full length on the rug in front of the fire.

"What an easy young man to entertain," said Tonia. "Where are his parents?"

"In bed, I expect."

She stared. "In bed!"

"Why not? Good old British custom. Tuck into a nice Sunday roast followed by steamed pudding, and then go and sleep it off. Mind you, on the Continent they put the afternoon to much better use—they don't waste time sleeping."

Her eyes danced. "So I've heard, but what makes you think the custom is confined to the Continent?"

"I don't. I expect you and Lover Boy had many a wonderful afternoon session."

"We did," she said. "And they were wonderful, Julian."

"I'm sure they were. Especially if you looked at him the way you're looking at me right now."

He grinned at her startled expression. "Don't mind me. It's Spring! What's the lilac doing? Let's go and have a look. Martin, take your nose out of that book and go climb a tree."

The little boy moved so reluctantly that Julian almost shoved him through the door.

"Always books! A little more fresh air is what he needs," he muttered, and Tonia watched, a little subdued, as he hustled the child down the garden path.

Uncle Julian. Another facet of this many-sided man. She'd seen him with children before, but never with one so young. She felt a dull hurt in the certain knowledge that if this little fellow had been hers, he would already be astride the loftiest bough of the tallest tree, laughing down at them with a dirty face and wide, impudent grin.

And that's enough of that, she told herself, and went inside to put the kettle on.

The child turned out to be shy and unresponsive and she found herself resenting his presence, for there was little opportunity to talk alone with Julian, and a long week loomed ahead until his next visit. However, the day was far from over. When the time came for them to leave Julian put the boy into the car, and then turned to her. "After I've taken him home, may I come back?"

Her face lit up. "For supper? Why, of course! I'd be delighted."

"No, not for supper. I'm taking a week off, and I'd like to spend it here. Any objections?"

"A . . . a whole week? Here? With me?"

"Forget it," he said.

"No! Why should you forget it? After all, this house is yours, not mine. In any case, I've been thinking, if I'm not careful I'll become a recluse! It's time Her Royal Highness got out and about in the gay swinging world again." There was a break in her voice.

"Yes," Julian agreed quietly. "You've hibernated long enough. The winter is over. It's time to wake up."

She was as nervous as a kitten awaiting his return. She cleared her things out of his room, made up fresh beds, added to the already adequate flower arrangement, and dusted unnecessarily. Then she tried on two dresses, and discarded both in favor of a third. Oh, for heaven's sake . . .

She donned an old sweater over even older slacks and went out to replenish the coal scuttle.

# ❋ 21 ❋

Tonia came quickly out of sleep and instantly laughed. She felt so happy that she experienced a sense of guilt, an obligation to apologize to poor unfortunate people everywhere who never expected miracles, and thus, of course, received only what they expected. But the guilt was ephemeral, and she leaped out of bed and spread her arms, containing between her finger tips the garden with the lilac tree and the fields and hills beyond.

"Oh, I do thank you," she exclaimed, wondering even as she spoke, whether she was addressing her Creator or the man who was making such an outrageous clattering in the kitchen. She decided to be scrupulously fair and apportion a fifty-fifty share to each, then reached for her housecoat and proceeded in the direction of the noise.

Julian, clad in bright red pyjamas, was peering into the depths of a saucepan. "About time," he remarked, without turning his head. "Some people would sleep all day if given half a chance."

"What, with that racket going on? Some people must be joking!"

"Come over here," he demanded. "The speciality of the house is almost ready, and I need a second opinion. Open wide." He held out a spoonful of some dubious concoction, the predominating aroma of which made her recoil sharply.

"Garlic," she said faintly. "Ugh! I can hardly bear it at the best of times, and definitely not before breakfast."

"Correction," he said. "This *is* breakfast. Sit down, woman, and stop complaining. It won't kill you to sample a little."

She backed away. "I haven't washed yet . . . "

"Neither have I. Garlic seems to go down better when you're unwashed." He grinned at her moue of distaste. "Besides, it's good for the bloodstream, although there doesn't appear to be much wrong with your blood on this bright and beautiful morning. Now what about it? Going to try some of this mishmash?"

"Only if it's a question of confidence."

"It is, so brace yourself. Here you are . . . one measly little portion plus one giant cup of coffee. One to cancel out the other. There's consideration for you!"

Holding the plate at arm's length, she seated herself at the table, watching as he whistled cheerfully while heaping an enormous serving for himself.

"You know," he said, sitting down opposite her. "We make a most convincing picture of cosy domesticity. You in your pyjamas and me in mine."

She forced down the first mouthful of food and nearly choked. "Thank goodness it isn't the real thing. I can't imagine anything more revolting than exchanging good-morning kisses with a man who reeked of garlic."

"How do you know until you've tried it? Personally, if we both reeked, I think it could be fun."

"Well, I don't. As for living with such a man . . . " She shuddered again as the vile taste lingered in her throat.

Julian lifted his eyes and looked straight into hers. "Don't stop. You have my undivided attention. You were saying?"

"I was saying that it was a heavenly morning . . . "

"You were not. Would living with me be so revolting?"

"No."

His fork clattered to the table. "Glory be! We progress! That's the first straightforward answer you've given me in years. Any moment now we'll have the answer to the other question."

Resolutely she steered away from danger. "It *is* a heavenly morning, so let's dress quickly and do something special. Very special, because . . . this might be our last day together."

He stopped eating. "Our last day together?"

"Yes." She tried to keep her voice steady. "When you leave here tomorrow, I'm moving out, too. No, don't interrupt. I'm well, Julian—wonderfully well—and now that I'm fit to work again, I no longer have an excuse to stay here."

"You don't need an excuse. I invited you here. You like being here. Look, we're wasting time. We'll discuss this tonight."

"I've tried to discuss this every night for a week, but you've always sidetracked me." With her old impulsiveness, she reached for his hand. "Julian, there's so much I want to say. Please let me, before I go. You've made me whole again—in the only way that counts. And because I'm no longer a cripple, I can't go on using you as a crutch. You do see that, don't you? But I'll be forever grateful . . . " She hesitated, searching for further words and, finding none, swiftly bent and kissed his hand.

He snatched it away. "Don't ever do that again," he said hoarsely. "Women don't do such things."

Her head came up proudly. "This woman does. Why are you so embarrassed? Julian, do you realize just *what* you've done? You've restored my pride, my courage, my faith in myself and in the future. On this lovely day I'm ready to laugh and live and lo . . . "

She caught the word just in time.

"Say it," he said. "You've earned the right to say it. A man is characterless until he's tried, and no one could have had a worse trial than you. Yet you picked up the pieces, stuck them together, and you're a better woman now than you've ever been. You were born under a lucky star, Princess. I hope you count your blessings."

"Every day," she said, wanting to add that he was one of them, but afraid of embarrassing him further.

She smiled happily at him but was disturbed to receive no answering smile.

"You know," he said slowly. "I would like Luke Howard to see you now."

Her smile became fixed.

"You do remember Luke? Of course you do. Silly question. Well, it's odd, but Luke appears to have done things in reverse. After you ditched him, he went to pieces for a while—which was understandable. But he got over it. In fact, when he came back from America, he looked a new man, and I wish you could have seen him. But then, that wasn't possible, was it?"

He paused and smiled and her skin prickled. The smile was too bland and there was a glitter in his eyes which reminded her forcibly of the old predatory Julian.

"Let's see now . . . how long *is* it since you've seen Luke?"

She managed a careless shrug. "All of ten years, I suppose. Reckoning by my age."

"Thirty-one," he said. "And you don't look a day over twenty-five. As ravishing as ever. Woman, you're distracting me. What were we talking about?"

"Luke," she said tautly. As if you didn't know, she thought. Get on with it, Julian. I recall all too clearly these cat-and-mouse games of yours.

"Ah yes, Luke. Well, he married Angela, as you know, and on the face of it has it made. Top of the tree professionally . . . lovely home . . . delightful wife . . . Oh, by the way, that red-headed tyke I brought last Sunday was his. Did I tell you?"

The scalding coffee stayed in her mouth and burnt it.

She couldn't have swallowed to save her life.

"Obviously, I didn't. There's a baby, too, but until she's out of nappies Uncle Julian isn't interested. Are you feeling all right? The garlic hasn't upset you?"

The coffee went down in one blistering gulp.

"Finish your story. About Luke. What's the matter with him?"

Julian sighed. "I wish I knew. He looks sixty instead of forty."

"Thirty-eight."

"So he is. What a memory you have! Makes no difference, he still looks sixty. He's as grey as a badger, stoops worse than ever, he's like a man carrying an intolerable burden. Sick to death of it, yet can't find anyone to lift it off his back. In fact, if I didn't know Luke Howard so damned well I'd say he was harboring a murky past."

"That's ridiculous," she said.

"Yes, isn't it?" he said softly.

The blood rushed to her head. He knew. *He knew!* The kitchen blurred for one giddy moment, and then she steadied herself. How could he know? It was not possible. Only one other person could answer the unanswered question. And that person never would. Which meant that Julian was bluffing.

"Oh, don't," she said involuntarily. "Please don't!"

"Don't what?"

She sat mute. There were too many incriminating don'ts. Don't revive the nightmare. Don't force me to speak. To hurt you. Not now, Julian. Oh, not now! This shining new relationship . . . don't spoil it. Not for Luke. Or anyone. Or anything. Please, Julian, don't . . .

Something leapt inside her. Something that had been sleeping. Something so preposterous that she hurriedly bypassed it and drove her thoughts toward Luke. Luke with grey hair? Unhappy? His marriage suffering? Surely this was part of the bluff?

In a flash, she realized that it was not and knew with sad perception the bitter way that Luke had trod. The way of the Puritan, contrite and stricken with remose, the burden of sin growing heavier as time magnified the guilt. The way of the penitent, seeking absolution. Absolution, which only she could give.

Poor scarecrow. Her mouth twisted as once again she recalled that morning of passion, the scent of lilac, and a man laughing . . .

Quite unlike the man in the red pyjamas. He looked as if he would never laugh again. Something in her face seemed to infuriate him, and ignoring her choked little cry, he fastened his hand over hers like a vice, clamping it to the table.

"Talk," he said. "Talk about *him*. This person who commands such loyalty. Who took over where Lover Boy left off. Whom you've protected over the years. Will you name him, Tonia, or shall I?"

The room was hushed as he awaited her reply. It came in a curiously ragged voice. "It wasn't like that at all. The man . . . I didn't keep quiet for his sake."

Nor had she. The truth was simple as that. But only now did she realize the incredible truth—that the silence, the loyalty, had been not to protect Luke, but to protect this man whose love for Luke was great.

The implication was staggering. Julian? Julian, of all people? But there was no refuting it. This, then, was why she was still in his house when her health was such that she could have left a month ago. She had lingered in the hope of a miracle with this man. This man whom she wanted but who did not want her.

She looked up dazedly to see him watching her with an expression he had worn only once before. The day he climbed the stairs to the bed-sitter. Oh, you fool, Julian, her heart cried. You haven't given it a chance. It could be good. I'd make it good. There's so much warmth and loving and giving piled up inside me, and it could be yours. *It could be yours!* But unbelievably, he didn't want it. Not now, not ever. And the substitute offered was pity.

Pity! In one swift moment, she swept from a sigh to the age-old fury of a woman scorned. It skittled the years aside, reducing her to the rude little schoolgirl of the dusty lane, and to her shame and horror, she heard a voice which was surely not hers, saying, "Stick it! That's what you can do!" But in the silence which followed, she distinctly heard Stephen's quiet chuckle and the sound of his hands applauding.

Julian looked at her closely, speculatively. "Were you addressing me?"

"I was," she said. "A most regrettable lapse. I used those words at the age of sixteen, when I met Luke Howard for the first time. Now they've turned full circle, and all that remains is for someone to pick up the ends and tie them neatly together. Which I think you have already done. Goodbye, Julian. I won't embarrass you further with my presence. But I do thank you. I do . . . thank . . ."

She wasn't as strong as she thought. She made a dash for the door, but Julian reached it first and planted himself firmly in front of it. All tension seemed to have left him, and he appeared remarkably relaxed.

"Any further histrionics, and I will thump you," he announced calmly. "Now kindly explain what that tantrum was all about."

"You're the one who's playing Sherlock Holmes. You're the great unraveler of knots. Place any interpretation you like on it. Now let me pass. I'm in a hurry to leave."

"Dear, dear! We are sixteen again, aren't we? No manners, not even one little 'please.' Tell me, Princess, how did friend Luke react when you threw that delightful phrase at him?"

"He went as red as a beetroot and vanished in a cloud of dust!"

"Typical! Whereas I'd give half my practice to have you before me as that cheeky young teenager. I'd put you across my knee so fast, and afterwards . . . "

He broke off, but something flickered in his eyes, and the demon Julian always aroused in her stirred. "Don't stop," she said very softly. "You have my undivided attention. You were saying?"

"Never mind," he said shortly.

"Oh, but we must, Julian! Just think of all we could be missing. Would 'afterwards' be anything like this?"

Grasping the lapels of his jacket firmly, she raised herself on tiptoe and kissed him gently, full on the mouth. She liked it so much that she kissed him again, hard. Then for good measure, gently again.

And that's what is known as going out in a blaze of glory, she told herself wryly.

Something in his stillness warned her to stop. To go no further. Her common sense told her to stop. But to stop in the middle of her act was unthinkable!

"The speciality of the house," she mocked. "A little sample of Her Royal Highness's mishmash, and Julian, you were so right! I didn't even notice the garlic. It was fun!"

He said quietly, "You chose the wrong man to play games with. I'm afraid you've asked for this, Tonia," and brought his mouth down hard upon hers in a bruising, punishing kiss.

When he lifted his head, her face was very tired, and she looked every one of her thirty-odd years. He kept her in his arms, looking down at her, until she said, "Please may I go now?" and he knew that only pride kept the tears from falling.

Neither of them heard the arrival of the car, and the ring at the door took them completely by surprise.

With a muttered expletive, Julian released her. "Who the hell's visiting at this time of the morning?"

The bell rang again insistently.

Tonia pulled herself together. "The milkman, I expect. I'll go."

When she opened the door the gray-faced man said, "I was told that Julian kept a princess here. I didn't believe it, so I came to see for myself."

It was the grayness that did it. After one incredulous pause, she was in his arms, hugging him fiercely, feeling her breath catch on the edge of tears. "It's all right, Luke. It's all right. Darling scarecrow, don't look like that! Everything's all right now."

Then from behind came Julian's voice, and the hardness of it chilled her to the bone.

"Charming," he said. "Hello, old son. I expected you today but not quite so early. We've finished breakfast, I'm afraid, but do come in."

# ❊ **22** ❊

So it has finally come, she thought. The moment she had dreaded and fought against and tried so desperately hard to prevent. It had come, and there was even a measure of relief in the sudden sag of her shoulders as she gently freed herself from Luke's grasp.

He looked over her head at Julian, and his gaze slid over the red pyjamas.

"Why couldn't you have told me?"

"Told you what?"

"That you were living with Tonia."

"Why should I? On the day you married Angela, your interest in Tonia ceased. At least, it should have done."

Luke stood dumb. Beads of perspiration stood out on his forehead, and his lack of color was alarming. He was not merely gray and dejected. He was a man rapidly approaching the end of his tether, and the deterioration was pitiful to watch. Tonia, unbearably distressed, was moving forward again to comfort him when Julian's hands descended firmly on her shoulders, and she could tell by his voice that he was smiling.

"I hope sincerely that it *has* done, because I'm afraid we've been holding out on you, old son, and I might have known young Martin would let the cat out of the bag. I'm not living with Tonia, but I plan to do so from now on. We're going to be married, and you're the first to know."

His fingers were digging into her flesh, willing her to understand, offering her the solution; and instantly she knew that this had to be the way of it. Luke needed more than absolution; he needed release. From the look in his eyes, she sensed that she could rebind him to her with very little effort—not with love, but with the cloying tentacles of pity and obligation. Instead, she had to set him free. One final act was needed to ring down the curtain and send him home whole, and she approached it calmly, knowing that Julian would share the act with her.

Swiftly, gratefully, her hand reached up to return the pressure, signaling her acceptance, and when she spoke to Luke, there was just the correct trace of embarrassment in her voice.

"We kept putting off telling you . . . we felt such clots, remembering the way we used to spit fire at each other. Also, Julian was a little nervous . . . because of you and me . . . but I'm so glad you came to see us for we couldn't have waited much longer. We're so happy, Luke. Will you be happy with us? Please?"

Luke stood as one petrified, his mind in utter chaos, his face a study. He stared incredulously at the cameo in front of him, the quietly radiant woman with the face and figure of a girl, the dark man looking down at her with pride—the primeval pride of a male in possession—and he was unable to restrain a prick of envy. Obviously bound up in each other, the two of them looked so right together—so intrinsically, utterly right.

But he was free. Free! It was true what she had whispered. Everything was all right, and five brief moments had wiped out all those intolerable years. The nightmare was ended, and Julian had been nervous . . . *nervous* . . . of telling him! The relief was such that, unconsciously, he straightened. Standing erect, he was a very tall man, and Tonia fancied that she could see the burden lying on the floor at his feet.

He said simply, "I am happy for you." But he was even happier for himself, and his sweet smile as he spoke was not for the woman who could have been his wife, but for the woman waiting at home, who was.

Julian exclaimed in sudden apology, "What inhospitable blighters we are, keeping you on the doorstep. Come on in, old son, and tell us what's brought you up here on a Sunday morning—and why Angela and the kids aren't with you."

He led the way into the living room, while Luke muttered something about having been asked to inspect new hospital equipment. Julian shook his head at him. "Overdoing the dedication bit, as usual. No such weekend nonsense for me."

"For us, if you please! Let's have the royal we," Tonia said severely, and Julian winked at Luke.

"Starting with the ball and chain early, isn't she? Woman, instead of nagging, what about offering our guest some coffee?" Then he smote himself on the forehead. "Coffee? When there's champagne in the fridge? I must be getting old! Darling, I think we should crack it while Luke's with us, then he can help us celebrate what I think are termed the coming nuptials."

He leered lasciviously, and Tonia said, "Oh, get off with you. Really, Luke, I just don't know what I'm letting myself in for."

"You will," Julian promised, "you will," and went out whistling, banging the door noisily after him.

The two left behind looked at each other.

Luke said, "You never told him. Obviously he doesn't know."

"And he never will. Let's not discuss it, Luke. It's forgiven and will be forgotten. That's all you really want to hear, isn't it?"

"I expected bitterness . . . "

"You won't find it. It's Julian, you see. There's no time for bitterness with him around. He's a fine man. Not by

Rivingham standards, maybe, but certainly by mine. If you're wondering how we met again, it was through his mother. I went to be interviewed for a job, and by a curious coincidence, the employer turned out to be Mrs. Goldberg. And because I was ill—I'd been a little careless with my health, Julian was brought in to advise and help. I suspect he did it for old time's sake, with you in mind. Afterwards, because I was penniless and too proud to return to St. Michael's, he offered me the use of this cottage."

She gave him a level look. "I've lived here all winter. Alone. Julian could have had me weeks ago, but he didn't, and knowing him and remembering me, I think you'll agree that makes him rather special. Just one of the many reasons why I've grown to love him so much."

"If he ever knew what really happened that night . . ."

"I think he would want to kill you," she said quietly. "One final word. My silence was not for you. Let me make that quite clear. I kept quiet to preserve the illusions of the finest friend you'll ever have. You might care to ponder over that occasionally. Now let's brighten up, or he'll walk into a heavy silence and wonder what's going on. All right?"

"You're very generous . . ."

"Life has been generous to me . . ." and then the thump of a knee against the door heralded Julian's arrival, and there was no time to say any more.

"Don't forget, our love to Angela," called Julian as he stood with his arm round Tonia, watching Luke edge his car out of the narrow driveway. A last wave and he was gone, and Julian's smile vanished abruptly. He took his arm away and turned Tonia to him.

"With apologies to Sinatra," he said. "I did it my way. I hope it met with your approval."

"It was the greatest demonstration of friendship I'll ever witness," she told him gently. "You're a very wonderful man, Dr. Goldberg."

"Don't mention it. I'll hang my halo up in the hall as we go in, and you can collect your Oscar at the same time. What superb bloody actors we are. What superb bloody liars. You'd been a little careless with your health, had you? Why didn't you tell him about his baby?"

He crooked a finger at her stricken face. "Come into the house." He halted outside the living-room door and pointed silently upward to the open fanlight.

She leaned against the wall. "You listened? Oh, you fool!"

"Of course, I listened," he said roughly. "I don't conform to Rivingham standards, and I thank God for it. The good ones are always the worst, aren't they? I may not want to kill Luke Howard, but I think I am going to hate him for quite some time to come."

"You are not." She straightened up. "That's my prerogative, and I refuse to exercise it. Besides, your halo would slip, and it's such a nice fit. Julian, please . . . what difference does it make now? It's finished, my dear, Leave it."

Silence.

Tonia said softly, "When you stood outside the door, did you hear anything else of interest?"

"I did. I assumed it was part of the act."

"It wasn't."

Julian digested this very carefully. "Would you care to repeat it? I'd like to watch your face as you say it. I don't see why Luke should get all the concessions."

"Certainly. You could have had me weeks ago, Julian. You still can. For as long or as short a time as you wish. Here, in this little house or in a flat in town. Wherever you say . . . whichever you choose. My only fear is that you won't choose. 'I have no desire to make you my mistress,' you said, 'not now—not ever.' "

"Quite correct," he said. "I've had my share of mistresses. Charming women, all of them, but merely substitutes for the real thing. That's why they remained mistresses."

233

"The years are beginning to fly, Julian. Maybe you've lost sight of the real thing. Would you recognize it if you saw it?"

"I'm looking at it. I recognized it years ago when you came walking toward me hand in hand with Luke Howard. I've never lost sight of it, even thought at times it receded and became a little remote."

"My dear, *dear* Julian . . . all those years . . . " She was having difficulty with her voice. "But you can't possibly still want to marry me."

"I can. I do. And I intend to."

"You're forgetting. I can't marry anyone. I can't give you children."

He reached for her hand.

"Neither can I," he said. "So it doesn't matter, does it?"

There was not a murmur, not a sigh, Which made the silence seem more intense, as the missing piece of the puzzle called Julian dropped into place, and the eyes of her understanding were opened.

Poor Julian. Then she scorned the thought. One did not presume to pity such a man as this. Instead she gripped his hand and let her fingers speak for her.

At last she said, "When did you find this out?"

"During my first year in medical school. Charming discovery for a young man to make, wasn't it? Especially a cocky one who thought he was God's gift to women. Charming to have the most eligible Jewish daughters paraded before you and know you were capable of plucking the flower but unable to plant the seed. My father said, 'What the hell, Julian. The way I see it, you've got two chances. You can either cut your throat or have yourself a ball.' " He shrugged. "I had myself a ball.

"Then one day I saw a girl. The one they called the Princess. A joyous bubbling broth of a girl who stopped me dead in my tracks—and that was long before I saw you with Luke. You were fashioned after my own heart, after my own style, and you were having quite a ball of your own, kicking around the hearts of the wretched would-be princes who flocked to pay you homage. If I'd felt free to enter the lists, I'd have sorted you out so smartly, but I hadn't the right to start something that couldn't be finished. So I was forced to watch from a distance and, believe me, some of your more regal performances put my teeth on edge.

"Then you set your sights on Luke Howard. Poor devil, he hadn't a clue how to handle you. The affair was doomed from the start, and it was a blessing in disguise that Stephen Marais appeared before the wedding instead of after.

"When he chanced along, I hated his guts. Not because my instinct told me he was good for you—or because it was curtains for Luke—but because in a strange vicarious way, it was also curtains for me. You see, to reconcile myself to your coming marriage, I worked out a clever compensatory scheme. Luke Howard was going to be my proxy. He would stand up as the bridegroom and make the vows—for me. He would create a home and be the happy husband—for me. And later he would become the proud father, the ideal family man . . . because, my dearest, dearest Tonia, in the cleverness of my ignorant finite mind, I had planned that Luke would give you a child. For me."

"Oh no! No! No! . . . " This was surely the most cruel irony of all. Shaking her head wildly in disbelief, she tried to pull her hand from his, to turn and run, to run and never stop running from the knowledge that the wanton waste of the precious seed, the anguish and the shame, need never have been.

She cried out again, desolate beyond measure, but Julian's hands were gripping her, steadying, reassuring, upholding her with the same calm strength another had once supplied.

"Why did I tell you? To take this particular load off your shoulders, or at least to help you carry it. For I should never have let you walk out of my rooms that day. I wanted a child, didn't I? I wanted *your* child—so what the hell did it matter who the father was? But I let you go. My dearest love, the years that I've squandered because I let you go . . ."

He took her hands and raised them to his lips with a humility that took her by surprise and tightened her throat. " . . . which means that we must pack twice as much living in the years ahead. Don't you agree?"

Tonia was still trembling, and the tears were far from dry, but her voice was clear and steady.

"With all my heart, because that means twice as much loving, doesn't it? Could we start right away, Julian? I desperately want to put my arms around you."

"What's stopping you?" he asked. He spread his own arms wide and said simply, "Come."

Such an ordinary little word. But it hurled her into the waiting man's arms with a joyousness that took his breath away, and not until later did Julian learn that unconsciously he had pronounced a benediction.

At the moment, however, he was only concerned with the present. With the sight of the shining fair head pressed against his heart.

"So help me, woman, but I love you," he said. "I've waited such a long time for you. I'd almost given up hope."

Wasn't life funny? Julian waiting for her all this time. Just around the corner, so to speak. There had been many corners, many ways. But she had the sudden, sturdy conviction that this would prove to be the most marvelous way of all. The tears miraculously dried, and she began to laugh.